continued . . .

BEYOND CONTROL

REBECCA YORK

BERKLEY SENSATION, NEW YORK

THE BERKLEY PUBLISHING GROUP
Published by the Penguin Group
Penguin Group (USA) Inc.
375 Hudson Street, New York, New York 10014, USA
Penguin Group (Canada), 90 Eglinton Avenue East, Suite 700, Toronto, Ontario M4P 2Y3, Canada
(a division of Pearson Penguin Canada Inc.)
Penguin Books Ltd., 80 Strand, London WC2R 0RL, England
Penguin Group Ireland, 25 St. Stephen's Green, Dublin 2, Ireland (a division of Penguin Books Ltd.)
Penguin Group (Australia), 250 Camberwell Road, Camberwell, Victoria 3124, Australia
(a division of Pearson Australia Group Pty. Ltd.)
Penguin Books India Pvt. Ltd., 11 Community Centre, Panchsheel Park, New Delhi—110 017, India
Penguin Group (NZ), Cnr. Airborne and Rosedale Roads, Albany, Auckland 1310, New Zealand
(a division of Pearson New Zealand Ltd.)
Penguin Books (South Africa) (Pty.) Ltd., 24 Sturdee Avenue, Rosebank, Johannesburg 2196,
South Africa

Penguin Books Ltd., Registered Offices: 80 Strand, London WC2R 0RL, England

This is a work of fiction. Names, characters, places, and incidents either are the product of the author's imagination or are used fictitiously, and any resemblance to actual persons, living or dead, business establishments, events, or locales is entirely coincidental. The publisher does not have any control over and does not assume any responsibility for author or third-party websites or their content.

BEYOND CONTROL

A Berkley Sensation Book / published by arrangement with the author

PRINTING HISTORY
Berkley Sensation edition / August 2005

Copyright © 2005 by Ruth Glick.
Excerpt from *Shadow of the Moon* copyright © 2005 by Ruth Glick.
Cover photo by James Cotier, Getty/Stone.
Cover design by George Long.

ISBN: 0-425-20442-1

BERKLEY® SENSATION
Berkley Sensation Books are published by The Berkley Publishing Group,
a division of Penguin Group (USA) Inc.,
375 Hudson Street, New York, New York 10014.
BERKLEY SENSATION and the "B" design are trademarks belonging to Penguin Group (USA) Inc.

PRINTED IN THE UNITED STATES OF AMERICA

10 9 8 7 6 5 4 3 2 1

PROLOGUE

TEDIUM DID STRANGE things to a man's senses.

Mark Greenwood jerked toward the monitor as a shadow flashed in front of the security camera. It looked like a man crouching.

No. Impossible.

It had to be a deer—because nobody could get that close to Maple Creek.

He and Hernando Cordova were in the tomblike security center, each of them scanning ten of the twenty monitors that gave rotating views of the buildings and grounds.

The thirty-acre reserve, tucked away in an obscure corner of Prince George's County, Maryland, looked like a hush-hush agricultural research facility, with rectangular plots of soybeans, cabbages, and strawberries clearly visible behind the three security fences.

The joke among the guards was that the plants were genetically engineered with carp genes to withstand the humid Maryland summers and skunk genes to ward off pests, particularly of the human variety.

Mark sneaked a look at his watch, counting the twenty-eight monotonous minutes left on his shift. Still, it was a great job for someone who'd never been to college. He'd leave this place with enough money to go back to Howard County, Maryland, and open his own security company.

He pushed a button, then spoke into the microphone attached to his headset. "East perimeter, report."

"East perimeter secure," Donaldson answered from the gravel walkway along the fence.

The six men on topside duty checked in.

Like everyone in the twenty-five-man guard unit, they came from elite-force Army, Navy, or Air Force backgrounds, although they now wore plain black uniforms with no insignia. But they carried standard M16 rifles and Sig .40s.

Everybody lived on base, but there were a couple of bars in nearby Waldorf where you could negotiate a roll in the hay for under fifty dollars. A blow job was even less. But it was too late for any action tonight.

He was thinking about the surgically augmented breasts of the current *Playboy* centerfold when he saw another deer. Or maybe the same one. They were all over the woods. If you hit one, you could total your car.

The view switched to the parking lot. The vehicles belonging to the security staff were at the far edge. The research scientists got the better spots, closer to the Quonset huts, the only buildings visible inside the complex.

Other screens showed the interior. If you didn't know what you were looking at, you'd wonder how all those rooms could fit inside the two rusting buildings. In fact, only the control center where he sat and a few offices were upstairs. Most of the facility was in the Well, the forty-thousand-square-foot complex located three and four stories below the soybean fields. Only forty-five minutes from D.C., it had been built in the paranoid fifties as a bomb shelter for the families of privileged senators and congressmen.

When the steel-clad guardhouse flashed on the screen, Mark saw Ken Rota standing at attention under the fluorescent lights—his body ramrod straight, just in case the brass reviewed the tapes.

The view changed, and Mark was looking at a sign that said:

STOP AND SHOW IDENTIFICATION.
PROCEED SLOWLY. METAL BARRIER
MAY DAMAGE VEHICLE TIRES.

The cameras went through another cycle. Two minutes later he was back to the guardhouse. Rota was still standing beside the sliding glass door, but something about the glassy look in his eyes made Mark take the cameras off automatic scan.

"What?" Cordova questioned.

He gestured toward the screen, then zoomed in for a close-up. Rota's posture was stiff, his gaze fixed, his mouth rigid—as though he'd been flash-frozen as he stood at his post.

"Mr. Iron Jaw," Cordova muttered.

"I don't know," Mark answered, feeling a tiny worm of alarm slither down his spine. He'd seen action in Iraq, and he knew that feeling when something wasn't quite right. Eyes fixed on the screen, he spoke into the mike positioned in front of his mouth.

"Rota?"

The man didn't answer—or twitch a muscle, although Mark had effectively shouted directly into his ear via the headset he was wearing.

"Rota?"

Still no reply.

There had never been a Code Red at Maple Creek. The facility was too obscure to be a target and too secure to be penetrated. Yet as Mark stared at the man in the guard-house, he acted without hesitation—his finger jabbed down on the alarm button.

Instantly the grounds were flooded with light as a siren began to wail.

"Jesus," Cordova breathed.

A green light flashed on his console. When he switched comm lines, a sharp voice demanded, "What the hell is going on?"

The speaker was Major Showalter, the head of the security team.

Mark's answer was crisp and to the point. "We have a possible perimeter breach. At the main gate. Rota's on duty, and he appears to be immobilized. Maybe he was hit with some kind of tranq spray."

"On my way," the major barked, then issued a clipped order over the comm units to all security personnel.

Moments later five armed men poured from the Quonset huts and fanned out, rifles at the ready. They were joined by the four men on perimeter duty.

On one of Cordova's screens Mark saw fifteen more men clatter up the stairwell, including the major, who stayed in contact with the command center.

"What's Rota's status?"

Mark switched the view to the gatehouse again. Against all logic, he'd been hoping to see something different, but the man inside looked like a discarded robot. "He's standing up as though he's on duty, but he's not moving, and he doesn't respond to my hail."

The next question was more urgent. "How long has he been out of commission?"

Mark kept his voice crisp, focusing on the facts. "He looked okay on our last sweep. He can't have been down for more than a couple of minutes."

"Did you see anyone approach the guardhouse?"

"I thought I saw a moving body out by the road. I assumed it was a deer." Mark cleared his throat. "It could have been a man crouching over." His adrenaline was pumping now as he listened to the reports coming in over his headset.

"No contact."

"No contact."

He wanted to be out there—on the move with an M16 in his hands. But he knew his position was vital.

He heard the door open behind him.

"Sir—"

He swiveled his chair, expecting to see Showalter.

But it wasn't the major coming to take over the command center. Instead he saw two men standing in the doorway—holding hands. They were dressed in black, much like the

Maple Creek security staff. But Mark knew every man in the unit, and these weirdos weren't any of them.

"What the fuck!" he exclaimed, already reaching for his sidearm. Beside him, Cordova was doing the same.

The intruders' gazes flicked between the two of them. Sweat beaded their foreheads, and their skin was pale with nerves. But there was something else on their faces—a determination that Mark recognized. The determination of the fanatic—the suicide bomber, the nutcase willing to risk everything because he thinks his cause is worth it.

Before Mark could unholster his weapon, a terrible pain shot through his skull.

CHAPTER
ONE

THE LONG DRIVEWAY made a graceful curve, and Jordan Walker slowed his Mercedes sedan near a mound of tasteful white azaleas as he stared at the Tudor mansion that had been hidden until now by artfully placed stands of trees.

If he wasn't mistaken, the residence was a copy of a palace owned by the Prince of Wales.

He'd made excellent time on the two-hour drive up from D.C. Which was good, because he knew Leonard Hamilton gave extra points for punctuality. He also liked men who spoke frankly, delivered value for money, and had the guts to stand up to him.

Over the past several days Jordan had done considerable research on the billionaire. He knew his age—sixty-eight. His state of health—poor. His passion for opera, his famous collection of American art, from Copley to Whistler to O'Keeffe. His fondness for orchids.

The background check was standard operating procedure for Jordan because he'd learned that preparation often meant the difference between success and failure.

But careful research was only part of what had earned him the Pulitzer Prize. He had something more: a facility for reading people—for knowing when the subject of an interview was blowing smoke like a criminal defense lawyer with a guilty client.

The paving surface changed from concrete to cobblestones as Jordan reached the circular driveway in front of the house.

He parked, then stepped out beside a neatly mulched

bed of white and yellow tulips, planted in careful rows like soldiers guarding the entrance.

The sun was bright. The air smelled as clean as his mom's fresh laundry drying on the line. And the security camera high on the wall tracked him as if it were a jungle predator.

After stretching the kinks out of his arms and legs, he climbed the three brick steps to the double-wide doors. Seconds after he rang the bell, a tall, thin man in a dark suit opened the right-hand door.

"Jordan Walker."

"Yes, sir. Come in. Mr. Hamilton will meet you in the conservatory," he said with a very upper-class British accent.

Jordan stepped into a vast foyer that would easily have swallowed the first floor of the modest house where he'd grown up.

His footsteps echoed on two-foot-square marble slabs as he followed the man down a wide hall past silent reception rooms to a vast glass enclosure lush with the earthy scent of tropical vegetation.

It took him a moment to recognize the trees. Mostly he'd seen them as smaller specimens in large pots. These schefflera, dracaena, and ficus trees sprouted from enormous in-ground squares scattered around the terra-cotta floor. They alternated with carved rock formations holding jewel-like orchids.

"Make yourself comfortable. Mr. Hamilton will be right with you. Can I bring you something to drink?" the butler said.

"Just water," Jordan said. When the man had departed, he strolled around the room, looking at the trees and flowers, enjoying the ambience. Once he would have felt totally out of place in this rich environment. He'd passed the intimidating stage long ago.

He was inspecting a yellow-and-white orchid when the sound of a motor made him turn.

Leonard Hamilton, silver-haired and stoop-shouldered, rolled into the room on a one-seat electric cart and fixed him with a piercing look, then said by way of greeting, "With the work schedule you've been keeping over the past few years, I expected to see some gray in that dark hair of yours. But you look younger than thirty-two."

"Clean living," Jordan answered.

"Sit down so we're on the same level. As I told you in my letter, I want to discuss a book project."

Jordan pulled out a chair and sat.

Before Hamilton could elaborate, the butler reappeared, carrying a silver tray. There was a tall glass of ice water and a blue Wedgwood teapot and a matching mug, along with a silver cream-and-sugar set.

The butler made a fuss of fixing the old man's tea. Through the little ceremony, Jordan sat with uncharacteristic tension twisting in his gut—willing Hamilton to get on with the interview.

"Thank you, Griggs. That will be all," Hamilton said. He waited until the man had left before saying, "My health is poor. I don't have a lot of time to waste, so I'll get right to the point. I want a definitive biography. The man who writes it gets my complete cooperation."

Jordan fought to hide his surprise. Leonard Hamilton had always been as secretive as an Olympic athlete on steroids. He preferred to stay in the shadows, letting other men with equal wealth get their names splashed across the papers. Why had he finally changed his mind?

Leaning back in his chair, Jordan took a sip of water. "You'd make a fascinating subject, but if you're expecting a whitewash job, I'm not your man."

"You'd get the whole story."

Jordan set down his glass. "So you'd be candid about why your wife left you after thirty years of marriage? And how you kept your son out of a juvenile detention center after his series of arrests in his teens?"

They sat across the table staring at each other for several charged moments. He'd cracked the old man's veneer. But he hadn't gotten what he wanted—yet.

Hamilton shifted in his seat, then changed the subject abruptly. "I thought your book on the AIDS crisis in Africa was very well done. How long did it take you to write it?"

"The research took over a year—including six months traveling around the continent. The writing I did in nine months."

"You've always gotten information that other people missed. Even when you were just starting out at the *Baltimore Sun*."

"You checked that far back?"

"Further. Including your grade inflation exposé for the *Daily D*."

Jordan hid his surprise with a shrug. Apparently the old man had poked into his college days at Dartmouth.

"I'm prepared to be brutally honest about myself and my family," Hamilton continued. "And I'm prepared to pay you far more than your last few books earned out. You can tell the public whatever you want about me. I'll make sure it's worth your while."

"I can't be on your payroll, if I'm going to be free to write an honest book," he said, keeping his voice even. "I'll get my money from a publisher's advance. One of the big publishers should be willing to pay top dollar for a candid, authorized bio of you."

Hamilton smiled. "Good. Because if you'd jumped at my largesse, you'd be out the door before you could take another sip of water."

"So you were testing me with that offer?" Jordan clarified.

"I want to know what a man will do for money before I make a deal with him. You can work it any way you like. I'll cooperate fully. But I'm asking something in return."

Ah, the punch line.

"In exchange I want you to find out what happened to my son."

Although Jordan had a talent for throwing an interview subject off balance, he could take lessons from Hamilton. After a moment he said, "He and a friend . . . died in a boating accident recently, didn't they? On the Chesapeake Bay."

The gnarled old man studied him from across the table. "According to the official report, he and Glenn Barrow took out a boat in unsafe conditions. I think that's bull."

Jordan sat forward. He felt it then, that edge of awareness that grabbed him when he knew he was on the trail of something hot—something startling. "You have evidence to the contrary?"

"Yes."

"What?"

"They told me there was an autopsy at the office of the Maryland State Medical Examiner. But when Todd's body was brought back from Baltimore, I had additional tests performed. I have the results."

"Why did you go to all that trouble?"

"My son was afraid of the water. He wouldn't have been in any boating accident. Not unless somebody dragged him out to the middle of the bay kicking and screaming."

The old man sounded tired as he continued. "At first I thought some of his lowlife friends could have killed him."

"He was a disappointment to you?" Jordan asked, unable to keep thoughts of his own disappointing father-son relationship out of his mind. If he were dead, his dad would probably just shrug and go on.

"I loved him. I tried to understand him. But I could never . . . connect with him. Do you know what I mean?"

Jordan nodded, identifying with the sentiment all too well. He'd always felt out of place in his own family—like a baby bird accidentally dropped in the wrong nest.

The billionaire's face turned sad, then relaxed again. "I

invested a lot of money in my son. But it didn't turn out the way we expected. Todd never fit in with other kids."

Again, Jordan flashed on his own memories, then ruthlessly drove the thoughts from his mind, wondering why he was letting this interview get so personal. He wasn't here for a self-analysis session.

Hamilton was still speaking, his voice thickened by emotion. "As you pointed out a while ago, Todd got into trouble with the law. And other trouble, too. I wanted to find out if there was some medical reason for his strange behavior. And I wanted to know if his death was drug-related."

"Was it?"

"Not in the way I imagined."

"What's that supposed to mean?"

The old man gave him a direct look. "Why don't you read the pathology report. Then, if you think it's worth the time, find out what the hell he was up to that got him killed."

"He was a homosexual, right?"

Hamilton glared at him. "And you're supposed to be straight, but you haven't had a lot of relationships with women. You've never even come close to marriage. You've never lived with anyone. You've plowed most of your energy into your career." He looked like he might be about to say something else but refrained.

"How is my personal life relevant?" Jordan asked carefully.

"How is my son's sexuality relevant?" the multimillionaire countered.

"It may have something to do with his death."

"I doubt it," Hamilton snapped.

Jordan waited for several seconds before saying, "Let me understand. You'll cooperate with me on a no-holds-barred biography of you, if I investigate your son's death. Are we supposed to include what I uncover in the biography?"

"It depends on how dangerous you think the information is."

Jordan was still digesting that as the old man reached into a canvas bag that was attached to a carrier on the side of the go-cart. "Here's a copy of the pathology report. The original's in my safe-deposit box. And I had the computer files at the hospital where the tests were done altered."

"Oh, yeah? By whom?"

"Never mind that. The important point is that the request can't be traced back to me."

Jordan didn't bother saying that computer files could be recovered—if you had the skill and the time.

"Do some digging into the material. If you accept the assignment, I'll talk to you about my son. About the circumstances of his birth."

"Which are?"

"We'll get to that later. We'll talk about anything you want. Let me know by the end of next week what you decide."

"And if I don't want to take the job?"

Hamilton's eyes turned crafty. "I'll contact somebody else. Someone not too chicken to find out why Todd Hamilton had to die."

CHAPTER
TWO

RETURNING FROM A meeting at the Pentagon, Kurt MacArthur strode inside the converted mansion that housed the Crandall Consortium.

Until a few years ago, his office had been in downtown D.C., but he'd scooped up an old estate on the Virginia bluffs above the Potomac River and had it converted at taxpayers' expense.

At fifty-eight Kurt was still lean and trim, thanks to sensible eating and daily sessions at the state-of-the-art gym in the basement. But the liberal sprinkling of silver in his once-dark hair and the lines etched in his face testified to the rigors of his thirty-five-year career.

He'd met Calvin Crandall when he'd taken a night class in Political Ideology at The George Washington University. He hadn't known at the time that the adjunct professor was recruiting operatives for his own private power base. When the older man had invited him for drinks at the Cosmos Club, he'd been flattered. And he'd been eager to join Crandall's team, once he'd learned something about his organization.

Until then, Kurt had never gotten close to power. Not in the backwater western Maryland town where he'd grown up. Not in his unexciting years at Shepherd College where he'd waited tables to make up the tuition money his parents couldn't afford. And not in his lowly job answering mail for a nothing congressman from Oklahoma.

The "can do" atmosphere at the Crandall Consortium had energized him. He'd lapped up lunches and dinners with his boss at the capital's power spots. And he'd been eager to please. Which was why he'd taken on clandestine assignments that might have raised doubts in the minds of other men.

When the news media mentioned the Crandall Consortium, they called it a think tank. Insiders knew the agency was as much about murder, torture, and blackmail as about policy papers.

Getting your hands dirty changed a man, of course. Either you cracked under the pressure or you grew stronger.

Kurt had become an expert at rationalizing his activities as he acquired the trappings of power and prestige. There was always a reason why the American people needed a man on their team who was willing to make the hard choices. In the seventies and eighties all he'd needed to stay on the right course was to visualize a mushroom cloud rising over the U.S. Capitol or the San Francisco Bay Bridge. Lately he energized himself with mental pictures of airplanes crashing into skyscrapers or anthrax spores wafting through the New York City subway system.

Over the years he'd learned that doing the hard jobs gave him power and prestige. He'd also learned enough about Calvin Crandall to put him in jail.

He never would have betrayed his mentor to the legal system. But three years after Kurt stepped into the number-two spot, Calvin balked at sending operatives into Iraq on a suicide mission. Kurt had realized then that his boss had lost his nerve. So Kurt arranged for the older man to have a fatal heart attack while on a skiing vacation in Switzerland.

After he'd moved into Calvin's dark-paneled office, he'd made damn sure that nobody could get the jump on *him*.

As he strode into the reception area, Mary Ann, his executive assistant, looked up. "Good afternoon, sir."

She was a stunning blond, in her mid-twenties, not one of those skinny-assed model types who were in fashion now. He'd picked her because she had excellent secretarial skills and because she had enough meat on her bones to make her a comfortable bed partner. But at work they always observed the proprieties.

"Any calls?" he asked.

"Senator Borton wants to talk to you. He wouldn't leave a message."

"He's probably trying to wangle a job for one of his constituents. If he calls back, tell him I'm tied up." He paused for a moment. "Did Jim Swift call?"

"No, sir."

"Okay. Thanks."

For ten years Kurt had been absolutely secure in his position of power. Like J. Edgar Hoover before him, he had enough dirt on the right people to stay at the top until he died. Today he was fighting a queasy feeling as he strode into his own office and closed the door.

Once he'd settled into his custom-made chair, he tapped in the password—Jehovah101—on his computer keyboard, then scanned the e-mail that had arrived in his absence. When he found nothing from his senior field officer, he drummed his fingers on the broad walnut desk, then reached for the secure phone.

"Swift here," his man answered after three rings.

"Where the hell are you?" he barked in response to the fuzzy transmission.

"Still in Wilmington, Delaware. I've just been talking to some of Todd Hamilton's former teachers from his fancy prep school," he answered.

"I was hoping for a report by now," Kurt said, modifying his tone.

"As you know, since Hamilton was carrying no ID, we lost time figuring out who he was."

Kurt sighed. "Yeah. Right."

"I'm proceeding as fast as I can, but a thorough background check takes time. You don't want a half-baked job, do you?"

"Of course not," he answered, controlling his impatience. Swift was a good man. Some would have called him a psychopath. Kurt preferred to think of him as devoted, dogged, effective, technologically savvy. And he understood the adage that the ends justified the means.

"There won't be any problem collecting his grades and other pertinent information from his permanent record."

Translation: Swift had checked the burglar alarm at the school and was confident that he could get in after hours to photocopy the records.

Kurt tightened his hold on the phone and asked, "Have you found anything that might explain what happened in March?"

"Nothing yet. I'll try to get a report together as soon as I can."

Kurt hung up and rocked back in his chair, staring out the window at his panoramic view of the river, feeling like he was working in the dark. All he knew was that Todd Hamilton and his friend Glenn Barrow had somehow broken into Maple Creek and caused a fucking mess.

So who the hell was Todd Hamilton, really? Besides the son of a billionaire, for Christ's sake.

Were he and his boyfriend working for a foreign terrorist organization? Did they belong to some homegrown protest group? And why had they targeted Maple Creek?

LINDSAY Fleming never felt comfortable ducking out of the office early. Usually, she was one of the last staffers out the door.

Today she was too nervous to sit still. An odd state of affairs for her.

Martha Rinker, the receptionist at the front desk, raised an eyebrow when Lindsay marched past. But she knew better than to comment.

And Lindsay refrained from saying, "I'll make up the time in the morning."

She didn't have to justify herself. Instead she took the elevator to the first floor of the Dirksen Office Building, then walked down the hill to the Union Station metro stop, thinking that her early departure was an affirmation.

She'd finally made up her mind. She was going to Senator Sam Conroy's reception. Because she wanted to pay her respects to the man who had tutored her as a wet-behind-the-ears intern.

That was what she told herself. But she knew deep down it wasn't the real reason she was going to his farewell party. Something else was tugging at her. And if she didn't find out what it was, she'd go crazy.

She reached the station, already crowded with Capitol Hill staffers on their way home, and waited for a Red Line train to Tenleytown.

In actual distance her McLean Gardens apartment wasn't far from her ultimate destination this evening— Chevy Chase Village.

But there was all the difference in the world between her chosen lifestyle and the old money affluence just across the District line.

She picked up her own groceries at Whole Foods and used the washing machine and dryer in the remodeled kitchen of her apartment. As often as not, the society matrons just across the District line had their orders delivered from Magruder's upscale grocery emporium and had the maid do the laundry. That was her mother's lifestyle.

Lindsay enjoyed the challenge of living on her congressional staffer's income, although she *had* dipped into her trust fund to buy her apartment.

Eight years ago she'd felt compelled to live down her reputation as a spoiled rich kid who'd gotten her first job on the Hill as a favor to her politically connected stepfather.

Now she attended few of the power events laid on by the rich and famous—because she had the guts to admit that parties tied her stomach in knots. She hated the crush of people, the noise swirling around her, and the buzzing undercurrent that was always below the surface, making her nerves jangle, making her feel like she was catching snatches of people's thoughts.

But when she'd opened Senator Sam Conroy's invitation, she'd felt oddly compelled to attend the party. As the ranking member of the House Judiciary Committee, Conroy had gone out of his way to praise her work and give her pointers. Though she hadn't worked with him in years, she'd been disappointed when he'd lost his long-held senatorial seat to a brash young neocon. And she wanted to tell him so.

And find out who or what was waiting for her at his house.

The premonition made her breath catch in her throat. But she wasn't going to run in the other direction—even when that was what she wanted to do.

CHAPTER
THREE

AS LINDSAY TURNED onto Delaware Street, it flashed through her mind that she could still turn around and go home. Immediately she canceled the thought. She'd come this far, and it would be foolish to turn around now.

Lindsay found a parking space less than a block from the senator's redbrick colonial. In the front hallway she stood for a moment smoothing the black silk of her cocktail dress as she surveyed the well dressed guests and acclimated herself to the familiar buzz. The crowd was a cross section of the capital's power structure. Senators and congressmen. Ambassadors and administration officials.

Like a gazelle sniffing the grassland for danger, she scanned the faces in the crowd looking for someone. Someone she knew? Or another man? And why was she sure it was a man?

Struggling to keep an anxious expression off her face, she looked around for her host and saw him deep in conversation with Congressman Loman. She'd wait to greet him until he was more available. After taking an offered glass of champagne from a waiter bearing a silver tray, she moved toward the hum of conversation.

"Hey, Lindsay."

She knew the voice instantly. "Sid."

Was he the man she had come here to meet? Maybe.

Sid Becker had been a Marine colonel. Even in a dark business suit, he had the ramrod-straight bearing and short haircut of a military man, although now he worked for the Institute for Military Studies downtown in D.C. He'd been a good source of information, and they'd gotten to be friends.

She knew he wanted to take that relationship to a more personal level, but she'd always resisted. She and Sid worked well together, and she didn't want to spoil things with the rush of disappointment that always came on the heels of sex. Deep down she sensed there should be something more, some profound connection between two people who had joined their bodies in the most intimate of acts. But that "something more" had always eluded her.

They hadn't seen each other in several weeks. Now, as she studied his chiseled face, she thought she detected signs of strain.

"What have you been up to?" she asked.

"Nothing special."

"You look like the rat race is getting to you," she said softly.

"Yeah, maybe I need a vacation." He wiggled his eyebrows suggestively. "Want to spend a long weekend with me in St. Michaels?"

Last year they'd both attended a conference at a posh resort in the town on the Eastern Shore of Maryland. He'd been trying to get her to go back there with him ever since.

She shook her head. "Senator Bridgewater keeps me too busy taking care of the public interest." There was no point in adding that she knew in her heart she was destined for spinsterhood.

At that moment a feeling of being watched made Lindsay look over Sid's left shoulder. Standing at the side of the room with his eyes fixed on her was a tall, broad-shouldered man. An overall impression registered first. Handsome. Confident. Alert. Then her eyes took in the separate details that made up the total picture. Thick black hair tamed by an expensive cut. Brows that would have been severe on a less forceful face. A square jaw. The suggestion of furrows between nose and mouth that spoke of maturity beyond his years. But there was a touch of humor—or was it cynicism—around the dark eyes and well-shaped lips.

The man projected a strong sense of self that often accompanied celebrity status. She'd seen him before. Was it on the Hill?

Then it clicked. He was Jordan Walker. She'd read about him in the *Post*, then seen him on a local talk show when he'd done a series of articles for the *Atlantic Monthly* on behind-the-scenes maneuvering on the Supreme Court. Some of his allegations had cost Paula Grayson, a hard-working public servant, her job, and Lindsay had silently cursed him as a career-wrecker.

Walker caught the accusing look in her eyes, but his gaze didn't falter.

Then Sid said something that she didn't catch.

"Lindsay?"

Her attention had been focused on the author for less than a minute, but her concentration on the man had been so total that everything else had faded from existence. Now she realized she hadn't heard most of Sid's last few remarks.

She struggled to pull her attention back to him. "Yes?"

"There is something . . ."

"What can I do for you?" she asked, catching the worry in his voice.

"I may want to ask a favor."

"From Senator Bridgewater?"

"Maybe. We'll talk later. This isn't the place for a business discussion—but I saw you, and I thought . . ."

"No problem. Give me a call."

"Thanks."

Feeling unsettled, she moved on. Though the room was moderately crowded, there was an open stretch between herself and the brash Mr. Walker, as if he'd parted the Red Sea to make a path for her to join him in the Promised Land. Obediently she took several steps in his direction.

Then, realizing what she was doing, she stopped in mid-stride.

She felt an uneasy shiver start at the base of her spine and travel upward. For a long moment she stood very still. Then, making a quick about-face, she headed for the buffet table.

JORDAN'S eyes narrowed as he watched the slender brunette head for the dining room. Although many of the ladies here were more beautiful, he'd rarely seen one who captured his attention so intensely. As an investigative reporter, he was constantly analyzing people. Now he tried to come up with a reason for his reaction. Her dark hair was piled in a sophisticated upsweep with a few provocative tendrils framing her oval face and emphasizing the graceful carriage of her head and neck. She seemed outwardly at home in this environment of politics and power, yet there was something that set her apart. Maybe it was her eyes. Beautiful, yet analytically assessing. Their color was light. He wanted to know the exact shade.

He had been watching her for several minutes. When she'd returned his scrutiny, he'd allowed himself to engage in a little mental game he sometimes played—seeing if he could influence another person's behavior through the force of his own will. Sometimes it seemed to work. When she'd taken a step in his direction, his chest had tightened with anticipation—leaving him feeling let down when she'd turned away. On the other hand, the evening was young. There was still time to connect with her.

He'd been glad to get the invitation to Sam Conroy's party because he thought that some of the men here would have had dealings with Leonard Hamilton.

Now he was more interested in hooking up with the lithe brunette, which was unusual for him. While he enjoyed sex, relationships had never been his strong suit. And in the past few years he'd mostly lived inside his fantasies—as Hamilton had so kindly pointed out.

His work had taught him the importance of patience. For the next forty-five minutes he bided his time. He let Senator Appleton corner him and pump him for information about the publishing industry, then looked noncommittal when the senator let on that he was looking for a ghost-writer to do his autobiography.

Deftly Jordan excused himself to chat with a construction tycoon who'd been in a business deal with Hamilton. But all the time he was talking to the man, he knew where the mystery woman was and whom she was talking to.

His opportunity to meet her came when he saw her talking to Sam Conroy. Skillfully detaching himself from his own conversation, he moved in their direction. "Senator, you're a hard man to get a word with, even at your own party."

Conroy laughed. "At your service."

The woman started to turn away. Before she could flee, Jordan said, "I'd like an introduction."

Conroy grinned. "Lindsay Fleming—Jordan Walker. Probably doing undercover research for his next book."

"Now, Senator, even I'm off duty some of the time," Jordan insisted, although it wasn't true.

Their host kept the conversation going for a few more minutes before moving off to another group of guests, leaving him alone with Ms. Fleming.

"Conroy's a gentleman from the old school," Jordan observed. "I'm going to miss him. Do you work for him?"

"No."

Up close her eyes were green—and wary.

"Are you on someone else's staff?"

"Yes."

"Are we going to play twenty questions?"

A reluctant half smile flickered on her softly curved lips. He liked the effect.

"I'm with Senator Bridgewater. I started off as an intern with Sam Conroy. His encouragement meant a lot."

"Conroy doesn't hand out praise unless it's earned. You must have done a damn good job. You're a lawyer?"

"No. A sociologist."

"How did you end up on the Hill?"

"The way most people do. Idealism. The daily grind burns it off. But I'm sure none of this is very interesting to you."

"What have I done to get your back up?"

"Your writing is slanted to project a particular point of view."

"Oh, yeah?" he asked, wondering exactly what that crack meant.

She took a half step back, preparing to leave. Despite her put-down, he wasn't about to let her go so quickly. Acting on some primal instinct, he reached out and captured her wrist. She went very still, her eyes round and alarmed. He was aware of the pulse beating under her delicate skin, but that was simply one perception in a rush of sensations. During the moment his fingers encircled her flesh, he felt warm, dizzy, disoriented, and completely at a loss to explain the intensity of the reaction.

He saw her eyes mirror his surprise. They were dilated now, the pupils almost enveloping the green irises. For an instant all the normal barriers that separate individuals vanished. He was awash with profound emotions. Longing, desire, fear. Some supernatural force seemed to pull him toward her. It was coupled with a perception of danger that made his sharpened senses reel. For frantic heartbeats he was paralyzed, caught in his own trap, unable to draw a full breath into his lungs as he stood in the middle of the room with every nerve ending in his body screaming.

She was the one who wrenched her hand away, snapping the contact.

They both stood in the middle of the crowded room, breath coming in little gasps. His gaze swept the faces around them. Nobody was watching. Nobody was aware that something extraordinary had passed between them. In truth, it must have all taken place in a few brief seconds. The blink of an eye. Yet he felt as if his life had changed forever.

He heard Lindsay make a small sound, and his gaze locked instantly back to her. The color in her cheeks was high, as if she'd just finished a very satisfying session with her lover. He felt the same heat on his own skin.

Her chin tipped up defiantly. "That was certainly novel. How did you manage that cheap parlor trick?"

"Is that really what you think?" he asked, willing his breath to steadiness.

"You tell me."

When he didn't answer, she turned and walked away with her back straight and her head up, leaving him feeling more defensive and more isolated than he'd been in his whole lonely life.

CHAPTER
FOUR

GRADUALLY, LIKE MORNING mist evaporating from rocky ground, the fog in Mark Greenwood's brain lifted.

His mind still felt like one of the Jell-O salads his Aunt Jen used to make. But at least he knew who he was. Mark Greenwood. And he was pretty sure of his current place of residence. A private hospital. But he couldn't remember exactly what had happened to him.

Did it have to do with intruders at Maple Creek? Two guys who had invaded an impenetrable facility? Or was that just a bad dream? And he'd wake up in his cozy bedroom back at Aunt Jen and Uncle Eddie's house. Any moment now he'd catch the scent of her breakfast pancakes wafting up the steps.

No, wait—his adoptive parents were dead. And he was in the special forces. On a covert assignment in Iraq.

He squeezed his eyes shut. No. Not that, either.

"How are you feeling?" a man asked, his voice full of concern. But Mark sensed a hard edge below the solicitous tone.

He slitted his eyes and tried to look at the three people hovering above him. Their faces were partially covered by surgical masks. To protect against germs? "I feel bad. Are you a doctor?" he asked the man who had asked the question.

"Yes. I'm Dr. Colefax. I'm here to help you."

Somehow, Mark wasn't reassured.

"Can you rate the pain in your head on a scale of one to ten? With ten the worst."

"Now? Or when the guys burst into the control room?"

Tension gathered in the doctor's eyes. "Tell me about that."

Mark didn't like that look—a mixture of cunning and eagerness.

When he didn't reply, the doctor prompted him, "What happened to you? A spray? An injection?"

"Not sure."

"Tell me what you remember?"

"Need to sleep."

"Stay with me," the doctor urged.

"No." He wanted to escape into sleep, but a hand closed over his shoulder, the grip tightening, anchoring him to the hospital room.

"Tell me about the men who came into the control room. What did they do?"

"Don't know."

Was this some kind of psychological experiment? Was that it? He'd always believed there was a time and place for violence. This wasn't it, yet he was unable to control the surge of frustration and rage that knifed through him. Lunging off the bed, he went straight for the doctor.

The man jerked back—his hands slapping out like a girl's in self-defense.

"Hold him down, dammit."

He felt the prick of a needle in his arm. "Leave me alone . . ." he tried to shout. But the injection turned the pain in his head to raw fire. When he heard a scream, he wondered if it was him—or someone else.

AS soon as Jordan climbed into his Mercedes, he unknotted his tie, pulled it out of his collar, and tossed it on the passenger seat.

He was still stewing over the disturbing episode with Lindsay Fleming. His reaction tonight had been completely out of kilter. He'd never been the type to lose his

head with a woman, and the experience had challenged his
well-honed need for control.

No. It was more than that, he admitted as he felt his
scalp tighten. For a few moments, when his hand had circled
her wrist—and right afterward—he could have sworn that
something strange was happening between them.

He sighed. *Come off it, Walker. You just need to find a
willing bed partner. And it's not gonna be her.*

With an effort, he put the congressional staffer out of
his mind as he crossed the lobby of his apartment building.
His newly purchased penthouse was on upper Massachusetts Avenue, with a large extra bedroom that he could use
as an office. Until a few months ago, he'd been living in a
slightly shabby building off Sixteenth Street. But it was
scheduled to be gutted and rebuilt, so he'd had to find a re-
placement. And he'd decided that the royalty money he'd
been socking away in bonds and savings certificates might
as well go toward a mortgage payment rather than rent.

Once he'd moved into the new space, he'd liked
the amenities. Like the twenty-four-hour lobby staff and
the gym upstairs, where you could contemplate the city
while you sweated.

Though it was close to midnight, the desk clerk called
him over.

"Mr. Walker, there's a package for you."

"Thank you." Jordan accepted the red-and-blue envelope, then turned away toward the elevator.

As the car took him upstairs, he noted the return address
on the package. It was from Herb Goldman, his former college roommate. Jordan had formed very few close relationships in his life. Herb was one of the people he trusted
implicitly. Probably they'd bonded—as much as Jordan
Walker could bond with anyone—because they'd both been
shy, scared freshman at Dartmouth, neither one of them
with a prep-school background. And each had found it easier to face the brave new world with a buddy at his side.

Even when Jordan had focused on liberal arts courses and Herb had taken mostly science and math, they'd stayed friends.

Herb was married now, settled down with a wife and kids—providing Jordan a window into a world he had decided he could never enter. Not with what he looked on as his personality defect. He'd never been close to his parents. In fact, he'd earned his father's dislike early on because he'd had an overactive imagination. Every time he saw a scary movie or TV show, he'd pictured monsters and kidnappers lurking in the dark, waiting to scoop him up and slit his throat or worse. That made him a sissy in his father's eyes.

His interest in reading over sports had been another one of his sins. So had his devotion to his scruffy dog, Digger. He'd related to that dog better than he had to people because a dog's mind was so uncomplicated. If you loved him, he loved you back—twice as hard.

What did it mean when you felt closer to a dog than to people? Nothing good, he was sure.

Jordan had been twelve when Digger escaped from the house and got run over by a truck. And Dad had forbidden his bringing home another pet from the pound. Probably his old man had been the one to leave the screen door unlatched in the first place—to get back at his son for being such a damn dud.

Jordan had been lonely after that, although he'd been careful not to let the old man know about it. He'd told himself that he was just fine living inside his own mind. Yet, deep down, intimacy with another human being was something he'd always craved. At the same time, getting close inevitably brought an acute feeling of discomfort.

So he'd kept to himself. And focused on what he was good at. He might not be able to change his personal style, but he could damn well make sure his career was something to be proud of.

Since he didn't want to get caught like Dan Rather with radioactive fake documents, he'd express-mailed a copy of the pathology report he'd gotten in Wilmington to Herb. A research physician with the FDA, his friend had helped him out on a couple of projects and was in an excellent position to evaluate the material from Hamilton.

As he stepped inside his eighth-floor apartment, Jordan stopped and looked around. He still did a double take every time he took in the subtly textured tweed carpet, track lighting, onyx coffee table, and gray sectional sofa that were as dramatic as the view from the floor-to-ceiling windows.

The whole package was a lot grander than he was used to. In truth, his former apartment had been furnished with pieces he'd picked up at garage sales and the Georgetown Flea Market. But he'd thrown the old stuff out when he'd seen this place and been told he could get a good deal on the furnishings, because the diplomat who'd ordered up the decor was being recalled to Bolivia.

The only things he'd brought were his books, clothing, and a few mementos—like his Pulitzer paperweight.

He was antsy to get to the contents of the mailer, but the signal light on his answering machine was blinking.

When he pressed the Play button, he heard Leonard Hamilton's raspy voice.

"Any day next week would be convenient for us to meet. Get back to me with the particulars."

Jordan made a note on the pad by the phone. He was jotting down a few questions he was going to ask Hamilton when a completely extraneous image superimposed itself upon his thoughts. Lindsay Fleming, standing in front of a closet unzipping her black silk dress.

Jordan watched, mesmerized, as the creamy skin of her bare back emerged to his view. When she laid the dress on the bed, his pulse quickened. She was wearing a satin bra that exposed the tops of her creamy breasts and a half slip that draped seductively over the swell of her hips.

The erotic image made him instantly hard. As she reached for the catch of her bra, he murmured, "Come on, sweetheart, take off your bra and turn around. Let me see your nipples. I'll bet they're pink, right?"

Instead of turning, she froze. After several heartbeats she glanced over her shoulder, her face wary as though she knew he was watching her.

He drew in a shaky breath, half convinced that he'd stepped into the Twilight Zone.

Immediately he dismissed the notion. He'd met a woman who attracted him, and he was undressing her in his mind. But a fantasy was like a movie in which you were the producer and director, where the actors did anything you wanted. And she was resisting him.

My God, it was as though he were actually a voyeur, and she was somehow aware of his prying eyes.

A mental shutter snapped closed, breaking the contact, and Jordan was left with nothing but the same disoriented feeling he had experienced at the senator's when his hand had circled her wrist.

"Jesus, what's gotten into you tonight?" he muttered.

Needing to get out of the room, he strode past the king-sized bed to the walk-in closet, where he changed out of his party duds and into a comfortable pair of worn jeans and a dark T-shirt. Next he opened a kitchen cabinet, took a bottle of bourbon, and poured a double shot over ice cubes.

Too much alcohol dulled his brain. But he'd discovered that one drink helped him focus his thoughts when he was having trouble concentrating. Somehow the liquor blocked out the background noise in his head. At some level or other the interference was always there—like a radio station that wouldn't quite come in. There had been a time when he had desperately wanted to tune out the static and hear the transmission clearly. The attempt had only led to frustration. It was like trying to open a door without a knob—or climb a sheer cliff without a grappling hook. There had been no way to make any progress, and he'd finally given up trying.

As he'd matured, he'd learned to ignore the cacophony, except when it became so strong that he couldn't think about anything else. Once or twice, he'd tried to talk to Herb about it. His friend simply couldn't relate to what Jordan was trying to describe. The knowledge had been one more piece of evidence to support his secret thesis: that he was different from other people. Damaged. A freak, if you wanted to put a name to it.

After a few quick swallows, he set down the bourbon on a glass-topped end table, retrieved the package from Herb, and slit it open.

He discovered quickly that he didn't need the alcohol to concentrate. The material inside the envelope was enough to rivet his attention. On top was a letter in Herb's precise writing:

Walker, what kind of trouble are you in this time? The pathology report you sent describes a case of a fatal toxic reaction to a compound that, to the best of my knowledge, has never been available on the streets.

I notice you carefully deleted any facts that would tell me where this information came from or the individual it describes. I've searched our databases. Where in the hell did you get this material? By law it should have been sent directly to us from the coroner's office where it originated. But I can find no such report.

Jordan, I wouldn't go out on a limb like this for anyone else. However, after careful thought, I've decided you've got a better chance of figuring out what's going on than I

do. As you know, our records are confidential; but I'm
going to give you some background information. If
anybody asks, you didn't hear it from me. But please, for
Christ's sake, keep me informed.
    Regards,
    Herb

Jordan read over the letter again, feeling adrenaline
course through his system. Once in a while a journalist was
lucky and skillful enough to crack open a story the government was desperate to bury. Like his own exposé on excess
military spending. Tonight, he didn't need his sixth sense
to tell him he was on to something else big. Herb had prac-
tically spelled it out.

Okay, so what exactly did he have here? Quickly he
turned to the thick sheaf of reports and began to scan the
pages. They described an army chemical weapons project
designed to neutralize a large enemy force with minimal
risk to friendly troops. The project, called Granite Wall,
had supposedly been terminated in the early eighties. During the animal trials, a number of lab workers had accidentally been poisoned by a genetically engineered drug. And
the autopsies detailed how their organs had been affected.

To his layman's eye, the findings looked surprisingly
similar to the recent pathology report that Hamilton had
given him.

Jordan took another swallow of bourbon, this time to re-
lieve the uneasy feeling that suddenly squeezed his gut.
Leonard Hamilton had been right. His son hadn't died in a
boating accident. Either he'd taken an illegal substance
that was tainted with poison, or somebody had deliberately
doused him with the stuff.

But why?

Hamilton had said that digging into the circumstances
of his son's death could be dangerous. Which was why

Jordan hadn't asked Herb for anything more than an opinion on a medical report. Now he knew he'd better keep his friend out of the loop.

LINDSAY snuggled deeper under the covers. In her dream she was dressed in the T-shirt and panties she'd worn to bed, but she stood in the family room of her mother and stepfather's sprawling beach house. She'd played here as a child, turning a dozen dolls and stuffed animals into students in her schoolroom. She'd written spelling lessons and math problems on a chalkboard. And she'd read stories aloud and organized sing-alongs, because that way she was surrounded by a whole classroom of pupils, and she didn't have to try and fit in with a bunch of other children.

She looked around at the sailcloth-covered couches and rag rug warming the wide boards of the pine floor. Her toys were long gone, replaced by the computer and a wide-screen television set her parents had recently purchased.

"Mom?"

Her mother didn't answer, and she hurried down the hall toward the kitchen, where Mom had taught her to cook and bake. But she never reached it. The kitchen had vanished, and the hall stretched in front of her, dimly lit and endless. Heart pounding, she began to run—knowing she had to get away, even when she didn't understand what she was running from.

When she came to a fork, she stopped—confused. Whirling, she saw only a blank wall.

Fear constricted her throat as she tried to decide what to do. Going back the way she'd come was impossible. So she chose the left-hand fork and began to run.

Mist swirled around her, blocking out the walls. And her bare feet thumped against the unseen floorboards.

Then, somewhere behind her, other footsteps sounded, sending a shiver of dread down her spine.

How could anyone be back there? The hallway behind her had vanished. Yet she felt a man's presence behind her. Although he was trying to be quiet, she heard him. Not just with her ears. She sensed him on a subliminal level that was stronger than hearing—stronger than sight.

It was someone she knew and feared.

She wanted to hide. But there was nowhere to go but forward, into the unknown.

She wanted to believe the mist would conceal her. But that was a lie. Because she *knew* the man felt her presence, just as she felt his.

"Lindsay?" His voice drifted toward her down the corridor, wrapping around her body, sinking into her very cells.

She would have run then, but the floorboards had turned to spongy ground, slowing her steps.

"No," she whispered.

Behind her, the man spoke, his voice whispering in her mind. "You can't escape me. Don't even try."

She had stepped into the hallway wearing a T-shirt and panties. Now she was naked. Defenseless. He was behind her. No, somehow he was in front of her. She longed to run to him. Clasp him in her arms. Take his essence into her body. At the same time she knew she had to get away—or he would destroy her.

"I can rescue you from all the lonely days and nights." His voice wove itself into her mind.

She felt the promise. And the pain. His pain. His loneliness as well as her own.

She saw his face through a screen of mist. It was Jordan Walker. He stepped from behind a bend in the hallway, and she saw his body, as naked as hers. He was tall, muscular, very male. Challenge, anticipation, yearning all mingled in his blue eyes as he held out his hand to her.

When she'd come home after the party, she'd thought of him, then she'd felt him probing her mind, asking her to take off her bra and turn around for him. She'd resisted the order. Now she should run from him, but her feet were rooted to the spot where she stood.

Her whole body tingled as she waited for his touch. When it came, it was like a bolt of blue-white energy, spreading a newfound sensual pleasure over her skin. Stunned, she melted into his embrace, naked skin clasped to naked skin.

Her arms came up to circle his neck; her cheek settled against his shoulder as he pulled her close, held her fast. Then one long-fingered hand wove into her hair while the other caressed a hot, erotic path down her back to the base of her spine.

"Yes. Oh, yes." The words sighed from her lips. She had never felt anything so sensual. And she knew she had longed for his touch all her life. Needed it. And never found it.

She moved urgently against him, the hard points of her nipples pressing against his chest, increasing her arousal—and his. Liquid heat invaded her body. It was good. So good. More than she could ever have imagined.

Then all at once it was too much. The pleasure was so intense it hurt. Prickles of pain danced across her skin, sending sharp, probing darts into her mind. Gasping, she pushed against his chest and tried to wrench away.

He clasped her by the shoulders. "Don't fight me. It won't work if you fight me."

"What's happening to us?" she begged for an answer.

Instead of speaking, he lowered his head to hers, his lips a bare whisper from her mouth. In that charged moment she knew that if he kissed her, there was no going back. Her body would flow into his. Her mind would . . .

There were no words for the mixture of deep longing and primal fear that welled up from the depth of her soul. The fear was stronger, and she brought her hands up, pushing frantically against his chest.

"No. Please don't."

All at once, she was alone. Her mother's house had vanished, and she was sitting up in bed, her skin covered with perspiration, her heart threatening to pound itself though the wall of her chest. Her hands clutched at the tangled bedclothes as she fought to anchor herself to reality. To her bedroom.

She was awake, but the dream still held her in its power. Closing her eyes, she touched her own body, intensifying the erotic sensations from the dream. Her past experiences with men had been lukewarm at best. Yet here she was— turned on past endurance and building a white-hot fantasy about a man she didn't even like.

"Jordan Walker." She whispered his name into the darkness, then pressed her palms against the mattress. Taking several shallow breaths, she tried to bring her body and her emotions under control. It was just a dream, she told herself. It didn't mean anything. It hadn't meant anything when he'd touched her at the party, either.

Deep down she knew she was lying to herself, but she wasn't ready to deal with the experience.

Sighing, she glanced at the clock. Five A.M. She could have used another hour's sleep. But she didn't want to risk a repetition of the dream, didn't want to face the hot, sexual intensity or the fear.

Instead of remaining in bed, she swung her legs over the side and headed for a cold shower. As long as she was up, she could use her home computer to start digging into the Navy equipment records that Senator Bridgewater had requested in an e-mail from Florida. Apparently, he'd talked to a constituent who was concerned about accidents on aircraft carriers.

After dressing and fixing a cup of instant coffee, she sat down at the computer in the spare bedroom and pulled up the Navy record.

Bridgewater had said he wanted the report as soon as he got back, and she'd thought there was no way she could meet that deadline, given the other research projects already on her desk. But maybe she'd manage it after all.

She paused for a moment, thinking about her boss. He'd been on edge about this trip. And usually he shared his itinerary with the office.

But the schedule he'd distributed left out several blocks of time. Which could mean one of several things. Maybe he was seeing a woman, and he didn't want it splashed all over the tabloids. Or maybe he was on a fishing expedition for campaign money, and when he came back, he'd be closer to announcing a run for the presidency.

After noting research sources, she sent the list of URLs to her office address and turned off the computer.

She was just about to leave her apartment when a knock at the door made her freeze—suddenly caught in a swirl of emotions that she'd suppressed while she was working.

Was that Jordan Walker? Would he have the nerve to come here? Did he know she'd dreamed of him?

No. He couldn't! Yet she didn't believe the reassurance.

On legs that didn't feel entirely steady, she walked to the door. But when she looked through the spy lens into the hallway, she was surprised, relieved, and disappointed to see Sid Becker standing in the hallway.

"Sid?"

"Can I come in?"

Puzzled, she opened the door. Last night at Senator Conroy's party, Sid had looked like something heavy was weighing on his mind—although he'd denied it. This morning he looked several degrees more upset. There were dark circles under his eyes. And his lips were set in a grim line.

Stepping back, she ushered him into her apartment, then closed the door and turned back to him.

"What is it? Are you in trouble?"

Instead of answering, he walked to the window and looked out at the little patch of woods that shaded the apartment.

"Nice view."

"You didn't come to talk about the scenery."

"Probably I shouldn't have come at all."

"Why don't you sit down and tell me what's going on," she said gently.

He hesitated for a moment, then walked to one of her wingback chairs and sat down, his back Marine straight as always.

"How can I help you?"

He dragged in a breath and let it out before saying, "Lindsay, I think of you as a friend."

"Yes."

"I want to ask a favor. My cousin Mark Greenwood lived with us from the time he was ten—after his mother died of encephalitis and his dad started drinking. Mark is like a younger brother to me. We kept in touch until a couple of weeks ago. Now I can't get him on the phone. Every time I call, they tell me he's not available."

"Where do I fit in to this?"

"He's a security guard at . . ." He stopped and grimaced. "I guess I have to tell you the name. A facility called Maple Creek. It's supposed to be an agricultural testing station. But nobody would have a squad of armed men guarding string beans."

"Why do you think I can help?"

"You and I exchange information because Senator Bridgewater heads the Armed Services Committee. He might be able to find out if anything strange is going on at Maple Creek."

"What do you suspect?"

His expression hardened. "I suspect that they're testing biological agents out there—and something deadly got loose. I suspect that Mark's sick or dead, and they're saying he's unavailable because they're trying to keep a lid on the situation. Like—you know—when China tried to hide its avian flu epidemic."

Alarm leaped in her throat. "You . . . mean hundreds of people died?"

"Yeah, like that." He pressed his knuckle against his lip. "Well, that's my worst-case scenario. Probably it's not that bad. Probably they've got it contained. Like when the Russians had that anthrax accident at one of their labs. But if you can get Bridgewater to start asking questions, maybe you'll break through the cover-up."

"I'll do what I can," Lindsay murmured. "But the senator isn't coming back from Florida until tomorrow morning, and I may not be able to speak to him about your concerns until he's settled in."

"I understand." He cleared his throat. "Maybe you can do some digging on your own."

"Maybe."

"If you find out anything, don't call me from the office."

"All right," she answered, wondering exactly what she was getting herself into.

He reached into his pocket and pulled out a folded slip of paper. "This is my cell phone number. I'll leave it on."

Lindsay nodded.

"I don't want to get you in trouble," Sid muttered. "But I need to find out about Mark."

"Of course. Can you tell me any more? Do you want a cup of tea or something?"

"No. I'm going to do some Web searching."

"Do you know who's in charge at Maple Creek?" Lindsay asked.

Sid looked like he was holding a silent debate. "I'm not sure," he finally said.

"You mean you don't want to tell me."

"Maybe it's better that way," he said as he climbed to his feet. "Thank you, Lindsay."

"I may not be able to find out anything."

"Then I'll just thank you for trying."

"And it might be something completely different from what you think," she felt compelled to add.

"I hope so."

He looked like he might be about to say something more. Instead, he turned and exited her apartment—leaving her feeling like she was standing in a frozen wasteland wearing only a thin shift. Folding her arms, she rubbed her shoulders, trying to make the cold feeling go away.

CHAPTER
FIVE

SAXON TRINITY WALKED unannounced into his sister's boudoir. It was decorated like the princess's room in a fairy tale, with lots of purple and gold and crystal. He knew she loved the opulent setting, but he could see it gave her no pleasure this evening.

"I'm sorry, but it's almost time," he murmured.

"Okay," his twin sister Willow answered without enthusiasm.

"I wouldn't have set this up if it weren't necessary."

"I know." She gave her thick mane of platinum hair one last toss before swinging away from the mirror. In church she always wore white, in keeping with her virginal image. In the privacy of their stone fortress outside Orlando, she indulged in vibrant colors. Tonight she was dressed in a turquoise evening jumpsuit with a softly draped neckline and wide legs that swirled gracefully as she turned to her brother.

"We agreed that Bridgewater is our best option."

"Sorry. I'm just having . . ."

"Your usual stage fright." He finished the sentence as he often did.

She nodded and crossed the room to clasp his hand.

His grip tightened reassuringly on hers. They had planned this evening carefully, because it was important.

Something was in the air. Neither of them knew what it was, but Sax had felt it stalking them. A new danger. An unforeseen wrinkle in the fabric of the universe that might upset the comfortable life they'd carved out for themselves.

"Bridgewater is a man of strong will. Pulling him in so quickly won't be easy."

"You'll wow him," he murmured. "We both will."

He wasn't a modest man. He knew that he and Willow gave off a sense of rock-star energy. But it wasn't mere sex appeal that had made them the leaders of a New Age movement that had grown from a tent-show novelty to a successful upscale ministry in just a few short years.

"Together, we can move mountains," he murmured. They had invented the phrase during the bad times when every new foster home had held an unknown terror. And it was still the bedrock of their relationship.

Musical chimes sounded.

"Showtime."

Leaving the bedroom, Sax made his unhurried way to the massive stone foyer of the mansion they'd purchased from an oil billionaire who'd gone back to the Middle East. The servants had been dismissed for the evening. Only the twins and their guest would be present tonight.

"Welcome to our home," Sax greeted Daniel Bridgewater. Before setting up the meeting, he'd researched the man carefully. A former trial attorney who'd made a name for himself on several high-profile cases, he'd proved that he was as effective in the political arena as he had been in the courtroom. Even in his younger days he'd boasted a head of vibrant silver hair. Now that he was in his early fifties, it only added to his mature good looks. But the senator's short stature surprised him. He'd looked taller on television.

DAN Bridgewater glanced up and saw Willow Trinity standing on the steps. Despite his resolve to be cautious tonight, the sight of the beautiful blonde on the steps made his stomach muscles tighten. She and her brother were both striking. But while Sax projected masculine resolve, she was a study in feminine vulnerability.

A few years ago he wouldn't have risked any involvement with the Perfect Pair, as the press had irreverently dubbed them. But their success had made them respectable, and when they'd suggested they might make a large campaign contribution, he'd been interested. Now he needed to find out what they wanted in return.

The pair presided over a mother church in Orlando. And they staged intimate gatherings in various cities around the country. Although they'd been offered half a dozen lucrative television deals, they'd so far resisted—which made them more mysterious, as far as today's media culture was concerned.

Dan shook Saxon's well-manicured yet strongly masculine hand, then turned to his sister, who had joined him at the foot of the steps.

"Thank you for coming," she murmured, holding his hand just a few seconds longer than necessary.

"The pleasure is mine," Bridgewater replied, his gaze captured for a moment in the azure depths of her eyes.

"Let's go into the library where we can be comfortable," Sax suggested. Turning, he led the way down a hall past a spacious sitting room and a formal dining room that looked like it had been taken in its entirety from a baronial castle and relocated to Florida. The library beyond it was rich with dark wood paneling and the aroma of leather. Dan stopped for a moment to inspect the glass case near the door, which displayed an old Bible inlaid with gold leaf.

"This is a work of art," he commented.

"The only other one is in Saint John's College, Cambridge," his blond host informed him. "Perhaps you'd like to see my collection of first editions later. But make yourself at home now." Sax gestured toward one of the comfortable sofas flanking the stone fireplace, where real logs burned.

Dan and Willow took one sofa. Sax sat opposite them.

"My brother and I don't drink anything alcoholic. Can I offer you some herbal tea?" Willow suggested, nodding toward the silver tea service on the table.

"That would be fine," Bridgewater answered, although he would have preferred a martini.

They exchanged small talk while Willow served tea and almond cookies. As they sipped the pungent beverage, Sax stretched out his long legs and crossed them at the ankles. "You know, since we became interested in the Save the Ecosphere movement, we've come to see local and national politics as an important vehicle for change."

"Um," Dan acknowledged noncommittally, concentrating on his tea.

Willow slipped off her shoes, curled her feet up under her body, and leaned back into the cushions with an indolence that stopped just short of provocation.

"We've been impressed with your record in Washington," Sax continued. "And we hope you're thinking about a bid for the presidency in the next election."

"I haven't made that decision yet."

"We liked your message in the senatorial campaign two years ago. But you took a bit of a media beating—like those negative ads Governor Baker ran during primetime hours."

"Yes, well, he was drawing on a considerable family fortune, and his PR team was better."

"We know a very dynamic PR man you might want to consider."

Dan shifted in his seat. Saxon Trinity was talking like a political pro. His sister was communicating very effectively on a nonverbal level. "Thanks for the offer, but it's still very early in the process. I haven't even started fundraising yet. But I know it would take a lot of money to pull off a run for the presidency."

"Would a million-dollar contribution from us help on that front?"

Despite Dan's resolve to play it cool, the amount of

money made his teacup rattle in the saucer. A million dollars could buy a nice chunk of TV airtime.

"That's very generous of you," he allowed. "But, of course, legally there would be no way I could accept that much from you and your sister."

"Oh, we'll keep it strictly aboveboard. The contributions will be arranged through hundreds of our most trusted disciples."

Dan was impressed with the strategy. "You seem to have thought this through rather carefully."

"When an individual is deserving, we go out of our way to help him out." Saxon began a laudatory discussion of the senator's voting record.

Well, Dan thought, Trinity had done his homework and had a remarkable grasp of local and national issues. What's more, he understood the rules of the game.

Sax ended with a warm smile. "I believe our interests and yours match rather well, although I did notice you abstained on the vote last term on the Harwood-Gordon bill."

Ah, yes. Removing the tax-exempt status for questionable religious groups. So opposing the bill was what the Perfect Pair wanted in exchange for their money. The measure hadn't come close to passing. Though it was due to be reintroduced, his vote probably wasn't going to make any difference. "I certainly feel that worthy groups shouldn't be excluded from favorable treatment," Dan answered. "Perhaps you could provide me with some more information about your organization."

"Certainly."

Willow reentered the conversation. "Dan. I hope we're on a first-name basis."

"Of course."

"Well, Dan, it sounds as though we'll be able to help each other out."

His eyes swung back to her. For just a moment the million dollars had made him forget her very beautiful presence. Once more, however, he was enthralled. "I'm looking forward to it."

"But I do have a small request to make."

"Yes?"

"My brother and I often ask for spiritual guidance in our daily decision-making process. It's a very private communication, and we rarely invite outsiders to join us. But tonight I have a strong feeling that the three of us should ask for counsel from the universal mind."

Dan studied her earnest expression, silently admitting he'd been fantasizing about something a bit less spiritual. But Willow Trinity was a religious leader. Despite her seductive appearance, she was probably as pure as Mother Teresa. She was so firmly in the spotlight that if she'd been seeing anyone, it would have made the front page of the *National Enquirer*.

"I'm a Christian, of course," he hedged.

"Our beliefs are in harmony with all religions of the world."

"All right," Dan agreed. He was feeling a bit adventuresome, as though the herbal tea might have contained something a little more potent than mulberry leaves. The sensation was far from unpleasant. He had the sudden premonition that what this woman could offer on a spiritual level might be very exciting.

The Trinitys had already gotten up. Saxon dimmed the lights and moved toward a small round table at the side of the room. After setting a cut-glass bowl in the center, he poured in a cup of clear liquid. "Water is for purity, and the circle is the symbol of the never-ending universe," he explained, as they all took seats.

Dan looked from one twin to the other. Though their faces were tranquil, there was a coiled expectancy in their posture.

"Let us share our energy," Willow suggested. Dipping her fingers into the bowl of water, she pressed them briefly against her lips, her tongue licking out to catch a drop. After she repeated the ritual with her brother, her fingers plunged into the bowl again and touched Dan's lips, stroking across them with a slow sensuality. He tasted the water but at the same time felt a spark of carnality that had nothing to do with worship.

"We will join together," Saxon decreed. "Give Willow your hand."

Dan tensed as she reached simultaneously for her brother's hand and also for his where it rested on his knee. As her strong, slender fingers closed around his, he felt a sharp surge almost like an electric current. The energy seemed to flow around the table in a circle from one twin to the other and back to him.

Fighting a jolt of uneasiness, he looked up. Neither Trinity acknowledged that anything out of the ordinary was happening.

He might have leaped up and fled the room. But his body felt too heavy to move. He didn't resist when he felt Sax's grasp on his hand tighten.

Willow gazed at her brother, her face a study in beatification as she began to chant in a minor key. The words were a hymn to the spiritual kinship of all things, and their rhythm seemed to weave themselves through his consciousness.

"Light commands all," she murmured. "Let our collective living force bring us to the Way of the Light."

Dan felt a calm in the room like the quiet before an electrical storm. Then a tiny spark popped in the bowl in the center of the table. Another spark followed and then another. Suddenly the liquid burst into shimmering flames.

Dan knew there was only water in the vessel. He had tasted it. Had the force of their energy really set it on fire? Or was it some elaborate trick? He tried to wrench himself away from the circle. Strong hands that might as well have been links of steel held him fast.

Smiling slightly, Willow turned his palm up, her fingers

massaging a sensual pattern against the fleshy pad at the base of his thumb. His body relaxed; his mind swirled. Tendrils of pleasure snaked up his arm. The delight increased as her fingers moved down his body to the tweed-covered expanse of his thigh.

His mind was floating in the sibilance of her words; his body vibrating to the touch of her fingers. Golden threads of arousal wound around and through his being, stripping away rational thought, binding him to Willow.

There was only her touch, her voice, her commands, and his need to join himself with her. The desire to give of himself was overwhelming. Mental fingers caressed the very core of his essence as her hand stroked over the swollen erection behind his fly.

"Please," he gasped.

What do you want? Her voice spoke in his mind.

"You."

When she unzipped his fly, he breathed out a sigh of relief. He would have reached for her, but he couldn't move. He could only sit there, praying she would give him what he craved.

She freed his swollen red cock, stroked him with delicate fingers. He needed to be inside her. Or if not that, he needed her hand to tighten around him.

Please, he begged again, although this time he wasn't capable of speaking aloud.

As she stroked him, she spoke.

"The three of us are going to be very warm and close," she said, her words filling his head. "There will be an openness, a sharing among us."

"Yes," he gasped.

"We are going to be much more than mere associates, more than friends. Just as your body craves me, your mind is open to me."

"Yes."

"We want you to keep on the alert for us. Be on the

lookout for any incidents that seem strange, out of the ordinary, unexplainable by normal means."

"What incidents?"

"You'll know."

"I'll try."

"That's all we can ask. Come back to us with the information we need, and we will reward you."

"Yes," he answered. In his mind an image formed—Willow, naked and beautiful, holding out her arms.

The mental contact and her hand on his cock brought him deep pleasure, and the craving for more. He was like an addict who had gotten his first taste of an illicit drug and knew he would be back again and again. Because Willow Trinity—this woman who was like a goddess—could offer him more than any other female on earth. The longing for that ecstasy opened his mind more fully to her.

"In a few moments we will part."

Disappointment shot through him. "No! I need . . ."

She squeezed his cock. "I know you want me. We can't do anything more until you come back with information. But you must not tell anyone about this meeting. And when you think about tonight, you will not remember any intimate sexual contact. You will remember only the pleasantries exchanged over the tea and your business conversation with Sax. Say it."

"I will remember only the pleasantries exchanged over the tea and my business conversations with Sax."

"You are impressed with our offer. You trust us. You want to come back so we can talk again."

"I will come back." The pledge was engraved on his mind like an inscription carved into a gravestone.

"And you will report any strange phenomena you hear about."

"What phenomena?" he asked again, desperate to understand.

"Anything out of the ordinary. Anything to do with national security. Anything you hear in the defense community—or outside of it."

"Can you be more specific?"

"No. Just do your best."

"All right. But please . . ."

"Later. Much later."

He wanted to scream when she pressed his erection back into his pants, and zipped him back up, leaving him aching and unfulfilled.

Only her silent promise of more intimate contact in the days and weeks to come kept him from losing his sanity.

SAX ushered their guest to the door. When the senator had driven away, he returned to his sister, helped her to the couch, and cuddled her in his arms.

She was exhausted, and he stroked his lips against her cheek.

"Did he make you hot?"

She laughed. "Not hardly."

"Will he come through for us?" Sax asked.

"If he can. But we have to reinforce his resolve with campaign contributions."

"That will be the easy part," Sax answered, then sighed. "I just wish you could have been more specific about what we wanted."

"What you warned me of—it's still too vague?"

"Yes, but I think it has to do with other people like us. And national security."

"How?"

They had been over this territory before. All he could do was give her the same answers. "I wish to hell I could see the future better. Maybe I'll know more when the time gets closer."

"You said we were unique."

"I thought we were. But . . . I'm picking up . . . vibrations."

She laughed nervously. "You sound like a New Age guru."

He joined in the laughter. "I *am* a New Age guru."

"If there are others like us . . . they could be stronger."

"If anyone had gotten stronger . . . I'd know it. I'd feel it," he said confidently. "What we have to do is find them and kill them before they can become a threat to us."

"Yes," she murmured. They had been poor and weak for fifteen years. Today they had everything they wanted. But the fear still nipped at her heels.

Together, they had the potency to hold it at bay. And only by keeping the power for themselves would they stay warm and safe and comfortable in the new life they had built together.

CHAPTER
SIX

LINDSAY SAT AT her desk going over the Defense Department research reports. She had enough seniority to rate a small office to herself, but she could sense the buzz of tension around her.

The senator was due back any minute, and he would have notes for staffers demanding immediate answers to questions from constituents.

Although Lindsay couldn't see him from her room at the back of the complex, she knew the moment he arrived and marked his progress through the suite as he gave orders and exchanged greetings.

When he stepped into her office, she asked, "Did you have a good trip, Senator?"

"Very. Have you finished with the summaries of the weapons systems reports?"

"They're almost done."

"Anything unusual?"

"They're what you'd expect, if you expect the Defense Department to play fast and loose with the taxpayers' money."

"Uh-huh."

Lindsay looked up at Bridgewater. He was watching her, and for an instant she was caught by a strangely intent expression she'd never seen before in his gray eyes.

Then he no longer seemed to be focused on her. In fact, his features had turned flat and vacant, as if he'd stepped out of the room and left his body beside her desk.

"Senator?"

Bridgewater blinked, and his crisp demeanor returned. "Is there some problem, Lindsay?"

She swallowed. "Why, no."

"Then give the summaries to Margaret, and I'll get back to you in a couple of days."

He looked like he was about to leave. Lindsay cleared her throat. "If you have a minute, I had an inquiry about our chemical and biological weapons program."

She knew from his sudden sharp expression that she'd caught his attention. "What about it?"

"The information came from a confidential source worried that there might have been a flap at a secure research facility."

"Is the source credible?"

"Yes."

"Are we talking about Fort Detrick?"

"No. A place called Maple Creek."

He tipped his head to one side, watching her. "You ever heard of it before?"

"No, sir."

The look on his face made the skin on her arms prickle.

"Can we make some inquiries?" she said, reaching for a pad of paper.

"I'd better handle it myself," he answered.

Lindsay nodded, wondering if she would be able to get any of the information back to Sid Becker. Or whether doing that would be a bad idea. That depended on what Bridgewater found out. She thought about relaying Sid's specific concern. Then she decided it was a bad idea to get her boss stirred up about a nightmare disaster, when the problem at Maple Creek was probably nothing of the sort.

THE drugstore on upper Wisconsin Avenue was wedged into an old shopping center, and the narrow aisles were crammed with cosmetics, over-the-counter remedies, and an assortment of goods ranging from corn chips and Cokes to windshield wiper fluid and notepaper.

It was a lot like the five-and-dime store a couple of blocks from where Jordan had grown up in New London, except that there was a pharmacy in the back.

He had to step around a young woman on her knees stocking the shelves. She kept her gaze averted from him, and he saw that she was setting out boxes of condoms.

When he reached the pay telephone, he glanced over his shoulder, feeling suddenly as jumpy as a bullfrog on a stove burner.

Either one of his own phones would have given him more privacy, but he was gathering sensitive information, and some of the agencies he planned to contact kept electronic phone logs. Since he didn't want his inquiries traced to him, he was stuck with using a public phone.

That morning he'd made a list of all the sources that might be useful. The trick was to get information without tipping anyone off to his real purpose.

Lindsay Fleming was a good bet. As an aide to Daniel Bridgewater, she had the inside track on special Defense Department projects—which would give him a legitimate reason for calling.

In the three days since he'd seen her, she'd continued to invade his thoughts. He'd looked her up on the Net and found out a great deal about her. She was the daughter of Harold Fleming, a former Connecticut state congressman. She'd grown up on a big estate outside Darien, with all the advantages he'd never had. Servants. Riding lessons. Ballet lessons. Art lessons. A top girl's prep school. Harvard. The Ivy League background was one of the few things they had in common, although she'd arrived by a much easier route.

After college, while he'd sent out a hundred résumés to newspapers all over the country, she'd spent the summer touring Europe, then come back in the fall and waltzed into a paid internship on Capitol Hill, courtesy of the strings her father could pull. Three months later she stepped into a regular staff vacancy.

Of course, he had to give her credit. She'd earned the promotion on merit. Since then she'd racked up an admirable record—changing jobs several times as she solidified her reputation for reliability.

She was cool, confident, and intense. In some circles, she'd earned the nickname "Ice Princess."

That was consistent with the brush-off she'd given him two days ago. And in truth, he found her intimidating. Certainly not the kind of woman who was going to be impressed by a guy who'd clawed his way into the middle class.

No, be honest. He was more than middle class. So far out of his parents' league that his dad had used his "snootiness" as an excuse to break off relations.

He knew his mom was secretly proud that her son was a respected journalist. But that didn't mean she was willing to buck her husband's orders and invite the prodigal son to Thanksgiving dinner.

So he was one of those displaced persons who inhabited the nation's capital. One of the throngs who had come here from Connecticut or New Mexico or Iowa.

Most of them made trips back home to see the folks. He didn't have that luxury. He'd been forced to make his own life. He'd never pictured himself settled down into a stable relationship with anyone, but now he'd met a woman he wanted to know better. Except that she was like his father—unwilling to give him the benefit of the doubt. Ironically, for entirely different reasons.

Still, he felt compelled to break through the barrier she'd erected between them. Although he understood that the compulsion was a good part sexual, there was another element that he couldn't name. A need to connect with

Lindsay Fleming that was different from anything he'd felt before. Instinctively he knew that if he made any mistakes, he'd frighten her away.

The prospect left him feeling strangely empty. And edgy. He muttered a low curse. He was making a case of lust into something it wasn't. Still, he decided to wait on contacting her until he could think about his approach.

He shook his head. He knew how to get an interview with the Secretary of Defense, if he wanted it. But he didn't know squat about the fine points of male-female relations.

Looking down at his notes, he picked the next name on the list. Ed Wilkerson, who worked at the Classified Archives. Maybe he'd like to get together for lunch, talk shop, and give him some leads.

He reached Ed on the first try and chatted about work for a few minutes before making a luncheon appointment for Monday.

He skipped the next few names and went for something more direct—the physician who had handled the pathology report on Todd Hamilton.

A woman picked up on the first ring. "Dr. Charles Lucas's office."

"Is Dr. Lucas in?"

There was a pause on the other end of the line. "I'm sorry. Dr. Lucas passed away yesterday."

He heard himself saying, "But I have a report he wrote a couple of weeks ago. How did he die?"

"It was heart failure."

Stunned, Jordan mumbled, "I'm . . . sorry."

"We were all so shocked. He was such a young, healthy man. Nobody suspected he had a heart condition."

"Yes, I see."

"Would you mind holding for a moment?"

Jordan's hand tightened on the receiver. "Why?"

"We're transferring all of Dr. Lucas's calls to another extension."

"Oh, yeah?" Jordan stifled the impulse to fling away the receiver as though he'd accidentally picked up a poisonous snake. Instead he carefully replaced it into the cradle, turned, and strode toward the front of the store. Behind him, the phone he'd just used rang, but he didn't break his stride.

When he'd started this investigation, he'd thought that Leonard Hamilton was paranoid. The further he got into the subject of Todd Hamilton's death, the more he agreed that something strange was going on.

Controlling the urge to sprint down the sidewalk, he walked at a steady pace to the side street where he'd left his car. As he climbed behind the wheel and started the engine, he told himself that no one could dispatch an operative to a previously unknown location within seconds of tracing a call. Still, he felt the way he had when he'd been a small kid waiting for his father to punish him for some minor infraction. Those sessions were always after dinner. Dad would make him choke down food before taking him into the bedroom and pulling his leather belt from its loops.

As he drove, he clenched his teeth, struggling to wipe away that image. Instead of turning up Nebraska toward his home office, he kept going down Wisconsin Avenue, past McLean Gardens. Where Lindsay lived. He knew because he'd made a point of getting her address.

Glancing in the rearview mirror every minute or so, he continued down the hill into Georgetown. Finally satisfied that he wasn't being followed, he made a right turn on P Street and started uptown again on a side street parallel to the avenue.

As he drove, he thought about the drugstore. It was understaffed, with only one clerk working the front register, one pharmacist on duty, and the woman replacing the condom stock. She hadn't wanted to look at him. The pharmacist had been filling a prescription. The clerk at the counter had been busy ringing up sales. So probably none of them would be able to describe the man who'd stopped in to use the phone.

He hoped.

Deliberately he turned his attention back to pathology reports—and heart failure. He'd once read a murder mystery in which a doctor had told a detective that any death could be attributed to heart failure.

Of course, Dr. Lucas's untimely demise could simply be a coincidence. The phone ringing ten seconds after he'd put it down could be a coincidence, too. But Jordan was willing to bet his next royalty check that neither of those assumptions was true. Someone had decided that Lucas's information on Todd Hamilton's death wasn't going any further.

And whoever had taken out the doctor was having the dead man's incoming calls traced so they could find if he'd talked to anyone.

Paranoid conclusions? He didn't think so.

Jordan slapped his palm against the steering wheel. Probably the smart thing to do was drop the investigation right now. Yet he sensed he was on to something big. Todd Hamilton had been killed by a drug used in an Army weapons-testing program called Granite Wall that was supposed to have terminated years ago. And it looked like the doctor responsible for the Hamilton pathology report had been murdered to protect the secret that someone was still working with the poison.

Jordan wanted to know why. And how. And who. And he was damn well going to finish what Leonard Hamilton had started.

CHAPTER
SEVEN

JUST BEFORE THE phone rang, Lindsay felt a tingling anticipation.

"Hello?"

"This is Jordan Walker. We met at Sam Conroy's party."

"I remember." There was no way to forget, not after she'd conjured up an erotic dream about the man. Now her heart had started thumping inside her chest at the sound of his voice.

"How are you?"

"You didn't call to ask the state of my health," she answered, trying to make her voice brisk.

He sighed and continued with slow deliberation. "I think we got off on the wrong foot. I'm trying to observe the niceties, if you'll let me."

She'd hardened her features. Now they softened. "Okay."

"I have some business to discuss."

She didn't know whether to be relieved or disappointed. "What?"

He hesitated for a fraction of a second. "I'd rather not say over the phone."

"If you're digging into my boss's background for a stinging exposé, you're not going to get any help from me," she answered instantly.

"It's not about Bridgewater."

"Then who?"

Ignoring the question, he said, "Will you meet me for dinner after work?"

She should refuse. She hardly knew Jordan Walker. She

told herself she didn't want to know him, even when she realized that was a lie. But the tone of his voice told her he had something important on his mind.

"Lindsay, don't turn me down."

Now he sounded like a man asking for a date. Whether or not the business discussion was a ploy to see her again, she found herself saying, "Yes."

When she heard him expel the breath he'd apparently been holding, she felt a little thrill of elation.

"I made a reservation at I Ricchi."

"That was brash of you."

"Yeah, well, I figured I could always eat a solitary bowl of pasta puttanesca if you said no."

"You may still end up doing that," she answered, realizing that she was enjoying the sparring, then added, "Don't pick me up."

"How did you know I was going to offer?"

"You're observing the niceties," she answered quickly, telling herself that was how she'd anticipated the offer.

"Okay. You know where it is?"

"Yes."

"Six o'clock."

"If I'm not there by six-fifteen . . ."

"I'll figure you got stuck in traffic," he said.

Before they could continue the conversation, the light on her second line blinked. Welcoming the interruption, she said, "Got to go."

KURT MacArthur studied the notation on his computer screen, then dialed Jim Swift's cell phone, hoping they'd gotten lucky this time.

"I see there was a call to the doctor's office—from Washington."

"Yes," Swift answered. "From a public phone booth, as I noted."

"Where?"

"A drugstore on upper Wisconsin Avenue."

"Can the staff at the drugstore tell you who made the call?"

"Negative. All they can say is they think it was a man. That eliminates slightly less than half of the D.C. population."

"I want to know who it was and why."

"As soon as I have anything, I'll get back to you."

"I want to know who ordered that pathology report. Go in there and get it."

"I'm on it."

Struggling to master his frustration, Kurt signed off. If anybody could unearth the identity of the mystery caller, it was Jim Swift.

And what if that was beyond even his top investigator's powers?

Kurt repressed a shudder. He'd never looked back during his climb to the heights of Washington power. His work had become his life. His recreation. His mission. His fun.

And Swift and the others under him had become his family. He'd nurtured them, praised them, trained them, given them a sense of purpose. Like Calvin Crandall had done with him, he knew. Only he'd cultivated a more personal sense of loyalty. Nobody was going to sneak up behind him the way he'd gotten the drop on Calvin.

Anyway, there was no need for it. He wasn't going to lose his nerve—or his resolve. He was going to continue as Crandall's director into old age. And if he never got a medal for his service to the country, that was all right, because he was proud of his silent sacrifices and proud of the difference he'd made to national security.

The raid on Maple Creek had been a piece of bad luck. He would find out what the hell had gone wrong there— and set his world right again. He had no other choice. He had acquired too much power. Stepped on too many toes.

And if one of his enemies caught the scent of blood, he was done for.

LINDSAY stepped into the upscale Italian restaurant on Nineteenth Street and looked around. It was still early for dinner in D.C., and there were only a few people enjoying the elegant, understated atmosphere. Memories came back to her. Her mother and stepfather had taken her here to celebrate her first job. She knew they were proud of her career. They were still proud of that aspect of her life. And they'd given up asking who she was dating—because they knew there would be nothing new on that front. They'd taken what they could get. She should be grateful for that. Still, she couldn't stop herself from feeling guilty that she would never give them the grandchild they longed for.

She chopped off that thought as the hostess came hurrying toward her.

"Can I help you?"

"I'm meeting someone here." Looking around, she spotted Jordan Walker sitting at a corner table sipping from a tall glass. He looked preoccupied.

But he glanced up as though he knew she'd entered the door. Well, why not? He was waiting for her, wasn't he?

Crossing the handmade tile foyer, she walked up a step into the partitioned dining area.

The intensity of his stare made her heart start to pound—the way it had in her dream.

No. Not the damn dream again.

She didn't need fantasies from her subconscious to make her nervous. The piercing look in the man's dark eyes was quite enough. Still, she'd taken his invitation as a challenge—that she could have a meal with him without experiencing any of the feelings she'd found both frightening and exhilarating.

"Thank you for coming," he said as she pulled out the

chair opposite him. He was coatless, and she supposed his blue Oxford cloth shirt was meant to indicate that the meeting was casual. But the tight lines of his face told her otherwise.

She'd taken the Red Line straight from work, then walked from Dupont Circle. Now she felt overdressed in her navy suit and burgundy silk blouse. But she kept the jacket on as though it could serve as a barrier between them.

"What did you want to talk about?" she said.

"Let's order first."

Letting him set the pace of the meeting, Lindsay scanned the menu. Before she could make a selection, the waitress asked if she wanted a drink.

She glanced at Jordan's tall glass of iced tea, then ordered the same before going back to the menu. Any other time the Northern Italian specialties would have tempted her appetite. This evening she wasn't sure she could choke down more than a bowl of soup.

"The Italian bread soup is good," Walker said.

Her head jerked up.

"What's wrong?" He looked at her, then around the almost empty room.

"Nothing's wrong."

"Something."

"I was thinking about soup—just as you mentioned it."

"Maybe because we were both looking at the appetizers."

She nodded, then turned back to the selections as the waitress set down her drink.

At the corner of her vision she could see her dinner partner's fingers curved over the edge of the menu he held. At the party he'd touched her with that hand. The pressure of his skin against hers had created sensations within her that she'd never experienced before. What if she reached out and laid her fingers against his flesh? Would it happen again? Or had her memory blown the incident completely out of proportion?

When the waiter came over, she ordered an appetizer portion of homemade mushroom ravioli and a tomato-and-mozzarella salad.

"That's all you're having?" Walker asked.

"I'm not very hungry."

He ordered the bread soup and the mixed Italian grill.

"What business do you think we need to talk about?" she asked when they were alone again.

He lowered his voice and leaned forward across the table. "Bridgewater heads the Armed Services Committee."

"Yes."

"I was wondering if he's gotten any recent updates from Fort Detrick," he said in an even lower tone.

"You mean where they store the chemical and biological warfare agents?" she asked in a similar voice, wanting to make certain they were both on the same page.

"Not just store. Test."

"Okay."

"You'd know about it if Bridgewater had received a report on something new they were doing? Or an old project that's back on line. Maybe moved to another facility."

The recent conversation with Sid Becker leaped into her mind. He'd been asking about something similar. "Like where?" she hazarded.

He shrugged. "I'm trying to check out a tip from a confidential source. I was hoping you could help."

She felt like they were sitting across a poker table, not a dining table. He was doing the same thing she'd done with Bridgewater—asking a question, but asking cautiously. And she was being just as circumspect.

"You want me to do your dirty work for you?"

"Unfortunately, the source is dead. I tried to call him this morning. His office told me that he'd died of heart failure. Which is odd, considering that he was a relatively young man."

The information made her scalp tingle. Before she could

ask for more details, the waiter appeared with the salad and the soup.

She sat staring at the fat white slabs of mozzarella lying on top of tomato rounds, the red-and-white composition arranged on green romaine leaves suddenly astonishingly unappealing.

Walker hadn't touched his soup. He was looking down at the table—no, looking at her hand where it rested next to her plate. Lord, had he been thinking about touching her— the way she had?

"What's your motivation for telling me any of that?" she whispered.

"When I called my source this morning, I was trans- ferred somewhere else. I'm pretty sure there's a trace on his phone."

"Are you trying to scare me?"

"No."

Was that a lie? Unbidden, the thought popped into her mind that there was a way to find out. Before she could stop herself, she reached across the table and laid her fin- gers over his, knowing in that moment that this was why she had really agreed to meet him.

She had come back for more of what had passed be- tween them—fearing she would never get it and fearing at the same time that she would.

She felt the warmth of his skin. But that simple sensa- tion was buried below the swirl of awareness that en- veloped her.

The breath froze in her lungs as she grappled with con- fusion, elation, terror, and a sexual pull like nothing she had ever imagined in her life.

It was more than she had bargained for. Although she had initiated the contact, she sought to jerk away.

He was too fast for her—and too determined. His hand turned upward, closing around hers in a grip that was firm and possessive.

She saw his lips move. Maybe he mouthed the word "Don't."

She wasn't sure whether he had really given voice to the protest or even if she was capable of hearing over the ringing in her ears.

At the party the experience had been fleeting. And the surprise had added to the electric jolt of the connection. This time, as he forced her to prolong the physical link between them, the sensations fluttered, peaked, settled down to a buzzing in her body and in her brain that was as much physical as mental.

The sexual arousal was a steady background hum, transmitting itself along her nerve endings. Yet it was only part of the mix. Because even more overwhelming than the sexual component was the knowledge that it was happening to him as well.

She knew it, not just from the way his pupils had dilated. She knew it from the disjointed thoughts and emotions pouring off him like rain streaming down a windowpane.

An image flashed in her thoughts. She saw him dragging her out of her chair, pulling her into his arms, molding the length of his body to hers, so that she could feel the pressure of his erection against her.

The vivid picture was from his mind. A glimpse into the man's most private sexual thoughts. It was what he wanted to do. Here. Now. Yet the two of them remained where they were, sitting at the restaurant table—their hands the only point of contact.

Granite Wall. Along with the sexual image, a strange name leaped into her mind, burned itself into her brain.

She had never heard of it before. But she knew it was important.

The contact snapped, and she realized Walker had lifted his hand from hers. But this time she didn't turn and run. This time they sat breathing hard, staring at each other across three feet of white tablecloth.

"What's wrong with Bridgewater?" he said, his voice gravelly.

"What do you mean, what's wrong with Bridgewater?" she demanded, feeling her skin go cold.

"He was acting strange when he came back from Florida. You're worried about it."

"How do you know that?"

"You know how I know."

He had spoken the truth, a truth she didn't want to acknowledge.

"And what about Granite Wall?" she asked, trying to hold her voice steady.

It was his turn to blanch. "You picked up that name . . . from me?"

"Yes. You read it in a report, right?"

He nodded, then glanced around the restaurant. She did the same, relieved that no one was nearby. But still, they weren't alone.

JORDAN ran a hand through his dark hair. He wanted to get Lindsay out of here—where they could be alone. But he forced himself to sit quietly across the table from her.

She looked away, not meeting his eyes, and he knew she was deliberately distancing herself from what had happened between them moments ago. Whatever it was. All he knew was that touching her again had left them both dazed and shaken and vulnerable.

Under the table he clasped his hands, squeezing until the pressure was near to pain.

They were both balanced on a knife edge of tension, and he realized that he was going to lose her. Unless he was the one who stuck his neck out.

On some deep self-protective level, he wanted to pretend that nothing extraordinary had happened. But he felt desperation rising inside him.

He simply didn't know what he would do if she walked away. That truth made him reckless enough to moisten his dry lips and say, "Have you ever thought that you were different from everybody else?"

She had been sitting hunched over, her face averted. The question made her sit up straighter and focus on him again with an unnerving intensity, almost as jarring as the experience of touching her.

He needed some sign from her. She seemed to understand, because she gave him the smallest nod.

He swallowed hard and went on. "Have you watched the men and women around you pair up, and known that you were cut off from that kind of . . ." He wanted to say *intimacy*. But the word felt too loaded. So he settled for "sharing."

"Yes," she whispered, and he was sure she hated uttering the admission.

That one syllable and the way she spoke it gave him the guts to go on with a conversation that was so outside his experience that he was astonished at his own question.

"Have you ever felt like there was a buzz in your head? That you were being bombarded by radio signals that you couldn't quite tune in?"

The effect of his words on Lindsay was startling. Her face went from wary to shocked, to hopeful, then back to wary again.

"Are you talking about yourself?" she whispered.

"Can you identify with the description?" he pressed.

When she gave him another almost imperceptible nod, he felt a little thrill of something close to victory.

"And then you touch a stranger—and suddenly . . ." He shrugged, let the sentence trail off, watching her eyes, seeing that she was following his unspoken logic. Something monumental had happened to them. At Senator Conroy's party. And today. Well, perhaps not monumental in the grand scheme of wars and tidal waves, he corrected himself.

But in the small scheme of his life, it felt near to cataclysmic.

"Of course, you could get up and walk away from me," he added, his chest tightening painfully as he offered the suggestion. "Is that what you want to do?"

"No."

"Then let's try to figure out what the hell is happening. And why."

"If you're willing to tell me what someone named Todd Hamilton has to do with any of this."

"Jesus! You got that out of my head, too?"

It was her turn to shrug.

"Another dead man."

He heard her indrawn breath.

"We have to talk about it."

They sat staring at each other, and he knew that talking was the least of what he wanted.

He heard himself say, "Come up to my apartment after dinner."

"Why?"

"The papers you want to see are there," he answered, thinking they both knew that was only an excuse.

CHAPTER
EIGHT

LINDSAY'S MOUTH WAS so dry, she could barely talk, but she managed to answer, "If I do, I take a cab and meet you there."

"So you won't feel trapped?"

"Exactly."

To defuse the tension crackling back and forth between them, she asked. "Tell me about Jordan Walker."

"Like what?"

"Where did you grow up?"

"New London, Connecticut. My dad worked in the Groton shipyards. What about you?"

"Darien."

"So we're both from the same state," he murmured, although he'd already known the answer to his question.

"Coincidence."

"I stopped believing in coincidence when I was doing one of my first stories—on income tax evasion. The wise guy at the center of the piece turned out to be connected to another story—where a woman lawyer tried to poison her husband. When that didn't work, she hired the wise guy as a hit man. He was recommended by one of her tax evasion clients."

"You mean the Martha Blaine case?"

"Yeah."

Before she could switch the subject away from herself, he asked, "How was your childhood?"

She gestured helplessly with her hand. "You want me to

tell you I didn't know how to fit in? That I didn't have many friends? That I focused on schoolwork rather than social activities."

"Is that true?"

"Yes," she whispered.

"And your greatest pleasure was losing yourself in a book—pretending that you were living someone else's life—someone with warm, close relationships?"

"Are you reading my mind again?" she whispered.

"No. I'm describing myself. It seems that we're a lot alike—even if we come from different social classes."

"What? You asked where I grew up. But you already knew because you investigated me?"

"Just a Google search."

"I should have done that with you!"

"But you were trying to pretend you weren't interested."

"Yes," she admitted, then tipped her head to one side as she studied him. "I don't need to do a background check to see you're self-confident. In charge. You get people to say things to you that they wouldn't tell their mothers."

"Yeah. I taught myself to be pushy because I knew I could make a damn good in-your-face investigative reporter. If I only had the balls to do it."

She laughed. "That gives me kind of a strange image."

"Yeah. A badly mixed metaphor."

They laughed together, and for the first time she wondered if she could actually like the man.

She'd barely noticed when the busboy took their unfinished appetizers away. Now they paused in the conversation as the waitress set down their dinner plates.

She was glad she'd only ordered a small portion of the ravioli. She supposed it was excellent, but she could barely taste the filling or the sauce. And Walker didn't seem to be doing much better with his mixed grill.

When he put down his knife and fork, she looked at him inquiringly.

"I don't think either one of us is too hungry. Why don't we leave?"

"All right." She hauled her purse off the floor and got out her wallet.

"My treat. I invited you."

She might have argued. Instead she got his address. When he'd signed the credit card slip, they walked to the front together.

"It's silly to take a cab," he said.

"But I'll feel like I have more control. There's a front desk in your building?"

"Right."

"And they can call me another cab when I'm ready to leave."

"Yeah."

She should be reassured. But as she rode toward Massachusetts Avenue, she felt like she couldn't fill her lungs with air—because she understood that if she went to Jordan Walker's apartment, her life would never be the same.

MARK Greenwood awoke from a bad dream—only to find that reality was no better.

He had been in the control center, and someone had come in holding a blaster from a fifties science fiction movie—and hit him with a death ray.

That was a dream. Right? Or was that reality?

"What's wrong with me?" he croaked.

"You had a drug overdose. It's affected your brain," the man with the surgical mask answered. The same voice that had spoken to him before.

Fear twisted like knives in his chest. Was the guy telling the truth? It didn't feel right. He didn't take drugs. Ever.

Something had happened at Maple Creek—and they wanted him to tell them about it. But he was pretty sure that if he did, he was a dead man.

"How are you feeling now?" the doctor inquired.

"Did you ask me that before?"

"Yes. Does your head hurt?"

"Yeah. Why do you need a mask?"

"Just a precaution."

"Am I contagious or something?"

"What can you tell me about your delusion—about the break-in at Maple Creek?

"It didn't happen? It wasn't real?" he asked stupidly.

"That was all a drug-induced fantasy. We're going to get you straightened out."

"Who are you?"

"I told you my name before. But you're having memory problems. I'm Dr. Colefax. I'm here to take care of you. Everything is going to be fine."

He should be grateful for the steady voice and the reassuring words. But this whole setup just didn't feel right. Starting with the sharp, watchful look in the doctor's brown eyes.

"How long have I been here?"

"Don't worry about that."

Oh, he was worried all right.

"What about Rota and Cordova? Are they okay?"

"They're fine."

Sure. Because I'm the only one having the drug problem? The only one affected? No, I saw Rota standing like a department store mannequin. Or is that true? Is it a fantasy, like he says?

He tried to sit up. "Let me out of here."

"You need to rest."

"No. I want a lawyer."

"You don't need a lawyer. You need to let me help you."

A needle pricked his arm. And he floated away again—into a drug-induced safety net.

Some time later he woke again. It was dark, and he

could hear voices. In his head? No, he could hear people talking in the hall.

"He's sleeping."

"Is the new treatment working?"

"We won't know for several days."

"I want to know what happened to him."

"He's tough. He doesn't trust us."

"We need to get his story. He's the only one who came in contact with the intruders who's still alive."

God, no!

"Get him to talk. Then get rid of him."

The voices moved away. He strained to hear more, but they were out of range.

Oh, God. Oh, God. Was it true? If Cordova and Rota were dead, why was he still alive? He didn't know. But he understood one thing, all right. He had to get the hell out of here.

Cautiously he opened his lids a fraction, peering through his lashes. Once again he studied his surroundings.

Once again? He'd been here the whole time, since Maple Creek? Right? Or had they moved him from somewhere else? He still couldn't think clearly. And nobody in this funny farm was helping along the process.

He was in a small room with bars on the windows. The only furniture was a metal chair. Ahead of him was a door with a rectangular window filled with chicken-wire-reinforced glass. There was another door—this one solid. Did it lead to the bathroom?

He had to get out of this cage. But if he did, would it make any difference? Would he only find himself in a locked hallway?

Deliberately he tested his memory, casting his mind back—to a time when he'd been happy. With the Becker family. With Aunt Jen and Uncle Eddie and Sid. The Beckers had taken him in when his mother had died, and his real father been too paralyzed by grief to take care of him.

The Beckers had welcomed him like a son. They'd given him a warm, secure childhood. Sid had taught him how to use in-line skates and how to keep his eye on the ball when he was up at bat. Aunt Jen had helped him with his math homework. And they'd all sat around the TV in the living room watching Orioles games, because even Jen was a fan.

She and Eddie were dead now. But Sid . . . Sid would help him. Help him get out of this place? Maybe—if he knew. But how the hell would Sid find out where he was?

A jumble of emotions swirled through Jordan as he drove home. He wanted to focus on Lindsay—what he'd felt when he'd touched her. But the dinner conversation had called up a host of images from his past.

Like the time in seventh grade when he'd been the only kid who'd gotten one hundred percent on a surprise history test, and Mrs. Garland had assumed he had cheated. She'd made him stay after school, and she'd quizzed him orally on a bunch of questions—some of which hadn't even been on the test. He'd stood in front of her, spouting answers that came from his terrible determination not to have the school call his dad.

She hadn't been able to give him an F on the test. But after that, he'd caught her looking at him, and he knew he had given her the creeps because they both understood where those answers had come from—her head. She had thought of the answer, and he had pulled it right out of her soggy brain. During the test—and later when she'd quizzed him.

He wasn't sure how he'd done it. And he'd chalked it up to the strange things that sometimes happened inside his mind.

The experience with Lindsay had been similar—yet different. More tentative and at the same time more intimate.

The thoughts he'd picked up from Lindsay had been random and disorganized. And there was another big difference, too. He hadn't had any sexual feelings for Mrs. Garland.

He wanted . . . to make love with Lindsay. Not just the physical act. More. He wanted to fulfill the promise of intimacy that had bloomed between them.

He was afraid to find out what that meant. Terrified not to find out. And in agony that she was going to change her mind before she got to his apartment.

As soon as he stepped into his own living room, he started pacing back and forth across the carpet, clenching and unclenching his fists.

When she called from the lobby, he breathed out a sigh of relief—just before his heart started pounding so hard inside his chest that he was surprised he couldn't see his shirtfront moving.

Opening the apartment door, he stepped into the hall, then watched her get off the elevator and smooth her skirt. The gesture told him she was as nervous as he.

As she leaned down, her dark hair swung in a curtain in front of her face. He wanted to brush it back. Hell, he just wanted some excuse to touch her, stroke her, kiss her. His stomach knotted painfully, but he stayed where he was, then saw her glance up and spy him watching her.

She covered her look of surprise, then walked toward him, and he didn't need to read her mind to know she was pretending that her nerves weren't jumping.

When she reached the door, he cleared his throat and said, "So you didn't stand me up."

"It was a close call."

The way she said it made his stomach clench.

"Come on in," he managed.

They were careful not to touch each other as he moved aside to usher her into the small foyer.

As she stepped into the living room, she looked around

at his furniture, and he suddenly saw the room as sterile—
soulless. When she laughed, he cringed. "You think this
place looks like an upscale hotel room?"

She turned to face him. "No. I think we just discovered
another trait in common—neatnik."

He expelled a breath. "So why do you feel the need to
keep your environment orderly?"

"It gives me the illusion of control."

"The illusion?"

She answered with a little shrug. "You can phrase it dif-
ferently if you want."

He didn't want to stand here arguing with her, not when
her proximity had his body tingling.

He had never wanted a woman with such urgency—
such violence, if he was honest. But the need wasn't simply
physical. There was so much more below the surface of his
sexual desire that he could barely breathe. Yet he forced
himself to keep his arms at his sides.

"Do you want a drink?"

"No, thanks. You were going to tell me about . . . Granite Wall," she answered. "That's the weapons program you
think has gone back online?"

"Shit."

"And you have some papers to show me."

He shifted his weight from one foot to the other. It was
almost impossible to keep from reaching for her and wrapping her in his arms. But he had also been wondering what
he would say when she asked him about the secret project.
This was the moment when he had to decide how much to
trust her.

He knew he had made a decision when he said, "I'll be
right back."

He walked rapidly into his office and opened the locked
lower right-hand drawer, where he'd stowed the folder of
material that Herb had sent him. When he returned to the
living room and saw the eager look in her eyes, he knew

that giving her the folder would be as irrevocable as touching her again.

"Maybe you shouldn't get involved in this."

"It seems I already am."

His mouth hardened. "I didn't know you were going to pick up so much from my mind. I told you two men died because of this information, but the number is really three. Two in March. And the man I tried to call this morning— Dr. Charles Lucas."

He saw her swallow hard. While he had her off balance, he added, "If I show you this stuff, you have to agree not to tell anyone—that includes your boss, Bridgewater."

"No agreements in advance. I have to be free to judge what I do. Maybe it's something the senator needs to know."

"Yeah, well, I wouldn't want either of us to join the other three—because this information got into the wrong hands."

She blanched.

"I'm counting on your native intelligence," he added, handing over the folder.

She took it to the sofa and sat down.

He moved to the window, propping his hips against the ledge as he watched her open the clasp and sift through the contents before settling down to read Herb's letter.

When she lifted her gaze, her features were frozen in shock.

"Is this a medical report on one of the people who died?"

"Yes."

He watched her process the information. "So the chemical agent . . . called Granite Wall . . . killed this guy—and his friend?"

"Yeah."

"A chemical accident?"

"Or a deliberate attack."

"And a cover-up," she added.

"It looks like someone wants the threads clipped off."

She leaned toward him. "But you got away from that drugstore without being followed."

"I'm satisfied nobody picked up my trail," he answered, gratified that she'd been concerned for him.

Her next words and her tone of voice helped dissipate the warm fuzzy feeling. "And now you're hoping to use my connections." Closing the folder, she set it down on the coffee table.

"I wouldn't do it, if I had a choice."

"That's a lie, isn't it?"

He kept his features bland. "Why do you think so?"

"Because you get a bonus out of this. You like having an excuse to get together with me again."

He gave a little nod. "Yeah, I want to get to know you better. But I'm also worried about sucking you into something dangerous."

"Working on the Hill has taught me a lot about being discreet."

"Good." As he answered, he knew that he had postponed the other element of this meeting for as long as humanly possible—at least for him. While she'd read the report, the tension had been building inside him, and he felt like he was teetering on the edge of a sheer cliff. If he took a leap off into space, would he find out that he could fly?

Slowly he crossed the room and sat down on the couch. Not next to Lindsay but a foot and a half away. Deliberately he pressed his hand against the cushion between them, his fingers spread.

CHAPTER
NINE

LINDSAY HAD TOLD herself she was coming to Jordan's apartment for a business discussion. And she was still trying to decide whether to tell him about her talk with Sid.

As she stared at his hand, she figured he was finished with the business part of the meeting.

Something had happened when they'd touched. Something she couldn't explain. And he couldn't either—another masterpiece of deductive reasoning.

She'd assured herself she had a choice about what happened next.

Now she knew she'd been deceiving herself. Moving slowly, as though she were swimming underwater, she slid her hand across the sofa cushion, feeling the nubby fibers abrade her fingertips.

The action was deliberate, yet she had the sense that both her hand and Jordan's had become magnetized—that some invisible force was pulling her toward him. And him toward her.

As if they had made a secret pact, they both stopped millimeters from touching. This time she was more tuned to what was happening, and she had the strange sensation of energy leaping back and forth between them, like a spark jumping a gap between electrodes.

Her gaze shot to Jordan, and she knew from the shocked expression on his face that he felt it, too.

He made a low sound and closed the space, pressing the

side of his hand to hers. Only that. Only that small but significant point of skin-to-skin contact.

Thoughts flickered in her brain. None of them was clear.

When she'd read the letter in the folder, she'd noted that it was written by a man named Herb. Now she got a quick image of what she thought was his face.

Herb Goldman?

She felt Jordan's hand jump, the contact wavering for an instant before the pressure of flesh on flesh settled down again.

Yeah.

Another image flickered in his mind. An old man's face. But she couldn't bring it into sharp focus. He was important.

Don't go there.

She sensed his anxiety and did as he asked. Unfortunately, the next thing she thought of was Sid's visit to her.

He asked you about a chemical weapons accident?

I can't talk about it.

SHE snatched her hand away—breaking the contact. And she and Jordan were left staring at each other, breathing hard.

"You were in my head," she gasped. "Talking in my head."

"Yeah, well, you were in mine. It happens when we touch, in case you haven't figured that out."

"Of course I figured it out," she snapped, hating the sensation and at the same time craving it. "I don't like it," she whispered.

"Now who's lying? It made you feel . . . complete."

Her gaze shot to him. "How do you know?"

"Because I feel the same thing. I mean—inside myself."

"Why is this happening?" she murmured.

"I don't know." As he spoke, he reached toward her with deliberate purpose.

She might have scrambled away; instead she swayed forward as he gathered her into his arms. She gasped at the sudden intensity of emotions sweeping through her. Fear. Lust. Hope. Need. Not just for sexual gratification. For something so much more that she wanted to run and hide—from herself. From him.

"Don't!" she gasped.

"We have to see how far we can take this."

"I don't think so," she managed to say, then made a low, needy sound as he turned her in his arms, pressing her breasts against his chest.

She clung to him because his body was her only anchor in a wildly tilting ocean, where a large wave could sweep her under, choke off her breath.

Before she could speak, he brought his lips down on hers, and a jolt of hot sensation went through her.

It was like stepping from the real world into a blast furnace with flames licking at her skin and searing her nerve endings, yet the fire didn't turn her to ash.

She became one with the fire. One with the man who held her in his arms, his lips moving over hers.

She knew that if she didn't make love with him, she would die. Yet at the same time she understood beyond a shadow of a doubt that if his body joined with hers in the most intimate man-woman embrace, the contact might be the death of her. The death of them both.

Fear should have sent her running from the room. But if Jordan Walker was her downfall, he was her savior as well.

His mouth moved over hers, sending heat blazing through her. Heat she had never felt with any other man. She tried to tell herself it was only pure lust. But that was a lie. It was so much more. And not just on the physical level.

From deep in her mind a memory surfaced—a memory of terror from her childhood, when she'd awakened in a strange bedroom and had no idea where she was.

She'd cried out, but no one had come. And she'd lain there whimpering.

She whimpered now, and Jordan spoke against her mouth, his hands soothing over her back and down her arms.

She still felt the scorching heat of the physical contact. Now it was overlaid with another level of communication.

"You were so scared. But it was a long time ago."

"Yes."

What happened?

He didn't speak that part. But she heard the question in her mind, as she had moments earlier.

We had gone to my aunt's. Well, not my real aunt's. She was my stepfather's sister.

You have a stepfather?

Yes. I had never been to his sister's house before. I fell asleep in the car. So I didn't know where I was when I woke up.

He lifted his head and stared down at her. "They should have stayed with you."

She looked at him, blinked. "We were . . ."

"Yeah. Talking in our heads again."

"How?"

I don't know, he answered, then lowered his mouth once more. This time his lips were gentle, exploring, coaxing—calling forth a response that was no less sexual. Yet at the same time she felt the tender side of him. The side he kept hidden from the world. The side that had begged his father to let him bury his dead dog. But his father had put Digger into a plastic trash bag and left him for the garbage pickup.

She felt that small boy's emotion. Wept for them. As Jordan had wept, alone in his bed at night.

She barely knew this man, but she felt a connection between them that was stronger than she had to any other human being. Parents, friends, lovers.

She had come alive in his arms, every sense sharp and crystal clear.

She drank in the taste of him—new and yet familiar. The unique scent of his body. The pounding of his heart against her breasts. The low, satisfied sound that came from him—no, from both of them.

"I want to feel your weight on top of me," he growled, then eased back, stretching out on the sofa and taking her with him. She kicked off her shoes as she came down on top of him, ending up sprawled with his erection like an exclamation mark against her middle.

He adjusted her position, moving her body along his until that hard shaft nestled in the cleft at the top of her legs.

"Oh!"

His arms came around her, holding her to him, his ragged breathing mingling with hers.

When she moved against him, he stilled her. "Don't." His voice was low and urgent, and she obeyed.

"Why are you doing this?"

"To find out." His hands stroked up and down her back, pressing her breasts against his chest.

To find out what?

How far this goes. His lips teased hers, gently, erotically, as he reached to tangle his fingers in her hair. As he stroked his fingers through the dark strands, the sense of connection strengthened. And this time she deliberately reached out, diving into his memories—finding the time when he'd saved up to buy a used dirt bike. His father had said it was dangerous and forbade him to ride it.

She felt his sadness. His anger. His resignation. He hadn't defied the old man because he'd been smart enough to know that would only lead to further conflict.

"You had the sense to back down."

"I hated doing it. But I was always pragmatic."

He punished you—for not being the son he wanted.

Yeah. His lips nibbled at hers.

I couldn't do it, either. Be the daughter they wanted, I mean. Lucky for me, my family was different from yours. I guess my mom and my stepfather would have been embarrassed to admit that I disappointed them. So they put up a good front to their friends—and me.

But you couldn't explain that the way you were wasn't your fault. It was just the way you were made, and you didn't know how to communicate what you felt.

Yes!

His understanding was like a balm. But that was only part of the experience. His hand moved over her back, stroking her through her suit jacket and blouse, increasing her arousal but not the special sense of connection.

"The fabric makes a difference," he muttered.

"What do you mean?"

"Touching you through your blouse makes us both hot—but it doesn't increase the . . ." He grinned. "The Vulcan mind meld."

"I think you're right," she answered, astonished that they could still hold a coherent conversation when they were both as hot as molten lava.

He clasped the back of her head, bringing her mouth back to his, kissing her with lips and teeth and tongue, making her head swim with desire—and at the same time with an overload of thoughts and memories.

She struggled to blot out the thoughts and enjoy the sensations of arousal.

She knew he was doing the same thing as he reached under her suit jacket and tugged her blouse from the waistband of her skirt so that he could slip his hands under the fabric and press them against her hot flesh.

They both made a greedy sound as his hands stroked

over her skin. When he played with the sides of her breasts, she knew she would go up in flames if she didn't move against him.

The motion of her hips didn't quench the fire—it only increased her need.

The layers of clothing separating their lower bodies were intolerable. She wanted to feel his naked flesh pressed to hers. His wonderful erection where it belonged—inside her. Yet she felt another pressure—within her own head—like blood vessels threatening to burst.

The pain was almost as powerful as the arousal. Too much too soon.

No.

Ignoring his protest, she wrenched herself away, out of his arms, off the couch, then reached out to steady herself against the sofa arm as she swayed on unsteady feet, her temples pounding.

They were both gasping for breath as he sat up and ran a shaky hand through his dark hair.

"Christ!" he growled.

"We can't . . . make love," she managed. "Not yet. Not until we understand this better."

"Does your head feel like it's going to explode?" he asked.

"Yes."

"We'll take it slow."

"Not tonight. I have to go," she said, "before we do something . . . impulsive."

"You don't know how much I want to lock you in the bedroom . . . so you can't leave."

"Yes, I do know."

"Are you picking up my wicked thoughts?" he asked, managing a suggestive grin.

"No. I want to stay. Badly." She swallowed. "I want to get as close to you as . . . as two people can get."

"Jesus. Don't say that and walk away."

"I have to. For now. We have to take some time to cool off."

"Are you going to tell me about your friend, Sid?"

"He's worried about his cousin Mark. He's a guard at a secure facility called Maple Creek. Sid hasn't heard from him in over a week. He thinks there could have been a chemical or biological accident."

"Jesus," he said again. "Like that Stephen King novel, *The Stand*."

Suddenly the air inside the apartment felt thick. "We'd know if anything like that had happened," she argued.

"Would we?" he countered.

"You can't hide an epidemic from the press. Not in this country."

"But you can hide a few deaths."

They stared at each other in silence.

"I'll get back to you if I find out anything." Before she did something she knew was foolish, she scuffed into her shoes. "I'm going down to the lobby to call a cab."

"I can drive you home."

"Not a good idea," she said as she pictured the two of them locked in an embrace in the front seat.

"Yeah," he answered, and she was pretty sure the vivid picture had come from his mind.

He stood, stretched out a hand toward her, then let it fall back, again.

"If you don't call me, you may find me climbing in your window."

"I live on the second floor of a garden apartment."

"Maybe you've turned me into Spider Man."

She answered with a shaky laugh. "Maybe we can work up a mind reading act."

"If we learn to control . . . whatever it is we've got."

"Why do we have it?" she asked.

"I'd like to know."

She felt herself wavering—aching to try another experiment—more dangerous than the first. Before she could change her mind, she walked out of the apartment and closed the door behind her.

CHAPTER
TEN

DRESSED NEATLY IN a tweed sports coat, dark slacks, and a button-down shirt, Jim Swift waited in his rental car outside the Wilmington General Hospital parking lot. He'd paid with the credit card of one of his aliases, and he was planning to be out of the vehicle twenty minutes after he left the hospital.

When he saw a woman hurry to the employee entrance, he felt an inward surge of satisfaction.

But his own movements were slow and deliberate as he picked up his carry bag, climbed out of the car, and closed the door. Keeping his head down and away from the security camera on the wall above him, he ambled toward the building like a weary employee who wished he didn't have to go back on shift.

Even if a camera caught him, he wasn't worried about being recognized. Before coming to the hospital, he'd altered his face with his actor's kit.

His nose was more bulbous. His cheeks were fuller. Contact lenses lightened the color of his eyes. His brown hair was hidden by a gray wig. And nearly invisible, thin rubber gloves covered his hands.

Keeping his distance from the woman, he strained his ears and heard the sound of the lock clicking open. As soon as she had stepped into the building, he picked up his pace. Standing close to the door, he pulled a small computer from his carry bag. Attached to the machine was a rubberized paddle, which he pressed over the keypad.

The paddle sent information from the keypad to the computer, analyzing the recent heat signatures left by the woman's fingers—telling him not only which keys the woman had pressed but in what order. When he saw a sequence of five numbers appear on the screen, he duplicated them, then heard the lock click again. Seconds later he stepped into a dimly lit hall.

The woman had already disappeared. Probably she was a nurse, heading for the patient care areas of the hospital.

His destination was another location—the office of Dr. Charles Lucas, the man who had performed those tests on Todd Hamilton. The wimp had died of fright—keeled over before Jim could get any useful information out of him.

Since Lucas had been a proponent of the paperless office, his only copy of the report was on his hard drive. Now that the uproar over his death had faded, Jim was going to collect that information.

He had been here during the day, studying the layout. He had no trouble going right to the office, no trouble using a set of picks to unlock the door.

At the desk he turned on the light, booted the computer, and began making educated guesses about the doctor's password, based on the information he'd collected. The code turned out to be Lucas's sister's birthday. When he got into the files, he began downloading information.

The transfer was almost finished when the door opened and a security guard stepped into the office.

Jim's face remained impassive, but inwardly he was cursing. The hospital security staff was missing a couple of men tonight, and he hadn't expected anyone to challenge him.

"What are you doing here?" the guard asked.

"I'm with the State Department of Health, checking out the material on this computer."

"In the middle of the night?" the guard asked, his gaze fixed on Jim.

"We do this kind of work at night, so that we don't disturb the day-to-day work of the hospital," Jim answered, holding up the official-looking ID that hung on a lanyard around his neck. It was issued in the name of Ted Ryland.

While the guard inspected the ID, Jim considered contingency plans. Killing the guy was always an option. But then he'd have to get rid of the body.

He was glad when the guard nodded. "How long will you be here, Mr. Ryland?"

"Not long," he answered easily, thinking that this guy didn't know how close he was to death.

The guard withdrew, and Jim waited a moment before going back to work.

He had no qualms about killing in the line of duty. Long ago he'd decided that Kurt MacArthur should be running the country—if not from the Oval Office, then behind the scenes. And he was willing to do what it took to accomplish that goal.

After downloading the entire hard drive, he checked to make sure he had all the material, then wiped out all of the doctor's research reports so that the theft of the Todd Hamilton information would not stand out. He left the computer where it was. It might be days or weeks before anybody went into Lucas's files and discovered they had evaporated.

Forty minutes after he'd entered the hospital, he was back in his car and heading toward the airport where he would turn in the car and pick up his own vehicle from the short-term parking lot.

Kurt wanted to know who had requested the report. He was hoping he could dig that information out of the man's correspondence files—even if they had been altered.

*　*　*

LINDSAY had always prided herself on masking her emotions, but she'd been as open to Jordan Walker as the doors of a cargo bay.

The hour she'd spent at his apartment with him had shaken her to the core. By the time she got home, she'd convinced herself that the best favor the could do herself was to stay as far away from him as she could.

But now that she was alone, the business part of the conversation kept nagging at her. And sometime before dawn—as she tossed restlessly in her bed—a name popped into her mind.

Todd Hamilton.

She'd gotten it from Jordan's mind in the restaurant. Now she thought she knew who he was—the victim she had read about in that medical report.

And once she started focusing on him, she was also sure she had encountered him before.

In person?

Again she chewed on the problem.

Although she caught a few hours of sleep in the small hours of the morning, she felt like she'd been run over by a D.C. Metro bus when she climbed out of bed. The image in the bathroom mirror confirmed the opinion, but a hot shower helped her return to the world of the living.

Usually she made do with coffee until lunchtime. This morning she stopped at the basement takeout shop and treated herself to a latte and a blueberry muffin.

Sometimes there were advantages to being known as a loner. Since she didn't want to chat with anyone, she put on her "got too much work" look as she walked through the office to her desk.

While she drank her coffee and nibbled on the muffin, she checked her e-mail and phone messages. Nothing needed her immediate attention, so she went into the file room and opened the drawer where the "nutcase" folders were kept.

The names on the tabs sounded straightforward—like "Environment" or "Alternate Sources of Energy."

But they all contained letters from constituents and other citizens who had directed various off-the-wall complaints to Senator Bridgewater. For the record, the office kept the correspondence on file.

With hands that weren't quite steady, she thumbed through the folder on "Military Inquiries—Closed Programs." When she came across a letter from Todd Hamilton, her heart began to pound.

It had been sent three months ago and answered a few days later. Both pieces of correspondence had been produced on a computer and printed out.

Todd's letter was signed in bold black ink. The reply was also personalized, although the senator's signature had been produced by a machine.

Repairing to a chair in the corner, she read the correspondence.

> *Dear Senator Bridgewater,*
>
> *Although I am not one of your constituents, I am writing to you in your capacity as the chairman of the Senate Armed Services Committee. It is vitally important for you to be aware that a secret lab is hiding information from you and the other members of the committee, as well as from the public you serve.*
>
> *Several years ago U.S. chemical weapons programs were in full swing. In accordance with our treaty agreements not to pursue the development of such weapons, the projects were terminated at Fort Detrick, where most of this research is carried out. But I have recently come across disturbing evidence that several of these programs have resumed operations at a secret location in CONUS.*
>
> *Talking about this project is dangerous. This information must not get into the wrong hands. But I would be*

*glad to meet with you at your convenience to discuss this
matter.*

    Sincerely,
    Todd Hamilton

A reply was stapled to the letter.

Dear Mr. Hamilton,
    *As the chairman of the Senate Armed Services
Committee, I have had a continuing interest in the military
preparedness of this country including new weapons
systems, troop strength, appropriations, and intelligence
matters.*
    *Since my own service in Vietnam, military affairs
have been a prime focus of my career. In my capacity as
chairman of the Senate Armed Services Committee, I have
immersed myself in these issues and have been at the
forefront of making sure the public is kept apprised of
developments in these critical areas.*
    *I am always glad to hear from citizens with
information that is of importance to me. Your continued
support of my vital work is appreciated. Thank you for
writing to me. Feel free to contact me again with any of
your concerns. One of my staff members is reviewing the
matter.*
    Sincerely,
    Daniel Bridgewater

An intern had composed the answer, plugging in stock
paragraphs from the computer files. She knew from the
way the office worked that Bridgewater himself had not
seen either of these pieces of paper.

But Lindsay had taken a quick look at the material
before the answer had gone to the mail room and the copies
had been filed.

Because she had a good memory for names, she had put Todd Hamilton together with the letter.

Now she wondered if she'd made a mistake by dismissing what sounded like paranoid claims. She scanned the top sheet again, wishing he'd been more specific about where the secret facility was located. Then she checked in the H section of the drawer to see if Todd had rated his own folder. He hadn't.

So—should she call Jordan Walker and tell him about the letter? Should she do some checking first? Or was that a fatal mistake? He'd warned her about asking questions. Was that because he was worried about the consequences? Or did he want her to come back to him for answers?

When she felt the edge of the folder digging into her fingers, she ordered herself to relax. With the smallest excuse, she was thinking of Walker again.

No, not a small excuse. Something was going on. Something dark—and dangerous. It looked like Todd Hamilton had stuck his nose in the wrong place and gotten his head chopped off.

Not with a terrorist's sword, but with some chemical agent. He hadn't mentioned the name of the program he was worried about. But she was willing to bet it was Granite Wall. Had he been murdered just for asking questions about the project? Or had he accidentally exposed himself to the stuff?

And did Granite Wall have anything to do with Sid's cousin? Maybe not. But the alternative was equally disturbing—since it might mean that two chemical weapons programs had been jeopardized.

Although she felt like a sneak thief, Lindsay kept her expression unruffled as she carried the folder to the photocopy machine and duplicated both Todd's letter and the generic answer. Then she put the folder back.

Still trying to look casual, she put both letters into her purse. Once she'd hidden the evidence, she went back to her computer and plugged Todd's name into her favorite search engine. When she did, she got another surprise.

There were some small newspaper articles about the death of Todd Hamilton and his friend Glenn Barrow—in a boating accident in the Chesapeake Bay. From them she learned that he was the son of multimillionaire Leonard Hamilton. When she read his name, and saw a picture of Todd with his father and some business associates, another piece of the puzzle clicked into place.

She'd seen an old man's face in Walker's mind. Now she was sure the man was Todd's father.

She moved restlessly in her chair, burning with the need to communicate with Jordan Walker.

But she couldn't phone him from the office because there would be a record of the call.

At lunchtime she walked down to the business district on Pennsylvania Avenue, all the time thinking about Jordan's hair-raising drugstore story. And about Todd Hamilton, his friend, Glenn Barrow, and the doctor who had done tests on his body. The three of them were dead—the doctor to protect the secret of what had happened to Todd and Glenn.

She kept assuring herself that nobody could connect her with any of that. Still, she stopped to face a window display, then looked to the right and left to make sure she wasn't being watched.

Trying to appear like she was just running errands on her lunch break, she walked into an electronics store and up to the front counter and paid cash for a cheap cell phone, the kind that couldn't receive calls—only make them.

Walker had given her his phone numbers. When she tried to reach his home and his cell, she got a recording asking her to leave a message. Each time she hung up because she didn't want to speak to a machine.

Ten minutes after she got back to her desk, the phone rang, and she jumped.

CHAPTER
ELEVEN

"HELLO, THIS IS Jordan," a chipper voice said.

"How . . ." Lindsay stopped. She wasn't going to ask how he knew she had called and failed to leave a message.

"I enjoyed yesterday evening. I was hoping we could get together again after work."

He made it sound personal—like a man interested in a woman. It *was* personal—but she felt as though she were in the middle of a spy movie.

She dragged in a breath and let it out, then tried to match his light tone. "Sounds good."

"We can meet at the Woodley Park Metro. There are a ton of restaurants right there," he suggested. "Six-thirty again?"

"Give or take rush hour."

"I'll meet you at that weird little cement triangle with nothing but the Metro entrance. Across from the back door to the Marriott."

"I know where you mean."

She tried to be productive for the rest of the day. But she could barely focus on any of the work piled up on her desk. Finally she left early, walked over to Union Station, and wandered around the shopping hall before heading for the Metro.

Woodley Park was one stop up from the Dupont Circle area, where she'd met Walker the day before.

After she came up the escalator, she looked around, but he apparently hadn't arrived yet. When he still wasn't there ten minutes later, she tried to fight the tight feeling in her chest.

As a silver Mercedes pulled up to the curb, she tensed. Had someone found out about the meeting? Was she going to be hustled into a car and spirited away?

She took a quick step back. Then the window lowered, and Jordan called out to her, "Get in."

As soon as she climbed into the car and closed the door, he sped away from the busy intersection.

She stared at his set profile. "I thought we were going to eat around here."

"I have other plans."

While she fumbled with her seat belt, he turned right onto Connecticut, then right onto Calvert, heading in the direction of Wisconsin Avenue.

"What are we doing?" she inquired.

"Making sure nobody is looking for us."

When he caught her strained expression, he said, "I'm just being careful. The same way you didn't leave a message when you called my home and cell phones."

JORDAN spared her another quick look, then went back to watching the rush hour traffic, trying to relax his white-knuckled grip on the steering wheel.

The temptation to reach out and press his hand reassuringly over hers was almost overwhelming. But he didn't touch her because he knew that with the contact, his mind would shift away from the traffic, and he didn't want to risk getting into an accident. So he only looked at the hands she'd knit together in her lap.

They had things to discuss, but he didn't ask her any questions yet. Instead, he drove toward Thirty-first Street, then onto the grounds of the National Cathedral, the massive stone structure rising like a medieval anachronism along Wisconsin Avenue.

Lindsay looked around as he parked beside the building. "Are we going to talk in the crypt?"

"The Bishop's Garden." He led her along the sidewalk to a wooden gate. Inside they took one of the paved walkways wandering among carefully tended beds of herbs and flowers. Only a few other people were taking advantage of the garden, so it was easy to stroll in privacy through the series of stunning outdoor rooms.

"This is beautiful," she murmured, bending down to pluck a sprig of lavender, releasing the fragrant perfume into the air. "I've walked past the cathedral, but I didn't know about this garden. How did you find it?"

He slipped his hands into the pockets of his gray slacks. "I used to do some freelance work for *Washingtonian Magazine*. And I made it a point to write about interesting spots in the city."

"So you went from gardens to character assassination," she observed dryly.

He swung toward her. "Are you trying to start a fight?"

"Maybe."

He wanted to wedge his hands on his hips. Instead he kept them relaxed as he said, "That's the second crack you've made about my work. Maybe you'd better explain it."

She hesitated a beat before saying. "Okay. In that series you did on the Supreme Court, you were unfair to a woman named Paula Grayson."

He felt his eyes narrow, but he spoke slowly and evenly. "Paula Grayson, the woman who was sleeping with one of Judge Wilson's law clerks?"

"I don't believe that!" she protested.

"She was using him to get ahead. I could have gone into a lot more detail, but I chose to focus on other aspects of how the justices reach decisions."

"I heard your article cost her her job," Lindsay shot back.

"Maybe it did. But I was only reporting the facts I'd dug up. I'm not in the business of character assassination. I don't put anything questionable into a book or an article unless I've checked it through more than one source."

"But you took the word of the law clerk!"

With someone else he might have shrugged and walked away. But this was Lindsay. So he said, "I checked his story with the staff at the hotel where they'd met. He ordered champagne sent up to their room. She was in bed, the covers pulled just high enough on her breasts to hide her nipples. He was wearing one of those white robes hotels have for guests."

He was gratified to see the red stain spread across her cheeks. "Oh."

"And she was the one who paid for the room, in case you're interested in that bit of information."

Lindsay swallowed. "I'm sorry I attacked you."

"You're nervous. So am I." He laughed. "One reason I brought you here was so I'd keep my hands off you. It wouldn't be very decorous to kiss you in a church garden."

"Are you always decorous?"

"I respect holy ground."

She snorted.

Instead of reaching for her, he reached for a nearby plant and broke off a sprig, crushing it between his fingers.

"That's thyme," she said. "My mom has an herb garden at home."

"Yeah. But we didn't come here to talk about horticulture. Stop stalling. Why did you call me?"

"I picked up something else from your mind."

His whole body went rigid. "What? My mind's like a TV screen to you?"

"No. But after I got home, I realized I'd gotten something important last night. A name. Todd Hamilton. It was *his* pathology report that you showed me—right?"

"Christ!"

"Sorry," she muttered. But now that she'd started talking, she plowed ahead. "When I remembered the name, I was pretty sure I'd seen it in another context. So I looked it up in the office correspondence files."

After glancing around to make sure that they were alone, she reached into her purse and pulled out the photocopies, being careful not to touch him as she handed it over.

He read it and whistled through his teeth. "So he had important information a few months ago. Only he didn't know how to tell Bridgewater about it without sounding like he had a screw loose. What did the senator do with this letter?"

"He never saw it. An intern answered it. But I went over the intern's work before the letter and the answer went into the 'nutcase files.'"

"Well, don't blame yourself for dismissing him. It sounds like it came from someone who was mentally unbalanced."

She nodded fractionally.

"I mean it."

"Okay." She cleared her throat. "I looked for further correspondence. And I presume that there was no additional communication, since if Hamilton had written to the senator again, he would have gotten his own file folder."

He gave her an appreciative look. "Good detective work."

"Thanks."

His mood sobered instantly. "And you haven't told anyone about this?"

"No. In light of your three-death theory."

"It's not a theory! And you don't think so, either."

"I guess that's right." She moved her shoulder. "I looked up Todd Hamilton on the Web and came across some articles. There was a picture of his father. I believe you were thinking about him last night, too."

He swore again.

"You met with him."

"Yeah."

A smile flickered over her lips. "Score one for me. That was a bluff. I didn't know for certain until you told me."

"Maybe you should get a job as an investigative reporter."

"I like the job I have."

"You like Bridgewater."

"I like and respect him. He has tremendous power, and he doesn't throw it around for effect."

"But you were worried about him. I know you don't want to talk about it. But you were thinking he was acting . . . strange," he said, going back to his observation of the day before.

"Stop pumping me for information."

"You started it. I mean by digging the Todd Hamilton connection out of my brain."

She gave him a look that was only partly apology.

Somehow, that look made the pressure building inside him too much to bear. He couldn't stand the feeling of separation. Of misunderstanding—when all he had to do to bridge the gap was reach for her.

He stretched out his hand. To his relief, she came willingly into his arms. Her small sob told him she was as needy as he.

He drew her into a small courtyard with high stone walls. Not that the place was really private. But at the moment he didn't care about anything or anyone else besides the woman whose body had molded to his.

Jordan. Don't. Not here.

You don't want me?

He felt her breath catch, heard the echo of his own thoughts in his mind. *This is insanity.*

Or salvation.

He lowered his mouth to hers, the hot, greedy kiss fueling a wave of sexual power. And thoughts. And emotions.

His and hers. Just like every other time he had touched her, the intimacy was overwhelming. Disturbing. Shocking.

We can go to your apartment.

No, she protested.

We both want . . .

We hardly know each other.

You're lying. You know me better than anyone else you ever met.

He drew her lower lip into his mouth, sucking, nibbling. He knew what she was thinking. That this garden protected her. He couldn't do anything more here. He shouldn't even be kissing her in such a place.

When he sent her an image of the two of them naked, holding each other, rocking together on the grass, she cried out.

He drank in the sound as he raised his hand and covered her breast, frustrated by the fabric between his skin and hers.

She moaned into his mouth, moaned again when he cupped her bottom and lifted her up, pulling her middle against his erection.

They both gasped at the contact, and he knew they really might end up on the grass. The drive for fulfillment fogged his mind, blotted out rational thought. Unable to stop himself, he began unbuttoning her blouse so he could thrust his hand inside and pull down one of the cups of her bra. The thought of his fingers stroking across her nipple rang a sob from her lips. He tugged her skirt up. At that moment a sharp female voice cut through the sexual fog.

"Have you no sense of propriety? Find somewhere else for your shameful consorting."

The intrusion on their privacy was so disorienting that it took several heartbeats for him to realize that someone was speaking to them.

Raising his head, he saw a middle-aged woman looking at them with outrage.

Oh, Lord.

His gaze went from the woman to Lindsay, whose face flamed as she tried to redo the buttons of her blouse. When she pulled away from him, he felt like a piece of his soul had been torn away. Or was it a piece of his sanity? He wasn't sure. He only knew that he must have her back in his arms. Now. And damn everything else.

She took a step back, then another.

Wait! We still have to . . . talk. I have to ask you . . .

The plea echoed inside his own head. And he knew she had heard him because of the way her shoulders stiffened. But she didn't stop running, and she didn't look back.

CHAPTER
TWELVE

"MAYBE WE CAN work up a mind-reading act."

Willow Trinity's low, throaty laugh echoed through the private room at the back of their white marble temple.

Sax cradled her in his arms as they pooled their energy, revving up for the meeting with their most faithful followers.

"I think we already have, my dear," he murmured.

"Or mind-controlling. That's better, isn't it?"

"Oh, yeah."

She let her head fall to his shoulder, enjoying the intimate contact, enjoying the warmth and closeness, the comforting knowledge that the two of them had faced the worst together—and come out stronger for their suffering.

As Sax stroked her hair, a scene from the bad old days drifted through her mind. From one of the foster care homes where there wasn't enough of anything—food, clothing, or love.

They had been living with a couple named Henry and Eve Duckman, who had fooled the welfare system into trusting them with the lives of little children.

Back then, the twins had been Patty and Billy Anderson. Willow liked their new names much better. Willow Trinity went along with making herself over—into a person of power, not a victim.

Patty and Billy Anderson had been at the mercy of D.C. Social Services, a dysfunctional agency with too many needy kids and too few employees.

Which was why their caseworker didn't know that when

Mr. Duckman went on one of his frequent business trips, the little woman hung out with her boyfriend, a lowlife computer salesman named Karl Hilton, who liked to booze with her on the sofa, then fuck her.

Only one day, right before he was about to unzip his pants, he looked up and saw eleven-year-old Patty, standing in the doorway, her eyes wide as she watched the show.

The beer-sodden jerk leaped off the couch, charged across the room, and started slapping her on the face for being a Peeping Tanya. She screamed, and her brother Billy came running.

By then Mrs. Duckman was railing at Karl, telling him to let the little girl go. But he was too far gone to pay attention. And when Billy pounded on his back, he turned and swatted the boy across the room.

Billy came back. Only this time he didn't go after Karl. He reached for Patty, grabbing her arm and closing the secret connection they'd discovered, then nurtured, when they'd huddled in bed together at night, touching and cuddling and giving each other comfort any way they could.

She felt a surge of power leap between herself and her brother. And along with it came a strange mental clarity. Nobody had to tell her what to do next. It just happened.

They sent an arrow of pain shooting from their minds into Karl Hilton's body.

He made a low, frightened sound and staggered back, clutching his chest. And Patty and Billy dashed from the room and out to the old toolshed in the backyard, where they'd made themselves a secret hideout.

They heard a siren wailing in the distance, then peeked out to see an ambulance pulling up in front of the house.

Hilton recovered from his heart attack. But Mrs. Duckman had some explaining to do to her husband. And Patty and Billy Anderson were sent to another foster home. One of the twelve they'd survived before they'd run away at the age of sixteen. They'd lived on the streets for a few days, protecting each other from the lowlifes who preyed on children.

But their talent had quickly gotten them into comfortable surroundings. They'd figured out a get-solvent-quick scheme. In the morning they'd hold hands as they stood shoulder to shoulder with passengers on a crowded rush hour bus or subway train—reading minds and finding out where cash was stashed in people's houses. Then, while the marks were at work, they'd break in and scoop up the dough. It had been like stealing cream from a kitten.

After that, they'd invaded the mind of the Reverend Horace Redman and persuaded him to make them part of his revival tent show—where they quickly became the stars of the act.

They'd gotten backers to finance a show of their own, accepting bigger and bigger contributions. They still traveled around the country—in grand style, now, their religious performances like a secret club available only to the fortunate few.

Last year they'd built their own temple here in Orlando. And now they were reaching for the stars.

A knock at the door made Willow look up.

"They're waiting for you," Michael called through the door.

"We'll be right there," Sax answered.

Then he lowered his head and pressed his lips to hers. Some people would have called the contact wrong. But Sax's strength had kept her afloat when life would have sucked her under.

She opened for him, welcoming the rush of heat, of thoughts and emotions. And when the kiss broke, she squared her shoulders.

"Okay?" he asked.

"No. But I'll fake it."

He squeezed her hand. Together they walked down the

short hallway and into the small chapel that they used when they weren't having a fully public service.

About a hundred worshipers were sitting in the rectangular room where Ionic columns soared to a high ceiling.

The chapel was reminiscent of the sanctuary in the Mount Vernon Place United Methodist Church, a famous house of worship in Washington, D.C., where one of their foster families had taken them.

The marble columns set off polished wood pews with red velvet seat cushions, built far enough apart so that there was easy access to every row. The huge stained glass windows at Mount Vernon Place had depicted scenes from the life of Christ. In the Trinity version, they were more like the landscapes of Louis Comfort Tiffany. At the front were the decorative pipes of a large organ.

The low hum of conversation cut off abruptly as the Perfect Pair stepped through the door at the side.

"Peace be with you," Sax and Willow murmured.

"And unto you, too," the congregation responded.

There was no railing at the front of the church. No lectern that separated leaders from followers. Sax and Willow always started the proceedings by wandering hand in hand among the faithful, stopping to touch a shoulder, or shake hands or even exchange a kiss with close supporters.

Right before a performance Willow always had the jitters. Probably she would have backed out if Sax had allowed it. But the moment she was "onstage," everything changed.

She found her serenity. Found her natural ability to draw people and hold them.

She and Sax made an unhurried trip through the audience, since the personal contact with the Perfect Pair was one of the high points of the service. They usually repeated it again at the end of the meeting to give others a chance.

Saxon stopped beside a sloppy blond woman with an alimony settlement of twenty thousand dollars a month.

"Thank you for coming, Bonnie," he said in a low voice. "We appreciate it."

Bonnie Darnell looked at him with adoration in her eyes, and Willow suppressed a small spurt of jealousy.

She moved a step away, letting go of her brother's hand as she touched one of the men on the arm, William Partlow, who had built his pipe-fitting business into a multimillion-dollar enterprise, then sold out.

"William," she said in a low, throaty voice. He sucked in a sharp breath as she made contact with him, probed his mind, and for a moment the two of them might have been the only people in the room. She felt the need coming off of him. The desperation to connect with her on a more intimate level. And she made him silent promises of a more private meeting—a promise that she might or might not keep.

As they returned to the front of the sanctuary, they turned to face the congregation, and she felt the hushed expectancy gather.

"Thank you for coming," Sax said in a quiet voice that always reminded Willow of the calm before a storm.

A murmur of acknowledgment ran through the room.

Willow smiled at the congregation, making contact with several people. "We call on the light of the universe to shine upon us," she said.

"We call on the currents that flow through the universe to nourish each individual soul in this room," Sax added. "We call on the best in every religion to fill our minds and hearts. Let no one in this room harbor unkind thoughts against his neighbor. Let no one here forget where we come from. In our personal lives, we have all survived tragedy and fear. As you know, Willow and I were left parentless at an early age, and we survived the worst child welfare system in existence. But we're stronger for it.

"The same strength resides in you. All of you have survived forces that sought to destroy you. But you walked through the fire and came out stronger."

"Yes," voices answered from around the room.

"Let us join our strength," Willow said. "So let us join our hands." She raised her right hand, bringing Sax's left with her. He stepped to the end of the first pew and clasped the hand of the woman sitting there. She took the hand of the woman next to her, and everyone in the room followed suit, those at the end of the row reaching behind or in front of them, until each person was part of a giant chain, and the man on Willow's left had risen to complete the circle.

A soft hum of energy pulsed through the connection and manifested itself visually in small sparks that flickered on the hands of the people who sat on the benches.

The energy sizzled as it raced around the room, coming back to Willow and Sax, flickering like a giant halo around their bodies. And in back of them the organ burst into the notes of a traditional Christian hymn—"Have Thine Own Way, Lord." As a child, Willow had hated the words that made her feel subservient to a higher power. Now that she was in charge of the service, she changed the meaning of the text in her mind.

They were no longer about Christ. They were about her and Sax, molding these sheep as they wished.

Though no one sat at the console at the side of the hall, the music swelled, keeping time with the flickering sparks.

The congregation swayed with the music. One woman called out in ecstasy. Then a man. An exaltation was on them. A feeling of sweet fulfillment that Willow knew how to kindle and fan.

She didn't need to look at Sax to know what he wanted now. She didn't need to move her lips to speak.

You all know that we have been looking for members of Congress who can help us achieve our goals of peace and harmony in the world. And we know that Senator Daniel Bridgewater has joined our team. We want him to remain strong in the Senate, and we want him to run for president. Please be generous in your contributions to him. Give him the same consideration that you would give us. Give him what you can. A thousand dollars would be a wonderful place to start. But if you can give more, we would be eternally grateful.

While she spoke, she and Sax kept the sparks flying over their skin. And she kept the energy flowing over her own body, knowing that when she finished she would be depleted—that she would need to renew her own resources.

It was exhausting work, swaying so many people at once. And when the music came to an end, she leaned back against the altar at the front of the room, her vision blurred, her breath labored.

"We must go," she said in a voice that barely carried to the first few pews.

Sax helped her through the door at the front of the room, shutting it behind them.

Michael was waiting, a muscular man with a broken nose and a deep scar on his soul. His childhood had been more traumatic than theirs. And he'd ended up in a juvenile detention center after he'd robbed a gas station at gunpoint. Incarceration had only hardened his resolve to get even with the society that had failed him. His life of crime had continued once he was on the streets again—with armed robberies and muggings.

One evening he'd tried to rob Sax and Willow Trinity on a street in downtown Chicago. That had been the luckiest night of his life. They'd stopped him cold with a surprise jolt of psychic energy. But Willow had seen something tender and vulnerable in his mind, qualities that had her begging Sax to go easy on him.

They'd taken away his desire to hurt them, then brought him back to their hotel suite and found the right buttons to push. He was completely devoted to them now. One of their most trusted employees, happy to serve for the joy of staying close to them and receiving their emotional balm.

He walked on the other side of her now, down the hall to the private "retiring room."

"How did it go?" he asked.

"Very well."

"I'm so happy about that."

She gave him a kiss on the cheek. "Thank you for taking care of us."

His eyes were worshipful as he answered, "You know I found my purpose in life when I met you."

"It's our pleasure to help you find your way."

They parted at the door. Then she and Sax stepped inside the retiring room, and he reached to snap the lock closed as he gathered her close and brought his mouth down on her.

The service had fed the basic need for intimacy with each other that was at the core of their existence.

They had discovered the connection between them when they were very young, two children who only had each other for comfort. That connection had grown and flourished. Now it was everything—their reason for living. Sometimes they might disagree on how to run their lives, but they had learned early that no other relationship could compare to this one. They were like Siamese twins, not joined at the hip but joined by a mental bond they had never tried to describe to anyone else.

"Bridgewater should be impressed when the money starts flowing in."

"Yes. The money . . . will reinforce his bond to us."

"He wants more than money."

She let her head drop to his shoulder. *He wants to help us. He's our spy in the government.*

He stroked the length of her back, and she silently asked, *You think he'll find anything that could harm us?*

I hope not. But the premonition is strong. Something is in the wind—like a hurricane spinning our way. I can't see it clearly. But just because it hasn't gotten here yet doesn't mean it's not coming.

A shiver went through her. Sax was the one who could sense the future. And when that strong intuition overtook him, he was usually right. But not always.

It may not be true. I'm just being careful.

I know.

She didn't want it to be true. Not now. Not ever. She wanted her life to go on the way it had since they'd broken free of their past and taken charge of their own destiny. Together, they had made something bold and beautiful out of garbage. And they had to hold on to that goodness at all costs.

We'll be fine. I promise we'll be fine.

Blind to everything but each other, they clung together, feeding the connection that had changed them from losers to winners. From victims to the gods.

MARK Greenwood lay with his eyes closed, hoping that he looked relaxed as he contemplated a fortuitous set of circumstances.

He was coming out of his fog, the way he did when his shot was wearing off.

So he could think almost clearly.

Was it a dream, what he'd heard the head bitch say?

Her name was Brenda, and she was in solid with the chief monster—Dr. Colefax.

She'd been talking about a new nurse named Emmeline, who was coming on the evening shift. Brenda was hoping the rookie wasn't going to screw up—since this was heavy-duty work.

Or was any of that true? Had he just made up the conversation?

One thing he knew; he'd been in this damn bed for

weeks. At least it felt like weeks, although there was no good way to tell the time. Another fact he'd picked up— they were holding him in a private mental hospital, not a medical facility.

Since he'd started thinking straight, he'd been careful not to give the staff any trouble. Mostly he daydreamed—about sitting in Jen's kitchen eating chocolate chip cookies and milk with his cousin Sid. Or about the future—about the security company he was going to open. He had spent a lot of time stocking the shelves with a great selection of rifles, baseball equipment, clothing. All the guy stuff he loved.

While he soothed himself with a mental trip through a selection of mail-order catalogues, he worked his muscles, trying to keep them in reasonable shape. And when they'd walked him down the hall, he'd tried to study the layout of the facility.

If this Emmeline person was really coming on duty, then she was his best chance. So he pulled at the sheet and light blanket, making them fall off the side of the bed, then lay with tension coiling in his stomach as he waited for her to come in and give him his evening shot.

When the door opened, he cracked an eyelid.

Yeah, she was new, all right. A little brunette with a cheerful blue-and-green uniform top and a pinched look on her ivory features.

He hated to hurt her, but he didn't think he had much choice. Talking to her wouldn't do any good, since she'd been told he was a dangerous maniac.

"I see your covers are falling off," she said as she strode toward him.

He waited until she was within striking range, then jack-knifed his legs, hitting her square in the stomach with his feet.

He heard the air whoosh out of her lungs as she fell back. He leaped after her, coming down on top of her hard.

She struggled against him, but he knocked her out, then

tied her hands behind her back with the strips he'd ripped with his teeth and torn from the side of the sheet. Next, he stuffed more sheeting in her mouth and tied it in place. Finally he secured her feet and dragged her into the bathroom.

"Sorry, sweetheart," he murmured as he left her in a heap on the tile floor. "I hope I don't get you fired," he added. "But my need is more urgent than yours."

He had already checked the closet. His shirt and trousers were missing. But the light cotton robe would cover his ass where it hung out of his hospital gown.

He slipped on the robe and peeked into the hall. When he saw no one, he stepped out of his room and hurried toward the Exit sign.

His heart was pounding, and so was his head. He fought a wave of nausea as he went down the stairs—not to the ground floor, since the door at the bottom might be locked.

Praying he had time to get the hell out of Dodge, he opened the door, then darted back when a man came around the corner. The guy disappeared into another room along the hall.

Mark waited a beat then stepped out—and leaped into an office. With a window. And, praise God, no bars. A short drop led to a flat roof. He scrambled out, then hurried across the gravel surface. This time the drop was a whole story. But he lowered himself by his hands, hanging for a moment before letting go and landing in a flower bed.

The facility had a fence. He headed for the guardhouse at the gate. He was breathing hard, his heart racing. If he'd thought he was in shape, he'd been kidding himself.

The farther he got from the building, the more hopeful he felt—and at the same time more terrified that somebody was going to figure out he'd flown the coop.

But he told himself he was going to get out of this hellhole or die trying. He'd been trained in stealth warfare—which gave him an advantage over the rent-a-cop manning the guard station.

He got the guy from behind in a choke hold, then bashed him over the head with his own nightstick.

The guard had a couple of other things he could use, too. Like the keys to the Jeep Cherokee sitting next to the gate—and a pair of pants and a shirt that were large but better than the hospital gown and robe.

He had opened the gate when he heard a bell begin to clang inside the building. At the same time the gate started to close again.

His heart stopped, then started thumping in double time.

Behind him he heard pounding feet.

Cursing he gunned the engine, bashing the front bumper into the wire mesh.

The gate made a grinding sound, and he floored the accelerator. Metal ground against metal, but he plowed forward because that was his only option.

The gate tore off the back bumper as it clanked closed like the jaws of a prehistoric monster. But he kept going into the night—praying that he could make it just a little farther down the road before he had to get rid of the vehicle.

CHAPTER THIRTEEN

UP IN THE private quarters above his office, Kurt MacArthur was nuzzling his lips against Mary Ann's neck and pulling down the zipper at the back of her dress when the phone rang.

He cursed—then cursed again when he turned his head and saw the number on the caller ID.

Dr. William Colefax was on the line.

Snatching up the receiver, Kurt growled, "This had better be important."

"Mark Greenwood has escaped."

"What the shit! You're supposed to be running a secure institution. You said the new treatment was working."

"He assaulted his nurse."

"He's still in the building?"

"He also assaulted the guard at the main gate. He's gone."

"Find him!"

"We're trying. We need more men."

"Okay. I'll have a team down there in"—he looked at the clock on the bedside table—"forty minutes."

"Can we have a helicopter with a searchlight?"

"He's on foot?"

"He stole a Jeep. But we found it abandoned down the road."

Kurt grunted. "I'll get back to you on the chopper deal."

"Do we try to take him alive?" Colefax asked.

Kurt spoke through his clamped jaw. "He's our only witness, but he's resisted every attempt you've made to get him to tell you what happened during the break-in. I still want to try and get something out of him. But that may be impossible. If you can't take him alive, bring him in any way you can."

After clicking the Disconnect button, he looked into Mary Ann's worried eyes.

"Trouble at Colefax's loony bin?" she asked.

"Yeah."

He liked the way she snapped instantly back into work mode. As she fumbled with her zipper, Kurt thought about some of the emergencies he'd handled over the years. Including some incredible cover-up operations. Like hanging one of the biggest commercial air disasters in history around the neck of a supposedly suicidal Egyptian co-pilot. And Kurt had pulled that off right under the noses of the Transportation Safety Board.

Sending the plane crashing into the Atlantic Ocean had been the only way to get rid of master terrorist Ali Al Zahir, since the chances of convicting the bastard on any specific crime were nil.

But with that assignment and the others, he'd had adequate facts. With the Maple Creek fiasco, essential understanding was still beyond his grasp.

Dammit!

Now Greenwood was on the loose. And Greenwood at large was a big fat problem. How unstable was he? Would he go to the police? The newspapers?

Kurt stroked his chin. Should he pull Swift off his present assignment? Not until tomorrow. Maybe they'd get lucky and nail the escapee tonight.

AFTER cracking Dr. Lucas's correspondence files, Jim Swift had parked behind a thick stand of pines where he could see the entrance to the Hamilton estate. When a call from headquarters came in, he reached for his cell phone.

"Swift here."

"This is MacArthur. We're having a flap down in Maryland. I need you to join the search team."

He'd never heard MacArthur lose his cool—until now. "What happened?"

"Mark Greenwood escaped from Colefax Manor."

Jim whistled through his teeth. Bad news. But he wasn't going to state the obvious. "When?"

"Last night. I thought they'd have him by now. But he's managed to elude capture. I want you on the scene—calling the shots."

"On my way," Jim said.

He was about to pull back onto the road when he saw a flash of motion. Raising his head, he watched a silver Mercedes stop at the gate that spanned the entrance to the Hamilton estate. A man's arm reached out to press the button on the intercom, but his back was to Jim, and he couldn't get much of an impression of the driver.

Snatching up his binoculars, he focused on the license plate. The car was from D.C. He got the first three letters and two of the numbers. But he wasn't quite fast enough to get the last one.

"Shit," he muttered as the vehicle disappeared beyond the gates. He'd like to know who was visiting Hamilton. A friend making a condolence call to the grieving father? Or someone wound up in the case?

He'd find out. But he couldn't do it now—not when MacArthur needed him somewhere else.

JORDAN got out of his car and stood for a moment staring at the massive pile of brick and half-timbering that Leonard Hamilton called home. The estate looked the same as when he'd come here a few weeks earlier, except that the white and yellow tulips in the flower beds had been replaced by red and white geraniums.

Then he'd thought he had a choice about accepting

Leonard Hamilton's offer. Now he felt like a flounder on the end of a hook. And he couldn't wiggle off.

It wasn't simply because Hamilton had offered him a story too juicy to refuse. The investigation had become personal—as though his own fate were wound up with uncovering the truth.

He'd come up here to put the screws to the old man. Unfortunately, he couldn't get Lindsay Fleming out of his mind. He kept imagining himself turning around and driving back to Washington—because when he was away from her it was difficult to draw a full breath.

He clenched his hands into fists, fighting the pressure building inside him. When he'd pulled himself together, he pushed the doorbell and heard the chimes sound inside.

The same butler led him down the wide hallway to the back of the house. As he stepped into the conservatory, he was struck once more by the lush, expensive atmosphere of the room. This time Leonard Hamilton was already waiting for him, sitting on his motorized cart, sipping from a tall glass.

"Get yourself a drink from the bar," Hamilton said. "And a sandwich if you want."

Apparently they'd passed the stage of needing the butler to serve them.

Jordan poured himself a glass of water from a crystal pitcher. Sitting next to the drinks was a selection of small sandwiches. Roast beef, ham, tuna, egg salad.

He grabbed a couple and brought them to the Victorian-style table and chairs. But instead of eating, he said, "How about playing straight with me for a change"

"I have been."

Hoping to jolt the old man, he said, "Dr. Charles Lucas is dead. You got him mixed up in your private investigation, and he paid with his life."

Hamilton's face drained of blood. "What happened?"

"His office told me he had a heart attack. Then they transferred my call to another number. Lucky for me I was calling from a public phone."

"You think they had a trace on his phone?"

"Yeah. And I think the faster I figure out what happened to your son, the safer we'll both be. Because we're sitting on a time bomb. So stop playing games and tell me what you know."

The old man's expression didn't change. "First, tell me what you've found out."

Jordan fought the urge to throttle the man. Instead he kept his voice even as he said, "Okay, just so we're on the same page, I know that the drug that killed Todd was part of an Army research project from the eighties called Granite Wall. It was supposed to have been terminated. Either someone has reactivated the program, or they're drawing from a secret stockpile. And I have a letter Todd wrote to Senator Daniel Bridgewater."

He took a copy from his briefcase and handed it across the table.

Hamilton read the letter from his son. "This says Todd knew about a project that was resurrected. And not at Fort Detrick."

"Somewhere in the continental U.S.," Jordan answered, thinking that he might have a more specific location.

"That's a big help!"

"It's interesting that Todd used military terminology. CONUS—continental United States. Was he ever in the Army?"

"No. But his good friend Glenn Barrow was—before he admitted his sexual preference, and they kicked him out."

"He lived with Glenn?"

"They kept separate residences."

"Did Todd come home often? Would he have hidden anything important here?"

"He knew I disapproved of his lifestyle. But he'd always made a point of being dutiful. So he came up here every few weeks—to make sure I was still alive."

"Well then, I'd like to search his room."

"You have a nice way of putting that."

"Yeah. It justifies a trip up from Washington—since you're still holding out on me."

"How do you know?"

"My instincts are excellent."

The old man hesitated for a moment. He was watching Jordan carefully as he said, "Have you ever heard of a Dr. Henry Remington?"

Jordan searched his memory. "No."

"He ran a fertility clinic. My wife and I had problems conceiving. Remington was doing advanced work—maybe work that was revolutionary for the time."

"Like what?"

"In vitro fertilization."

"And Todd was conceived as a result of your treatment by Remington? Were drugs involved?"

"For my wife? Yes."

"You're telling me this because you think that somehow Dr. Remington's treatment could have been a factor in Todd's childhood problems?"

"It's worth investigating."

"Is Remington still in business?"

"He died of a heart attack when Todd was two," Hamilton said, his voice flat. "Like Dr. Lucas, apparently."

"Are you drawing a connection between the two deaths?"

Hamilton shrugged. "That's your job."

"Where was the clinic—in Delaware?"

"No. Connecticut. Darien, Connecticut."

Jordan felt goose bumps pepper his skin, but he chose to ignore them. Connecticut again.

"Do you have any information on the clinic?" he asked.

Hamilton reached into the carry bag hanging from the arm of his electric cart. "This should get you started."

LINDSAY stood staring into the pantry, thinking she should be making a grocery list. Yet she couldn't even do something that simple. Instead she was picturing Jordan sitting in a conservatory filled with lush plantings. He was facing a white-haired old man who sat on an electric scooter. A man whose lined visage spoke of his determination and his pain—physical and mental. Leonard Hamilton.

She hadn't pictured the millionaire's private Eden until now. With her eyes closed, she tried to focus on the scene, struggling to hear what they were saying. But she couldn't bring it into focus.

She huffed out a breath. Did she really think she could listen in on what Hamilton and Walker were saying?

No. That was impossible. Yet she couldn't shake the feeling that the words were real—and just beyond her reach.

Gathering every scrap of her attention, she tried again to tune in the conversation. But the static in the background made comprehension impossible.

Finally, in frustration, she went back to the notepad she'd left on the kitchen table.

She wrote down *bacon,* then stared at the sheet. Bacon was fattening. She hadn't planned on buying any. So who was it for?

Gripping the pencil, she began to write again, letting the hand guide her. Bacon, Fuji apples, eggs, imported Stilton cheese, gourmet coffee, hummus, pita bread, basil spaghetti sauce.

A list of foods that Jordan Walker liked. And she wasn't even sure how she'd come by the information.

* * *

JORDAN skimmed through the material Hamilton handed him. It included a thirty-year-old address for the Remington Fertility Clinic and a phone number—along with the names of some of the nurses who had worked there.

"I believe the doctor had a government research grant. So he could take low-income families in addition to the well off."

"Charitable of him," Jordan murmured. He was thinking there was more to this discussion than had come to the surface. But demanding answers didn't work with Hamilton. Instead he said, "Maybe I should take a look at Todd's room now."

The old man's hands clenched on the arms of his chair, and Jordan watched him consider his next words carefully. "We started off talking about a biography of me. Are you working on that?"

"We both know we've got to deal with Todd first."

Hamilton looked relieved. "Yes."

"You knew how to bait and switch," Jordan observed dryly.

The old man chuckled. "Yes, I did, didn't I?" He pressed a button on what looked like a remote control.

Moments later the butler who had showed Jordan to the conservatory appeared.

"Yes, sir?"

"Take Mr. Walker up to Todd's room. He is to have complete access to the premises."

"Very good, sir."

ALMOST faint with exhaustion, Mark pulled his stolen car up the long driveway. How many degrees of separation were safe? He didn't know. But he had to rest somewhere secure, so he'd made his way to this vacation house near

St. Marys, Maryland. It belonged to the parents of a kid named Tim Edgers he'd been tight with at the community college back in Howard County. But Tim's father had died, and his mom rarely came here by herself. Which was why Tim had brought his pals down here to party.

Mark just hoped she hadn't sold it to someone who wanted to take up more permanent residence.

There were no other vehicles in evidence. So he pulled the car he'd stolen around back where nobody could see it from the road.

He'd taken it from a house not far from Dr. Colefax's asylum. An older model that he could hot-wire. He'd learned the skill as part of his Special Forces training. He contemplated that irony as he stared at the darkened house, praying no one was home.

He climbed out of the car, then gritted his teeth against a wave of pain in his head. Probably from equal parts raw nerves and the damn drugs that asshole Dr. Colefax had given him.

At the back door he looked around carefully, hoping that nobody had noticed his arrival.

When he'd come here as a teenager, Tim had gotten the key from under a rock beside the stoop. It was still there, and Mark mouthed a small thank-you.

Once inside he made a quick trip through the house, satisfying himself that it was empty. Then he grabbed a knife from a kitchen drawer, laid it on the table beside him, and collapsed onto the sofa.

As he sat with his head back, breathing hard, he wondered what the hell he was going to do now.

He needed money. A gun. And a more secure hiding place.

· When he felt a little better, he got up and staggered back into the kitchen. There wasn't much to eat, but he found an unopened box of sugar-coated cereal. After tearing off the top, he started eating out of the box.

The only reason he'd gotten this far was that he'd been born and raised in Maryland. He'd been able to take some back roads Colefax's men wouldn't have known about.

But now what? He'd been lucky to escape the goon squad. Staying out of their clutches was going to be dicey.

He remembered a book he'd read about a guy who'd kept the government from coming after him by telling his story to the *New York Times*. A great idea in fiction.

But it would be difficult for him to pull that off—when his most recent address had been the loony bin.

CHAPTER
FOURTEEN

IN THE COURSE of his career, Jordan had never flinched from an illegal search. He'd given the police a tip that led to the arrest and conviction of a serial killer who had kept jewelry from the women he'd murdered.

And he'd found hidden records that proved an accountant was stealing funds from old ladies who trusted him to manage their financial affairs. He'd even gone Dumpster diving outside a famous Washington, D.C., men's club and come away with evidence that someone inside was selling controlled substances to the members.

This morning he couldn't suppress the feeling that he was violating Todd Hamilton's privacy as he stood in the doorway to the dead man's childhood bedroom.

Todd hadn't listed his father's house as his home address for six or seven years. But he had come here regularly, and maybe he'd hidden materials here that he didn't want discovered in his own apartment.

Shrugging off his reluctance, Jordan started with a quick inspection of the room—which was huge—perhaps twenty by eighteen. It looked like it had been redecorated sometime in Todd's teens. The furniture was dark, expensive, and well cared for, nothing like the scratched and dented bedroom set from his own youth. Floor-to-ceiling bookcases spanned one wall. Along with books, board games, CDs, and VCR tapes were expensive model cars that Todd had apparently collected as a boy.

The stereo system was state of the art. And a flat-screen television graced the wall across from the bed. Either Todd had a lot of money to spend, or his father had decided to make the living quarters as appealing as possible.

There were some interesting touches in the room. A couple of trophies sat on the middle shelves of the bookcase. Jordan picked them up and discovered that Todd had won them both in spelling bees at the Winthrop Academy. He'd also saved ribbons he'd won for horsemanship. Apparently, he was proud of his adolescent achievements.

On the top shelf were two plastic cups—one from a snowcone shop on Tchoupitoulas Street in New Orleans. The other was from a bar on Bourbon Street.

Jordan turned away from the bookcase and stepped into the adjoining bathroom. Lifting the lid on toilet tank, he looked for a plastic bag hiding government secrets. No dice.

And the medicine cabinet yielded nothing besides the information that Todd had sensitive skin, used tooth whitener, and suffered from allergies.

Repressing his frustration, Jordan began a methodical search of the bedroom. None of the baseboards or floorboards was loose. And Todd hadn't fallen back on the traditional "under the mattress" hiding place.

In fact, he'd used the Purloined Letter method.

In plain sight on his desk was a metal rack with colored file folders. One held directions for the various electronics equipment in the room. Another was stuffed with Caribbean travel brochures.

A third had some clothing catalogues. In one the page advertising black sweatpants and shirts was bookmarked—with a folded piece of printer paper.

If Jordan hadn't been pretty methodical himself, he would have left the paper where it was. Instead, he unfolded it and found a handwritten map showing what appeared to be a government agricultural research facility called "Maple Creek." It was located near Waldorf, Maryland, less than fifty miles from the Chesapeake Bay, where Todd's body had been discovered.

Maple Creek!

Suspicion confirmed. Lindsay's visit from Sid Becker was connected to the Todd Hamilton case.

Todd had saved this map—and hidden it in plain sight. Because he'd wanted it to be found if anything happened to him?

Jordan stuffed it into his own briefcase. And kept looking. He unearthed notes on some research projects at Fort Detrick in a similarly unlikely place—a textbook Todd had saved from his prep school days.

So, would Lindsay know about these projects? Would she share the information?

Lindsay again.

He'd been trying to keep his mind off of her. Finally that was impossible.

Sitting down on the bed, he allowed his thoughts to wing back to her—and saw her standing in the produce department of a grocery store. He recognized it. Whole Foods on Wisconsin Avenue. Was she really there? Or was he just trying to feel closer to her?

All at once the separation was intolerable. He had to stop himself from racing down the stairs and out the door without saying good-bye to Hamilton.

Instead, he sought out the old man, who was leaning over the handlebars of his motorized cart—dozing. He snapped erect, looking embarrassed, when he heard footsteps on the tile floor.

"I'm going back to D.C.," Jordan said.

"Did you find anything?"

Jordan hesitated. "Maybe it's safer if we don't share information on a regular basis."

The old man's eyes narrowed. "Safer for whom?"

"Both of us."

"Maybe. But I can see you found something. And I want to know what you unearthed in my son's room!"

"I found a list of projects at Fort Detrick."

"Where?" Todd's father demanded.

"In an old chemistry book."

Hamilton snorted. "An ironic place to hide information on Defense Department chemical and biological warfare projects."

"Yeah."

"Did you find anything else?"

Because he knew Hamilton would note any hesitation, Jordan went on quickly, "That was all. And speaking of sharing—when you decide to tell me what you're hiding, give me a call."

Hamilton's lips firmed.

Jordan waited for a moment to see if the millionaire wanted to say anything more. When he kept silent, Jordan turned and walked out of the conservatory.

MARK had slept for a few hours, then scavenged for food again. Maybe he was paranoid, but he'd wiped up any fingerprints he might have left initially, then found a pair of leather gloves in the coat closet and pulled them on.

He'd just chugged down a can of room-temperature Coke when he heard the sound of a car in the driveway.

"Shit."

Glad he'd taken precautions, he hurried toward the window and carefully pulled a curtain aside. A large man with thick blond hair had gotten out of the car. He was dressed in a yellow knit shirt and well-worn jeans. He stood in the driveway looking at the car Mark had stolen.

"Aw, shit," he repeated. He didn't recognize the guy out there. Was it one of Dr. Colefax's goons? Or somebody connected to this house?

Whoever he was, he returned to his car, popped the trunk, and pulled out a hunting rifle.

Mark's heart was pounding as he retrieved the knife

from the coffee table. He could run out the front door. But he wouldn't get far on foot.

And he wasn't going to let them take him again. Yet at the same time he felt nausea bubble in his throat as the guy approached the house. This man might be an innocent bystander. Which didn't mean he wasn't a jerk if he intended to go up against an intruder himself, instead of doing the smart thing and calling the cops.

The throbbing in Mark's head surged as he closed his hand around the knife handle. With his supercharged state of awareness, he thought he heard the guy outside cock the rifle.

So what did he think—that kids had broken into the house—and he was going to scare them shitless—or maybe blow their heads off and claim self-defense?

Mark moved to the side of the door and flattened his shoulders against the wall.

From his hiding place, he heard keys jingling on a metal ring—before one slipped into the lock.

He hated hiding like a sneak thief. But he stayed where he was until the intruder stepped into the room, crouched over like he thought he was a goddamned SWAT team leader.

Mark stepped forward, thrusting the point of the knife against Mr. Macho's back. "Move a muscle and you're dead!" he growled.

Instead of being smart and freezing, the man started to turn. As his hand jerked on the trigger, the rifle discharged, blowing a hole in the wall—and blowing Mark's improvised plans to bits. He had only a split second to react. He still had the knife. He could jab the guy in the ribs—which might be a fatal move. Or he could drop the knife and try for the rifle—which would give him the upper hand.

The blade clattered across the floor as he reached for the rifle barrel, yanking hard.

But the other man kept a death grip on the weapon. They struggled for possession, turning in a circle, both desperate to end up with the gun. As Mark spun past the open door, sunlight flashed into his line of vision. Instinctively he blinked.

Mr. Macho grunted and gave a mighty tug. Mark tried to compensate, but lost his footing.

The rifle fired again, and Mr. Macho screamed, the toe of his boot blown away.

Mark shoved him backward, and he landed in a heap on the floor.

Both barrels of the rifle were now empty. The man looked down, staring at the blood leaking from the toe of his shoe.

His face had gone gray. Beads of perspiration bloomed on his forehead. Feeling sick, Mark leaped on him, scrabbling through his pockets, grabbing his keys and his wallet before fleeing outside toward the car still in the driveway.

JORDAN had rented a motel room in Wilmington, where he'd planned to spend the night. Instead he checked out and headed back to D.C. Back to Lindsay.

He'd only met her a few days ago. He barely knew her. Well, if you thought in conventional terms. But there was nothing conventional about the way her mind had opened to him—or his to her.

As he drove south, he kept picturing himself folding her into his arms, ravaging her mouth, ripping her clothing from her body so he could feel his skin pressed to hers.

The sexual fog made driving difficult. To keep some semblance of sanity, he tried to focus on another problem— the puzzle of Leonard Hamilton.

The old man knew something important. Something he wanted to keep hidden.

If he were acting normally, Jordan would have turned around, driven back to the estate, and demanded that the old prevaricator come clean.

He focused on the Hamiltons—Senior and Junior—for as long as he could. But after he drove through the tunnel just north of Baltimore, he couldn't prevent his fevered thoughts from zinging back to Lindsay.

The need to connect with her suddenly gripped his chest like an iron band. Where was she? In her apartment?

She was in her kitchen. She was going to put the groceries away. Only she had decided to leave them in the bags.

Or was he just glomming onto that picture to calm himself down?

He didn't know. But he couldn't turn off the picture, either.

He almost pulled off at a rest stop so that he could sit in the car with his eyes closed and try to bring her into focus. But that would be a waste of time. Better to speed up and ask her to meet him. He could call her on his cell phone. No, he'd gotten paranoid about leaving a trail.

Could he just send a message to her through the ether?

He snorted. Sure. And next he could put Jonathan Edwards out of a job.

The idea of sending her a . . . telepathic . . . message made him feel light-headed. But that's what you called it—didn't you? What he and Lindsay had been doing. When they touched. When they kissed. When he turned her on. And she made him so hard he thought he might explode.

The erotic images in his head fueled a rising tide of urgency—part sexual need. Part something he couldn't name. The need to connect with her on the most basic level? And what was that—exactly?

The frustration bubbled up, spilling out into words he spoke aloud into the closed compartment of the vehicle: "Lindsay, can you hear me?"

He waited tensely. Shit! What was he expecting? That he'd hear her voice coming from the empty passenger seat?

He managed a strangled laugh. But now that he'd started the mental game, he couldn't quit.

"Go to the Bishop's Garden," he whispered into the silence of the Mercedes. "Lindsay, go to the Bishop's Garden. Wait for me there."

He realized after he'd said it that the last time they'd been there, they'd been locked together on the grass.

No. They'd been standing up. The part about rolling naked on the lawn had simply been his fantasy.

But maybe she was too embarrassed to go back there. Maybe . . .

"Shit." He was already worried that she wouldn't get his Twilight Zone message. Changing the meeting place was only going to confuse her. And maybe the damn garden was the best alternative—since both of them had very vivid thoughts of their last encounter.

His hands gripped the wheel as he sped toward D.C., desire and uncertainty warring inside him. He had no idea if his message to Lindsay was going anywhere besides into the fluffy clouds he could see wafting across the sky in front of him. But he knew he had to make her stop running from him. He knew he would go mad if he didn't make love to her.

He also understood deep in his gut that there was a flip side to the coin. Because pressing his naked body to hers might be the last sane thing he ever did.

Yet simply contemplating the tantalizing possibility was enough to make his blood boil. He wanted to grind down on the accelerator—to take the car up to eighty. But he forced himself to stay a few miles above the speed limit because he knew the cops loved this stretch of I-95.

ALTHOUGH it might be Saturday, Kurt MacArthur could direct the search for Mark Greenwood better from his office.

But after he'd arrived at his desk, he found he was simply

sitting around waiting for new information on the escapee. So he decided to tackle the Maple Creek problem from a different angle. Todd Hamilton.

He'd received a couple of folders full of material from Jim Swift with information pertaining to the millionaire's dead son. His MVA record. His phone calls. His school transcripts. His medical history. The material went all the way back to nursery school.

Kurt hadn't had time to go over any of that in detail. Now he took the folders to the comfortable sitting area in the office complex. Settling onto the sofa, he laid the folders on the coffee table, then shuffled through them.

He started with the most current information. Phone records were usually interesting. But Todd had been careful—or paranoid. He hadn't revealed anything Kurt didn't already know in the calls from home or his cell phone.

He went on to credit card records. Todd had purchased a Glock eight months ago.

Kurt snorted. Apparently the guy had bought into the he-man Glock myth. And he'd been concerned about concealability—so he'd purchased the model 27. He hadn't bothered to take it to Maple Creek, though. It had been in his Baltimore apartment when they'd searched the place.

He'd also bought clothing that was suitable for undercover work. And he'd wasted his inherited money on big contributions to Greenpeace and other environmental groups.

Mary Ann looked in the door, and Kurt glanced up. "Anything on the Greenwood problem?"

"No, sir."

"Have any teams reported in?"

"Yes. But there's no new information."

"Make me a Reuben sandwich with the low-carb rye bread. And bring me more coffee."

"Yes, sir."

He stood up and stretched, unwilling to reveal his disquiet by pacing back and forth across the Berber carpet. He also resisted the urge to make some personal phone calls to the men out searching for Greenwood.

Mary Ann brought in his lunch and set it on the round table in the corner. He carried the research material to the dining area and thumbed through more documents while he ate—still frustrated in his mission to figure out how Todd Hamilton and his friend had overpowered the security team at Maple Creek.

With a sigh he shoved his sandwich aside and shuffled through the folders, picking one at random. It had photocopies of records from Todd's elementary school days.

He'd arrived in first grade already able to read, Kurt noted. His math skills had also been good. He'd been smart, but he'd been a loner kid with few friends.

The teacher, Mrs. Jacobson, had made a notation in his permanent record speculating that his social problems had something to do with his background. He was the son of a very rich man. And his parents were always pulling him out of school to take him to somewhere called the Remington Clinic.

Kurt's breath went still.

The Remington Clinic. What the hell?

Standing, he strode across the room and booted up his computer.

He waited impatiently for the security systems to do their thing, then typed in his password—Jehovah101. His little joke.

When the menu came up, he called up "Old Business."

He was looking for a project from the days when he'd first come on board at the Crandall Consortium—back when the U.S. government had thought they were in a race with the Soviet Union for world domination. They'd known that the Commies were willing to try all kinds of nutball strategies to get ahead. The Kremlin had authorized projects that tried to find psychics who could remotely view faraway locations. They'd delved deeply into the use of "truth serum" and other chemicals as part of interrogation techniques. They'd had an extensive spy program designed to steal military and other technology from the West. And they'd tried to use genetics to breed children who were superior in various ways.

Calvin Crandall had gone looking for similar projects. And the Remington Clinic had been one of them—although relatively late in the game.

Kurt could still hear the doctor's supercilious voice echoing in his mind when he'd sat in on sessions with Remington and Crandall.

"Eight hours is the optimum time for the genetic manipulation of a human embryo."

In the late seventies human embryos had been in short supply. Not like today, when in vitro fertilization was common. So Remington had come up with an ingenious method for obtaining them. He'd set up a "fertility clinic" where couples having trouble conceiving could take advantage of the latest techniques.

But really, his goal had been to produce superintelligent children who could beat out the Soviets in the race for scientists to run the space program, military weapons programs, and all the other programs considered essential for grinding the Soviets into the ground.

Remington had received ongoing grants from the Crandall Consortium. He'd also charged big bucks to couples who could pay for his fertility services. But he'd taken on others for reduced fees—if he'd thought they were suitable for his purposes.

The results had never been what Calvin had hoped for. Remington had been highly successful in establishing pregnancies and bringing them to term. But as far as Crandall could determine, the babies had been only modestly more intelligent than their counterparts conceived in the normal fashion. On the other hand, a surprising number had ended up being taken to shrinks. At least the upper-class ones whose parents could afford the best for their little brats.

He called up the ancient files on the clinic—files that had been converted to current computer technology because Kurt believed in documenting anything Crandall had done in the past—especially operations in which he'd been personally involved.

The records were very complete. Calvin Crandall had insisted on that. And Kurt went right to a list of the children conceived by the clinic's methods.

Sure enough, Todd Hamilton had been born of the sixty-seventh successful pregnancy. His birthday and the names of his parents and hometown were also listed.

Now they were getting somewhere!

On a hunch, Kurt scrolled up higher and found another familiar name—Glenn Barrow.

Son of a bitch! They were both in the program. So what the hell did that mean? That Remington's half-assed experiments had produced a group of emotionally disturbed kids who would grow up to be troublemakers? And how had these two subjects gotten together? Had they met in the Remington waiting room when they were in diapers and kept in touch?

He went back to the list, stroking his chin, looking for other names he recognized. He saw several. The women were a problem, though. They were listed under the last names they'd been born with. But he'd expect many of them would have married by now.

Pressing his intercom, he snapped, "Mary Ann."

She was at the door in moments. "What do you need?"

"I'm sending a file of names to your computer. Start doing a Google search on as many of them as you can find. Look for people born in the late seventies or early eighties, probably from Connecticut or a nearby state."

"How deep a search?"

"Just a paragraph on each one." He leaned back in his chair. "It's a long list. If you can't find anything interesting on one guy, go on to the next."

"Yes, sir. What do you consider interesting?"

"Use your judgment. No—wait. Look for antisocial and criminal activity." He went on rapidly. "With the women, try and see if you can figure out any of their married names."

"Yes, sir."

When Mary Ann had departed, Kurt stood. He hadn't thought about the fertility clinic in years. Now he brought back the scene when Calvin had called him in and told him that Remington was looking for other sources of funding. His boss had asked him to evaluate the viability of the project.

He'd reported his findings on the children. They'd discussed the fussy little doctor with his arrogant demands. Finally, Calvin had asked him to terminate the research operation—with extreme prejudice.

CHAPTER
FIFTEEN

DANIEL BRIDGEWATER HAD brought no luggage with him to Orlando, but Willow and Sax were expecting him. He had called from a pay phone at Reagan National Airport to tell them he had business with them. And they had told him that some of the campaign contributions they'd promised were already on the way.

Taking off on the spur of the moment wasn't his customary style. But he needed to see the Trinitys in person. That's what he told himself on the way down. But he kept wondering if that was the real reason for his obsessive behavior.

And he understood deep down in his consciousness that he should turn around and go home. He had no business getting mixed up with this pair of charlatans. But they had promised him money. Money he needed for his campaign for president, so he drove to their mansion.

At night it had looked rich and impressive in the glow of warm yellow spotlights. In daylight it looked a little tacky—like an extension of Disney World.

Again, he questioned what he was doing here—even as he parked and rang the door chimes.

The last time he had been to the mansion, Sax had greeted him personally. This afternoon a guy who acted more like a bouncer than a butler showed him into a small but comfortable room that looked out over gardens of too-bright flowers.

As he cooled his heels, he thought about why he had really come here. To see Willow. She had the hots for him, and maybe she would meet him alone this time.

When the pair walked in together, he had to contain a surge of disappointment.

He wanted to ask Sax to leave. He wanted privacy with the woman whose heartbreakingly beautiful face and feminine body called to him.

"On the phone you sounded like you had some important information," his blond goddess said, sitting beside him, her knee pressed to his.

"Yes," he answered, knowing that he had come here to make love to her—and the promise of information had only been a ruse. Or had he come here for money? He couldn't remember.

Really, the idea that he was going to babble military secrets to her or her brother was unthinkable.

He watched them sitting beside him, holding hands like lovers, and he felt like barbed wire was twisting in his gut.

Then he reminded himself he was a powerful U.S. senator. She was just an upstart religious nut. And he'd come all the way down here to Florida to see her?

A wave of panic gripped him. He wasn't thinking rationally. He should get out of this room. Out of this house. What the hell was he doing here?

But when she laid a hand on his knee, his jumbled thoughts became clear.

He heard her make a small exclamation. Then her gaze bored into his.

"What about Maple Creek?" she asked.

Alarm leaped inside him. "Where did you get that name? It's supposed to be classified."

"I got it from you. You just told me. I asked you to let us know if you heard anything . . . unusual, and you were good enough to come to us with the information."

He saw the intensity of her expression—and her brother's.

"No . . . I . . . I was just thinking it."

"Yes." Her hand slid up his leg, pressed over his fly, making him instantly hard.

"I want you," he gasped out.

"I know. And I want you, too, Dan. So much. But first you need to tell me about Maple Creek. Why did it stand out in your mind? Why is it important?"

He wanted to pull her into his arms and ravage her mouth with his. He wanted to be alone with her. But when she pushed him back into the sofa cushions, he knew his knees were too weak to allow him to stand.

"Tell me what you know about Maple Creek," she whispered.

"It's a research facility. I'm not sure what they do there. Well, I know it's defense oriented. But I've never—"

"Why are you worried about it?"

"A couple of weeks ago something strange happened."

She sighed, and he felt her exasperation. He didn't want to make her angry. He wanted to please her.

When she asked, "How do you know?" he answered promptly.

"There's a report. It's secret. But I have contacts. I got a copy."

"What put you on to Maple Creek in the first place?"

"Lindsay Fleming asked me about it."

"Who is Lindsay Fleming?" Willow demanded, her fingers caressing him.

"She's on my staff."

"Do you fuck her?"

In the background he heard Sax make a growling sound.

"Certainly not," he answered. "I never have sexual relations with anyone on my staff."

"Let's get back to Maple Creek," Sax muttered. "What happened there?"

He didn't want to answer. He wanted to speak to Willow alone—naked. In a bedroom. But she was keeping his mind focused on business. He wasn't sure how, since he was so hot he was near to going up in flames.

"Two men broke in. They overpowered the security staff. But not with any kind of conventional weapons."

"Are you sure?"

"It's in the report."

"How did they do it?"

"Nobody knows."

"Chemicals?"

"They're not sure."

"How did they do it?" she asked again, this time more urgently.

"They're trying to find out. Most of the guards who came into contact with them are dead. The one who survived had his brains fried. He's in a mental hospital."

"Which one?"

"Colefax Manor. Before they died, some of the other guards were talking about getting zapped with a death ray."

Willow paused and looked at her brother, then asked, "Who were they—the intruders who broke in? Do you have their names?"

"Todd Hamilton and Glenn Barrow."

"Two men?" she asked carefully. "You're sure it wasn't a man and a woman?"

"No. Unless one of them had a sex-change operation."

The questions stopped. He saw the brother and sister gripping each other's hands, eyes closed.

He felt something. A pain inside his skull, like needles piercing the flesh of his brain.

"No! Stop." He would have shouted, but the plea came out more like a croak.

They were digging for answers. Information that he couldn't provide. He longed to give them everything they wanted. All of it. Every scrap. But that was beyond his power.

He knew Willow understood because the pain inside his skull eased. Now it was only a dull throbbing.

"You did the right thing by coming to us," she whispered.

"I know."

"Find out more about Maple Creek. If you have to steal the information—get it for us."

"I . . . don't . . . steal."

"You do. For us. When you know more, come back down here, and we can make love together."

"I want that."

"Yes. But you have to earn the privilege."

IT was rush hour by the time Jordan finally made it to D.C. He struggled to hold back his frustration as he crept around the Beltway to Connecticut Avenue, then cut across to Wisconsin, heading against traffic.

Even if Lindsay had been at the Cathedral, she wouldn't still be waiting for him. Would she?

Inside the hushed grounds a massive stone wall kept him from seeing into the Bishop's Garden. Frustrated by the delay, he slammed into a parking space, then trotted toward one of the garden gates.

Lindsay, if you're here, don't leave now! he shouted. A silent shout. But it blared in his own mind like a trumpet sounding.

As soon as he stepped across the threshold of the garden, he felt a surge of relief.

She had waited for him! He felt her presence. At least he thought so.

Speeding down one of the stone paths, he stopped short when he saw her standing with her back to a small fountain, looking in his direction—her shoulders tense, her expression a mixture of longing and relief and anxiety.

They hadn't seen each other in thirty-six hours. It felt like decades.

He was instantly swamped with emotions. He wanted to rush forward and take her in his arms. But he stopped a couple of paces from her, his hands clenched at his sides.

"I kept worrying I was going to run into that lady," she whispered. "The one who—"

"Yeah." He swallowed. "Thank you for staying." The words sounded inadequate. What he felt was so overwhelming that he couldn't handle it. How the hell would he deal with the rush of thoughts and feelings mingling and coalescing in his mind—and hers? And at the same time act on arousal so intense that pleasure shaded off into pain.

He felt needs, confusions, fears, and longings pouring off her, threatening to swamp him.

She licked her lips, and he knew they were as dry as his.

"Why did you wait for me?" he managed to say.

She raised one shoulder. "I guess I had to."

They stared greedily at each other. But he knew that if he took a step forward, she would duck away.

"Not here," she finally whispered. "Don't touch me here. Not again."

But they were going to touch. Kiss. And a whole lot more. It was inevitable—because both of them were desperate enough to risk their sanity.

"Where?" he asked, his voice sounding like gravel.

"Somewhere safe."

He wanted to tell her that nowhere was safe for what they both had in mind. Although he didn't speak, she nodded.

He could barely breathe, barely put coherent sentences together. But his brain was apparently still working. Or he was desperate to find a place where she would feel secure enough to let him touch her.

When he'd been working on one of his books and needed a place to hole up, he'd rented a cabin in the Catoctin Mountains—not far from Camp David, the presidential retreat.

"Cunningham Falls," he murmured.

"Yes."

"Now."

She gave a small shake of her head. "I have to go in my own car."

"So you can escape if you need to?"

"No. I can't sit beside you for that long and not touch you. And we both know what will happen when we do."

He felt as if a steel fist had clamped around his lungs. He knew some of it. He knew he had to make love with her, before the pressure building inside him blew the top off his head.

Or would that happen anyway?

"Do you know your way around up there?" he managed to say.

"I went to a weekend meeting at Camp David with Senator Bridgewater."

"You move in high-powered circles, Ms. Fleming."

"My job was taking notes."

"I was up there a couple of years ago when I was on deadline. I stayed at the Mountain View Lodge in Thurmont, Maryland."

She swallowed. "I want privacy—not a lodge."

"They have cabins. Let me see if they've got one open."

He'd vowed not to use his cell phone unless absolutely necessary. Well, it was necessary now. Feeling like a diver whose air tanks were empty, he called information. Then he called the office, telling himself that nobody was going to pick up on a conversation between him and a backwoods motel in Maryland.

Through the brief conversation, he watched the play of emotions on Lindsay's face, wondering if she would back out. After clicking off, he said, "We have a cabin for tonight—and the next two days. It's the last one at the top of the hill."

Emotions washed over her face. Relief and longing. But they were still tempered with uncertainty.

"Are you okay with it?" he asked, unable to breathe until she answered.

"I'll be there." She looked at her watch. "I have to go home and pack some clothes—and some groceries."

"You don't have to do all the cooking."

"What's in *your* refrigerator?"

When he twisted his mouth ruefully, she said, "I'll bring what I bought this afternoon. I guess that's why I didn't unpack most of them."

"Don't forget the apples."

She answered with a tight nod, not even bothering to ask how he knew.

He gave her directions to the lodge, and she wrote them down on a pad of paper. Such an ordinary exchange, yet there was nothing ordinary about where they were headed. Together.

"I'll try to get there by eight," she said, then started toward the gate.

He itched to grab her hand on the way past. But he knew that would be a serious mistake, so he kept his arms at his sides.

AS she drove toward Cunningham Falls, Lindsay fought her way through a fog. Not a mist that obscured her vision. A fog inside her head that made her thoughts stick together like clumps of clotted cream.

She had packed in a rush, throwing clothing and toiletry articles into a carry bag and groceries into a cardboard box and a cooler. Now she couldn't remember exactly what she had brought—or why.

She was no coward. Yet she wanted to back out. And at the same time she knew in the depths of her soul she had to keep this rendezvous if she wanted a chance of hanging on to her sanity.

Two days ago she'd walked away from Jordan

Walker—and felt like she'd hacked off her own arm. No, that wasn't quite how to describe it.

She fumbled for words and didn't even come close. She'd always felt as if something was wrong with her— that she was missing a part of herself that other people seemed to take for granted. Tonight there might be a way to make herself whole.

An image of herself and Jordan, naked and entwined, sprang into her mind—sending hot currents coursing through her, and she gripped the wheel when she wanted to press her hand against her own breast—or between her legs.

What the hell was going on with her? Sex had always been a take-it-or-leave-it proposition for her. Now the need for contact—the need for release—clawed at her.

She reached the outskirts of Cunningham Falls Park, a forest primeval sixty miles from Washington, D.C.

It was dark by the time she saw a lighted signboard advertising the Mountain View Lodge. She drove past the main building, up a one-lane track carved into the hillside by countless automobile tires. On either side the headlights caught the dark shapes of trees. And once she stopped short as a doe and fawn crossed her path.

She had never taken this road in her life, yet she knew exactly where she was going. To Jordan. The man who would be her salvation or her destruction.

There were lights in a few of the cabins. She ignored them and drove past, up the hill, alongside a rushing stream she could vaguely hear above the pounding of her pulse in her own ears.

Jordan was framed in the doorway to the cabin at the top of the lane. He stood with his hands in his pockets. The light shining out behind him made it impossible to see his face in the dark.

She could have parked in front. She wasn't sure why she pulled around back of the cabin, then climbed out of the car, cool mountain air hitting her skin.

As she closed the door, Jordan joined her beside the car. His voice was low and rough as he said, "I was afraid you weren't coming."

"You knew I had to. You knew I couldn't stand it any longer."

"You mean the feeling of being alone? Or the sexual part?"

"Both." She swallowed. "I could tolerate being alone—until I met you."

"Yes." He took a step toward her.

Despite her resolve, she automatically backed up, her hips pressing against the car door.

"I wasn't going to . . . grab you . . ."

"Not yet, anyway."

"Can I help you carry anything out of the car?"

"The box with the groceries. And the cooler," she answered, struggling to hang on to her composure. Turning, she popped the trunk and stepped back.

He picked up the provisions. When he was out of the way, she grabbed her carry bag, then followed him inside. The cabin was small but comfortable, with a kitchen area at one side of the main room. Across from it a green corduroy sofa and chairs made a U around a stone fireplace—where Jordan had built an inviting fire.

She walked to the hearth, staring into the dancing flames, then turned toward the room.

But the details of her surroundings faded into a blur as she brought her gaze back to him. He wore old jeans and a dark T-shirt that made him look lean and dangerous.

Dangerous to her, she decided as she took in the almost predatory expression in his eyes.

A shiver traveled down her spine. She had agreed to meet him in this isolated place. Now she wondered if he'd hypnotized her into coming.

No. He answered the silent question without speaking. *Whatever it is—it's happening to both of us.*

They stood frozen in place, facing each other as she breathed in the tang of wood smoke. The buzzing in her brain made coherent thought almost impossible. That and the arousal that flowed through her body.

Is this private enough? he asked. Again he had spoken without words—his mind to hers.

CHAPTER
SIXTEEN

LINDSAY HAD LOST the ability to make her voice work. But that didn't stop her from answering Jordan's question.

Yes.

And she knew beyond doubt that he caught her answer.

When he took a step forward, her whole body tensed. She wanted to ask him to start slowly—with the touch of hands, so she could let the sensations build by manageable degrees. Instead he moved decisively, pulling her close and wrapping her in his arms.

She gasped at the contact, clung to his broad shoulders as his mouth came down, searing her lips, turning her blood to fire.

The rest of the world vanished. Only the two of them existed. Lindsay Fleming and Jordan Walker—caught in a whirlwind of sensation and swirling thoughts.

She was instantly so aroused that she had to clamp her hands on his shoulders to keep from losing her balance. And she knew he clung to her with the same desperation.

The thoughts and feelings radiating from him told her he wanted her with a force that bordered on madness. His madness. Hers.

Fear leaped inside her. When she tried to break away, he held her fast, moving his lips over hers, stroking sensitive tissue with his tongue, nibbling with his teeth, exerting the exact amount of pressure that would bring her pleasure instead of pain.

Please—don't go so fast.

Be honest. You're as hot as I am.

"Yes," she moaned into his mouth because lying to this man when he held her in his arms was impossible. That lack of privacy—inside her own head—was frightening.

Let me go.

We've gone too far for that.

She knew in her heart that he was right. Stopping now was impossible. Simply walking across the room was impossible. If she wrenched away now, she would lose her mind.

She understood that truth on a gut-clenching level. Yet she also understood she was walking along a narrow edge of safety. The danger might tip either way. Pulling away was beyond her power, but they could crash and burn if they stayed in each other's arms—if they took this physical and mental intimacy to its natural conclusion.

They were both trembling. Both coping with too much too quickly. Yet he was a man, and his sexual urgency pushed the rest of it to the background.

He spoke against her mouth. "I need . . ."

He didn't have to finish the sentence. She knew what he wanted, and she moved far enough away for him to cup her breast.

They both exclaimed in pleasure as he took the soft mound in his hand, shaping and molding it to his touch, then skimming his thumb over the button-hard tip.

She moaned in response, the small sound swallowed by his mouth.

Oh, God. Oh, God.

The plea was his. No, hers. Because the intimate touch brought them to a new level of silent communication. A new level of need.

She cried out when he broke the mouth-to-mouth contact. The separation was intolerable.

Her mind and body throbbed. But she knew why he had lifted his hungry mouth from hers. He ached to feel her breasts against his naked chest. She stepped away and pulled her knit top over her head, then reached around to unhook her bra.

When she looked up, she saw he had ripped off his T-shirt, exposing a broad chest with dark hair spreading in a fan pattern, then arrowing down toward his narrow waist.

Nice. And so damn masculine. She hadn't spoken. But he answered her with a question.

You don't mind a man with a hairy chest?

I like it. She reached to comb her fingers through the dark, springy hair, the contact sending prickles along her nerve endings.

She heard his breath catch, felt his pleasure at her touch—felt it in his mind.

As she raised her eyes to his face, she saw he was staring at her with such heat and need that her heart melted. No man had ever wanted her so much, never affected her so deeply.

When he reached out and took her in his arms again, the sensation was like no other she had ever experienced. The erotic surge stole her breath. But there was so much more than sexual need, because the new physical intimacy deepened the mental connection.

They had shared their thoughts. But never like this. Never so deeply. So fully.

Fine threads of sensuality wound around them, through them, pulling them together. At the same time, his mind opened to her on a level that she could never have imagined. And she knew it was the same for him.

I've been waiting for you all my life.

Lord, yes.

But even as they spoke to each other—mind to mind— she fought a terrible sense of disorientation that was as terrifying as falling through space.

She was losing herself. Slipping from her own grasp. When her body trembled, he steadied her.

Focus on the feelings. Feel this!

He swayed her upper body in his arms, and she gasped at the hot sensation of her naked flesh sliding against his.

But she felt more than her own response. As the points of her nipples stirred the hair on his chest, she felt the urgent messages from his nerve endings traveling downward through his body to his cock.

His cock. Not her word. His.

She dropped her head to his shoulder, her teeth against his flesh, trying to cope with the mixture of torrid sensations and tangled thoughts—his and hers. The pressure building inside her body, inside her mind, skirted at the edge of pain.

"Stay with me, Lindsay. Stay with me." This time he spoke aloud as he stroked his hands up and down the length of her back, cupped her bottom through her pants—so he could pull her against his aching shaft.

She had no choice. She had never had a choice, she decided. Or was that his thought?

It didn't matter, not now. His naked chest against her wasn't enough. She needed more. She needed everything, or she would go insane.

She reached down, fumbling with his belt buckle, then the fly of his jeans as he worked the snap at the top of her pants.

She freed him from his briefs, breathless as she closed her hand around his cock, loving the contact with his rigid flesh and at the same time feeling his pleasure leap as she wrapped her fist around him and pumped her hand.

They kicked away unwanted clothing, then fell together to the rug in front of the fireplace—rolling across the padded surface, their bodies locked together as they exchanged hot, desperate kisses. His erection pressed against her middle, and the need to have him inside her made her gasp.

Yet the sexual frenzy was only part of what surged

through her. Through them. Bursts of static crackled along the pathways in her brain—interspersed with information—some of which they had no intention of sharing.

Words and images snapped back and forth between them.

She saw the first girl he made love with—in a motel near Boston. He took possession of her computer password at work. She discovered where he had kept his secret stash of cinnamon candy when he'd been a kid. She found out why he hadn't talked to his agent about the Hamilton book.

And she knew he had brought a map of Maple Creek.

Maple Creek?

Later. We'll talk about that later.

She couldn't shut off the confusing flow of information—from him to her and the other way. But she found she could push it to the back of her mind.

She had to—because as their naked bodies moved against each other, the sexual need reached savage intensity.

They drank from each other, skimmed their hands over backs and buttocks—neither able to get enough.

Reaching down, she clasped his cock again, this time deliberately exploring what the intimate touch felt like to him.

Before she could savor the experience, his fingers parted the folds of her most intimate flesh, then dipped inside her. But that small invasion wasn't enough.

I need . . .

Yes.

He changed the angle of his hand, so that his fingers could stroke from her vagina to her clit and back again, sending jolts of heated sensation through her.

So that's how it feels for a woman.

Yes. And you're going to explode if you can't get your cock inside me.

Yes.

She rolled to her back, and he came down on top of her. There was no need to guide his erection to the opening made for it. He knew exactly where she was. Knew neither of them could wait a second longer for him to plunge inside her. Or was that her thought?

It didn't matter.

They must finish this.

Yet the fear was as great as the pleasure. As they made the most intimate of physical connections, her thoughts scattered, clashed with his, crackled through her brain like sparks flying from a damaged power line.

She had wanted this. Now she thought she would lose her mind if he didn't separate himself from her.

She tried to pull back. Physically. Mentally.

Fear and frustration leaped inside him. *Christ! Stay with me. Stay with me!*

The plea screamed inside her head as his hips moved in a frantic rhythm, pushing them both toward orgasm. Finally she had no choice. She had to follow.

As the physical sensations built, the static in her brain receded to a background buzz.

There was only room for the hot, urgent need pumping through her—through him.

She felt the delicious male knowledge that orgasm was only seconds away. Felt his penis jerk as the spasms took him. Felt hot semen pump through his cock—out of him—into her as her own orgasm washed over her, through her. Through him. Wave after wave of hot ecstasy—like nothing she had ever experienced, ever imagined.

He collapsed on top of her, both of them gasping for breath. It took hours before their surroundings came into focus around them. Or was it only seconds? Her arms and legs were limp, but she clung to his shoulders.

He moved his cheek against hers. Neither of them spoke. Words were no longer necessary. At least for now.

When he stirred, she locked her hands across his back, holding him inside her. *Stay.*

I'll crush you.

Don't leave me. Not when we finally know what this is like.
Yes.

He didn't have to ask what they'd discovered. Each of them had been afraid that they were different from other people. Damaged. Below standard.

Well, they were different all right.

Not less. More.

KURT MacArthur clenched his teeth, then eased up before he brought on a tension headache. Why in the hell couldn't the search team locate Mark Greenwood? The guy had escaped from a mental hospital with no money and no resources, yet he'd managed to stay on the run. He was either very smart or very lucky—or both.

It looked like he'd broken into a house in St. Mary's and holed up there for a while to catch his breath. At least, the police report matched Greenwood's description. Now they were looking for fingerprints. And checking to see who might help him. Which had led them to his cousin, Sid Becker, who was under surveillance now.

Meanwhile, Kurt was thinking of another piece of the puzzle. Maybe he shouldn't have yanked Jim Swift off his surveillance duties at the Hamilton estate.

Eyes narrowed, he called the operative who had been in Wilmington that morning.

"Before I pulled you away to join the hunt for Greenwood, did you see any traffic in or out of the gate at Hamilton's place?"

"Not much. A bottled water company sent a truck in. I checked on the vendor. Hamilton does use them. And a silver Mercedes sedan came in just before I left."

"Did you recognize the driver?"

"I got all of the license number—except the last digit. It was a D.C. plate."

"Give it to me."

Swift read the number, then hung up.

Kurt went back to the computer, tapped into the D.C. Department of Motor Vehicles, and started looking for possible owners of a silver Mercedes.

JORDAN eased to his side, rolling Lindsay with him, still inside her as he cradled her body against his, both of them savoring the delicious sense of connection.

What just happened to us?

Our minds . . . linked. They're still linked.

She nodded against his shoulder, but this was too new for her to understand the rules. She wanted to drift in the afterglow of their pleasure. She wanted to simply savor these moments.

When a phone rang, they both jumped.

Damn. It's my phone. In my purse. I don't want to answer it.

Better do it.

Why?

I'm not sure. But I think it's important.

He moved to the side and pulled his body from hers, so she could get up. As she scrambled to get across the room, she broke the physical contact between herself and Jordan. The mental link snapped like a rubber band pulled too tight. It felt like a part of herself had been ripped away.

A wave of fire swept through her brain, and she heard a scream gurgle in her own throat.

Blind, deaf, unable to think, she flopped against the edge of the sofa, gasping.

CHAPTER
SEVENTEEN

"OH, CHRIST!" FIGHTING a wave of sick disorientation, Jordan pressed his hand to his temple, trying to stop the knife points of pain shooting through his head. His vision blurred, and for a moment he was lost to the world.

Then Lindsay's face swam into view. He could barely move. Barely think. Reaching out blindly, he grabbed her arm, and immediately the pain lessened.

"Got to get the phone," he croaked, then gathered her up and held on to her as they staggered across the room to where she'd set her purse on the counter. Pulling out the instrument, he snapped the lid open, then struggled to find the Talk button.

"Who is it?" he demanded.

"Who are you?" a man's voice challenged.

"Sid Becker," Lindsay whispered, holding out her hand.

He gave her the instrument, and she brought it to her ear, still keeping the contact with him.

They were both breathing hard, but with his hand on her arm, he was able to function. And it looked like she was reacting in a similar fashion.

"Sid?" she asked, obviously struggling to keep her voice steady.

The transmission was loud enough for Jordan to hear both sides of the conversation.

"Who was that?" the man named Sid asked.

She glanced at Jordan. "A friend."

"Someone you trust?"

"Yes."

"Are you all right? I couldn't get you at home."

"We went away for the weekend."

"Oh," he said, and she remembered that he'd tried to get her to go away with him, and she'd always refused.

She was still struggling to control her breathing when she asked, "Why are you calling?"

"I heard from my cousin."

"Good."

"I'm not sure. I thought he had contracted some kind of illness. But it's not that. Somebody invaded Maple Creek three weeks ago."

"I don't understand."

"Neither do I. He's on the run. He wouldn't tell me much. But I'm going to meet him. So I wanted to say you didn't have to bother Bridgewater."

"I already asked him."

Sid was silent.

"Was that a mistake?"

"It depends on where he takes the information."

"Okay. Keep in touch with me."

"I'm not sure I can do that."

"Sid?"

"It's complicated, Lindsay. I have to hang up now."

The line went dead. She pressed the Off button and set the phone down on the counter. But she kept hold of Jordan's hand, squeezing tight. He saw in her mind the image of a man standing in a bedroom, staring toward the door. Then he exited the room. As he stepped through the door, the image snapped off.

"That's him?" Jordan asked.

"You saw . . . that? In my head?"

"Yes."

"Was it real—or my imagination?" she asked in a shaky voice. "I mean, was he really standing beside his bed?"

"I don't know. Have you ever been there? To his bed-room?"

She turned her head toward him. "Are you asking if I slept with him?"

"Yeah, I guess I am."

She tightened her fingers around his, and he knew the answer.

"Sorry," he muttered.

"My sexual relationships were few and far between," she whispered.

"Mine, too."

By mutual agreement they switched back to the subject of Sid Becker.

"Who is he—exactly?" Jordan asked.

"He works for the Center for Military Affairs."

He closed his eyes and saw the crude map of Maple Creek. He didn't want to think about the map. About Todd Hamilton or Sid Becker. Or his cousin. He only wanted to focus on Lindsay.

And he knew she felt the same way. But it seemed she had more resolve than he.

"Let's tie this up. I mean—tie up what we know," she said.

"If you let me get you into bed first."

She laughed. "Talk first. Sex later."

He groaned. "Okay. We know that Mark Greenwood worked at a secure facility called Maple Creek. And it was invaded three weeks ago. Just at the time Todd Hamilton died."

She dragged in a strangled breath. "And you found a map Todd drew of the facility."

He didn't bother asking where she'd picked up that information.

"We know that Todd was worried about a chemical weapons program being conducted in secret. Can we assume the base of operation was Maple Creek? And Todd and his friend Glenn Barrow broke in there to try and shut it down?"

"Based on the evidence, yeah. I think we can."

"How did they do it?"

"That's part of what we have to find out."

"And there was some sort of massive cover-up."

"Yes. Maybe we can figure out more if we . . . link again."

"Can you be serious? You just want to get me into bed."

He grinned. "Guilty. Come on."

He felt her resistance wavering. Pressing his advantage, he clamped his arm around her and was gratified to feel her melt against him. Sensing victory, he led her to the bedroom, keeping her against his side while he pulled back the covers.

They both slipped into the bed, clinging together, and he closed his eyes to shut out the world as much as possible, holding her, pressing his body against hers, his hand stroking over her silky skin.

It was a strange experience. He felt like he was merging with her, even as he felt his arousal build again. This time the sexual urgency was more manageable.

He had better control of the physical sensations. Instead of being ruled by them, he could use them.

Yes, she whispered in his mind, and he knew she had picked up the thought, that they were joining again in that unfathomable mental way neither of them could explain. All they knew was that it had happened. And it was happening again.

He felt a sense of completeness. But what if they wanted to break the connection? Would either of them feel whole again?

Not what you bargained for? she asked.

Did you?

Of course not.

He didn't want to think too deeply about what this new reality meant for himself. For Lindsay. For the rest of their lives. Instinctively he knew that this was what he had always missed—always craved. He felt like he'd found the other half of his soul. Still, uncertainty gnawed at him. At her.

It was easier to focus on the current of sensuality that wrapped them in a tight embrace.

He bent to delicately swirl his tongue around one of her taut nipples, loving the feel of that hard pebble in his mouth and knowing exactly how his caress affected her.

He sensed the heat gathering in her lower body. Felt his cock fill with blood, and knew that she felt it, too.

I see why guys think women should have penis envy. You like that feeling of your . . . thing . . . expanding.

My thing. That's a poetic way to put it. You don't like the way that feels?

I like it. But the sensation of being turned on is so concentrated in that one inflatable tube.

Yeah, you get aroused all over your body, don't you?

Yes.

But this part is good, don't you think?

To punctuate the question, he slipped a finger between her moist, engorged folds, then dipped inside her.

I thought a woman would like the inside stimulation best, he mused.

No, the outside.

Mmm. Yeah. Like this?

God, yes.

As he focused on her pleasure, she couldn't hold back a small, moaning sound.

He wanted her hand on his cock.

She reached down, clasped him with her fist, and he sighed. He wanted . . .

She moved up to the head, circled, caressed him in exactly the way he had imagined, her finger picking up a drop of semen to use for lubricant, then swirling around the rim.

She drove him toward the point of no return. And he drove her.

They both knew the time was exactly right when she opened her legs and he eased inside her.

They lay on their sides, intimately joined. The physical bond brought them to a new level of mental awareness.

You need to come.

God, yes.

Now, please.

The slow pace was no longer enough, and he thrust in and out of her, fast and hard, driving them both toward climax.

LINDSAY felt the storm take her first, and he followed her over the edge. And in those blinding seconds of pleasure, she knew more than she had moments earlier. She knew they were in danger.

She tried for coherent speech, as the urgency filled her mind—and his.

"We have to get out of here," she gasped.

"Yeah. Now."

He pulled his penis from her, and they both braced for the terrible feeling of disorientation that had hit them when they had separated earlier.

This time it was less. Maybe because he'd thought to hold her hand and ease away slowly. Maybe because she was ready for the wrenching sensation.

Her breath caught.

"Are you all right?" he asked, his voice hoarse.

"I guess I have to be."

"How long do we have?"

"I don't know. Not long," she answered.

She wanted to pretend that she'd made up the feeling of impending danger. She knew she'd be lying to herself.

Neither of them had unpacked. They ran to the living room, scrambled into the clothing they had discarded, and grabbed their hand luggage.

By the time they dashed to the door, she saw a pair of headlights down by the office.

CHAPTER
EIGHTEEN

THE HEADLIGHTS BEGAN moving slowly up the hill. It could be a late-arriving guest. Lindsay knew it wasn't, because she felt a wave of malevolence sweeping up the rutted roadway ahead of the car.

Panic bubbled inside her. Instinctively she reached for Jordan's hand, locked her fingers around his wrist. "What do we do?"

She sensed thoughts churning in his brain. Plans.

We'd better not take my car. They traced me.

How?

Not sure . . . talk about it later. We've got to get the hell out of here. Give me your car keys.

With fingers that felt like sausage links, she fumbled in her purse, found the keys and handed them over.

They both climbed into the car. She prayed that the flash of light when the door opened was blocked by the cabin.

The engine roared in her ears like an uncaged lion. Could the men in the other car hear it?

Men. She pictured their hard faces and gimlet eyes. Had they killed Dr. Lucas? And Todd Hamilton and Glenn Barrow?

And now they were coming for her and Jordan—two more loose ends in the Maple Creek affair.

She tried to calm herself down. The U.S. wasn't some totalitarian country where the secret police stamped around doing whatever they wanted. That's what she'd always believed, until the government had started holding people for months and years, using the Patriot Act as an excuse.

"Yeah. We're not going to try and make nice with them," Jordan muttered, apparently following her line of thinking.

He didn't turn on the lights as he drove around the back of the cabin, then kept going up the access road.

Her heart blocked her windpipe as she looked behind her and saw the other car closing in on them.

Jordan tried to speed up. The right front tire hit something solid. Cursing, he slammed on the brakes, reversed, and made a course correction.

As his vision adjusted, he picked up a little speed, keeping the car in the tire ruts.

They reached the top of the hill and started down. Maybe they had a chance to escape.

She had just breathed out a sigh of relief when she saw headlights in the rearview mirror and heard the roar of an engine right behind them.

"Shit," Jordan muttered, ramping up his speed to the dangerous range.

Without even stopping to check the traffic, he barreled onto the highway with his lights off. She gasped as they narrowly missed an oncoming pickup truck.

Swiveling around, she saw the vehicle in back of them shoot from the access road. But another car was coming up fast. To avoid an accident, the pursuers cut sharply to the right—and nose-dived into a ditch.

"They're out of commission," she cried.

"Thank God."

She kept her gaze to their rear as they sped on into the night, passing secondary roads leading into small communities.

"We have to get off the highway," she whispered, "in case they get back on the road."

"Not yet. I don't want to get trapped on a dead-end road."

"Turn on your lights before we get arrested—or killed."

"Right." He kept going into the nearby town before he made a left into a sleeping neighborhood, then took several more turns, ending up on a residential street where he pulled around back of a convenience store, then cut the engine.

She slid into his arms, burying her face against his shoulder. Feeling her whole body shake, she struggled to keep her teeth from chattering. "Who are they?"

"You mean—like what government agency?"

"Yes."

"I don't know. But somebody knows I'm poking into Todd Hamilton's death—and the break-in at Maple Creek."

"The dirty-tricks department?"

He laughed. "Yeah."

The laugh sent a shiver traveling over her skin. "How did they find us?"

He sighed. "I paid for the room with my credit card. When you use plastic, you announce where you are."

She winced.

"Let's hope to hell this didn't come from your office. Did anyone see you when you pulled that file with Todd's letter?"

"Not that I know of."

"But you asked Bridgewater about Maple Creek. Because Sid wanted information." His jaw tightened. "The senator could have turned us in—if he thought your knowledge of secret installations was a threat to national security."

"I'm sorry."

"You didn't know. You were just doing a favor for a friend."

The comment triggered another frightening thought, and she turned haunted eyes to Jordan. "If they came after us, they could be after Sid. We have to warn him."

"We can't. Not on the phone. It's too easy to tap into a cell phone. If we use it, they might find us." Grim-faced, he added, "Or they could have traced his call to you!"

She made a small strangled sound. "You mean like one of those spy movies where they listen in by satellite?"

"Yeah, like that." He dragged in a breath and let it out. "Maybe they just want us for questioning," he said, trying to sound reassuring. "Too bad we can't send your friend Sid a telepathic warning signal—because we sure as hell can't call him."

"Maybe we should try." She reached for his hand and held on tight. "Like when you told me to go to the Bishop's Garden. And I went."

"We can *try*. But I don't think it's going to work. The reason I could sort of communicate with you was that we had already started forming a bond."

"Yes." Her fingers clenched his more tightly. "But we have to do what we can. Let's sit here and send him a message—that storm troopers came to our cabin in the woods to scoop us up. We got away, but he should be careful."

"Okay," he agreed, but she knew he didn't think they had much chance. She slipped one hand under his shirt and kept hold of the other, then closed her eyes and pressed her cheek to his. She felt their thoughts merge, heard the words of warning echo in her head. They sent the message ten times, and when they finished she didn't know if it had done any good.

"Can't we call him on a pay phone?" she whispered.

"Closer to D.C., maybe. Somewhere we can make a quick getaway if we have to. But we can't head back there yet. In case they're watching the highway."

As if to emphasize their precarious situation, a car pulled into the parking lot in front of the convenience store, and they both went rigid. Apparently it was the guy opening up in the morning.

"Maybe he'll think we were here for a make-out party," Jordan said as he started the engine. "What we don't want is for him to tell the cops someone suspicious is hanging round."

Jordan drove away from the store, then down the street

at moderate speed, this time with his lights on, since other people were out and about.

The rural neighborhood had large wooded lots, with the houses spread far apart. He slowed when he came to a long driveway where several newspapers were lying on the blacktop.

"We can hide up there for a while."

She gulped. "You mean break in?"

"No. We'll go around back and stay in the car." He headed up the driveway, then around to the rear of a clapboard house, hidden from the road by pine trees.

"I'm a congressional researcher. You've written about bad guys. What do they do when the law is closing in on them?"

"Mostly, they get caught," he said in a gritty voice.

CHAPTER
NINETEEN

KURT MACARTHUR SNATCHED up the phone on the first ring. "Do you have them?"

"It looks like they were expecting trouble. They cleared out just ahead of us."

"They?"

Swift answered with clipped syllables. "There's a woman with him."

"How do you know, if they aren't there?"

"Telltale sheets. They were going at it in bed." Jim laughed. "Well, the living room rug, too, I suspect. And— for a homey touch—there are boxes of groceries on the kitchen counter—like they were planning to spend the weekend burrowed in there."

"So Walker took his girlfriend away for the weekend to have a good time. That's not so strange."

"He doesn't have a girlfriend."

"He met someone. And they got close—fast. Maybe you didn't find them because they decided to go out to dinner." Even as he said it, the observation sounded too quick.

"They went down the driveway with their lights off. We were in hot pursuit—and ended up in a ditch to keep from getting rammed by another car. We're looking for them. But they had a fifteen-minute start on us."

"Find them. I want Walker. And meanwhile, I want you to round up Sid Becker."

"You want to talk to him?"

"If possible. But do what you have to do to keep him from talking to anyone else."

"I'm already on it."

Kurt hung up, then scrubbed a hand across his face. He'd been with the CC for a long time, and he'd devoted his life to the organization. His methods might not match the conventional norms. But he'd been sure of his values, sure of the mission, sure of how to accomplish what he thought was best for the country.

Maple Creek had shocked him into quick action, and maybe he'd made some hasty decisions about the cover-up.

In retrospect, he should probably have used something besides the drug from Granite Wall to terminate Todd Hamilton and his friend, Glenn Barrow. But he'd had it on hand at Maple Creek. He'd thought it was untraceable. Then it had shown up in that damn pathology report from Dr. Lucas.

He hoped that bit of information wouldn't go any farther—now that Jim had wiped the computer files.

But he'd feel better when they had Mark Greenwood back in custody—or dead. And anyone else who got wind of what had happened at Maple Creek. Including Leonard Hamilton, who had ordered the pathology report. From his phone records, it looked like Hamilton had gotten Jordan Walker on the case. He just hoped he hadn't talked to anyone else.

He pressed his palm against the desk. The team in D.C. would find Greenwood. Maybe through Sid Becker. And Jim would find Walker and his girlfriend. Too bad for her—getting caught in the middle of a flap. But he'd always had a philosophical attitude toward collateral damage. You did what needed to be done to accomplish the mission, and you didn't sweat the civilian casualties.

A pink-and-orange glow set the eastern sky on fire. A beautiful dawn, but a bad omen.

"Something's going to happen," Lindsay whispered,

feeling trapped, her gaze swinging to the long empty driveway.

"Yeah."

"Are they going to find us?"

"I don't know. You're the one who can sense the future."

"Lucky me."

He laced his fingers with hers. "Tell me what you feel— exactly. Do we have to get out of here?"

She struggled to open her mind—to possibilities. "It's not us," she whispered. Seeking comfort—more than comfort— she shifted so that she was curled against him again, the way she had been when they'd sent the message to Sid.

He held her close, slipping his free hand under her shirt, increasing the skin to skin contact. Neither of them moved, and she closed her eyes as she felt her thoughts merging more firmly with his.

The process was becoming familiar now. More controlled.

When a vision formed behind her closed lids, she squeezed her eyes more tightly shut so that she could concentrate on the scene.

A meadow. Trees in the background. Not somewhere nearby, although the same pinks and oranges tinged the sky. At least she knew it was in the same time zone.

Is this a fantasy? A place where we can escape? she murmured.

No. I think it's real.

The picture wasn't quite clear. As she sharpened the focus, she felt a small surge of triumph. She and Jordan were working together, although she still wasn't sure how they were doing it.

She felt like she was looking at a television commercial—where the scene is supposed to be so real that the viewer can almost step into it.

Yeah, Jordan agreed.

She focused on the grass. It wasn't tall and weedy, the

way you might see it out in the country. It was more like a lawn that had been mowed in the past few weeks. In addition, she saw several picnic tables grouped around a metal grill. Nearby sat an overflowing trash can. And to the right was a large metal swing set and a row of seesaws.

"I know that picnic grove," Jordan muttered.

How?

I was on a team that played softball up there. It's off Military Road. Just past 27th Street.

She felt her stomach knot. The park looked peaceful enough. But she was almost certain that something was going to happen. Something she wasn't going to like.

A flicker of movement caught her eye. A man was hiding among the trees. His hair looked like it was growing out from a military cut. His eyes were haunted.

Who is that? Jordan asked.

Sid's cousin. She had never seen him in her life, yet she was sure of his identity. And sure that he was on the run from . . .

Sinister forces, he supplied.

Yeah, that.

A car pulled into the parking area near the picnic tables, and she felt her heart start to pound.

When the door opened, Sid Becker got out. He was dressed in jeans and a light jacket over a plaid shirt. A baseball cap partially hid his face. But she could tell he was checking out the area—looking around in all directions. Apparently satisfied that he was alone, he started toward the trees.

The other man stepped out into the early morning stillness. He was a few years younger than Sid.

They met at the side of a table and embraced.

"Mark, thank God you're okay," Sid said.

Lindsay's fingers dug into Jordan's hand. They were doing more than seeing this. They were hearing it, too.

"Are you sure you weren't followed?" Mark asked.

"I came down Linnean and took a bunch of winding roads through the park. And I looped around several times. I would have noticed another car in back of me."

"Okay."

"So tell me what happened to you? Why are you on the run?"

Mark looked around, as though he still wasn't sure they were really alone.

Does he know we're watching? Jordan asked.

How could he?

It was a strange question. Until today, she would have believed that what she and Jordan were doing right now—eavesdropping on two men who were seventy-five miles away in the city—was impossible.

Finally the fugitive answered the question. "Maple Creek was attacked."

Every muscle in Lindsay's body went rigid. Not just *her* body. The tension radiated from her to Jordan and back again.

"You screwed up?"

"No!" Mark shouted. "You've got it all wrong."

"Okay. Calm down and tell me what happened."

Mark dragged in a breath and let it out. "It's a little hard to stay calm—when I know my ass is grass if I get caught."

Sid nodded. "Start from the beginning. Tell me about the attack."

"It was a two-man invasion."

"I thought the base was impenetrable."

"I thought so, too. That's the weird part. Two guys dressed in black made it past the sentry at the gate—then into the control room."

"How?"

As though someone could hear the conversation, Mark lowered his voice. "I was on duty. They zapped me and Cordova with some kind of mind-control ray. Not just us. Rota. Maybe others." Once he had started to speak, the story poured out of him. "Rota was the one at the guard post. I saw him standing there, like he was in a trance—and I thought someone had hit him with a tranq spray or something. Then they came for us. They didn't have any conventional weapons. Not that I saw, but they zapped us. I heard the staff talking at the hospital. The others are dead."

As she listened to the impassioned words, Lindsay fought for breath. What Mark was telling Sid was impossible—unless . . .

Beside her, Jordan made a strangled sound. They were already gripping each other's hands. Their hold tightened to the point of pain.

"Mark, are you sure?" Sid demanded. "What do you mean by 'some kind of mind-control ray'?"

The younger man grimaced. "I don't know what I mean! Don't you get it? The English language doesn't have the right words for what I'm talking about! But that's what it felt like. Something hit me. Not something physical. In my brain. First it hurt like hell. Then I went unconscious."

"Jesus!"

Jesus, Jordan repeated, the exclamation echoing in Lindsay's mind.

"The others died from the death ray?"

"Or from what Dr. Colefax did to them in the hospital. He tried to make me tell what happened. With persuasion. With drugs. And he didn't care what happened to them—or me."

Even as she struggled to wrap her brain around Mark's revelation, she felt something else tugging at the corner of her consciousness.

The image of a gray car solidified in her mind.

Someone else is coming.

She felt Jordan's alarm—and surprise.

Here? he asked, his inner voice urgent.

No. There. Mark, run. Get out of there. Run. Run.

The young man paid her no attention. Instead, he addressed himself to Sid.

"I was pretty out of it at first. But I'm thinking straight again. No thanks to that bastard Dr. Colefax who ran the place. He pretended I was contagious or something. And he pretended like he was trying to help me. But really, he wanted to find out what I knew. Then he wanted to make sure I didn't blab to anyone else."

A vice clamped around Lindsay's chest, choking off her breath. *Run, Mark. Run. For God's sake, get out of there!*

But his full attention was on Sid.

"Isn't it your job to help them figure out how somebody got through security—so it can't happen again?"

Mark dashed a hand across his close-cropped hair. "You think this is *my* fault. You think I'm crazy?"

"No."

"But you think I should turn myself in. Like a good little soldier."

"I don't know."

Mark's expression turned angry. "You're not listening to anything I said. This is all about covering somebody's ass. They didn't report the break-in, did they? You didn't read about it in the paper, did you?"

"No."

"You say we've got to report it. Well, I think that's dangerous. For me—and you, too. So give me that information I asked for."

Sid hesitated, then reached inside his jacket and handed over several folded pieces of paper.

As Mark reached for them, the gray car slammed to a halt in the parking lot and a loudspeaker boomed out across the picnic area. "Mark Greenwood and Sid Becker. Put your hands in the air."

CHAPTER
TWENTY

MARK STARED IN horror at the vehicle. "Oh, shit."

"Get out of here," Sid growled.

"I can't leave you."

"Go! You can't risk getting caught. I'll hold them off."

Four men in sweat suits jumped out of the car. Lindsay watched helplessly as they ran toward the picnic area.

Sid reached inside his jacket again. This time he pulled out a gun. "Hold it right there," he growled.

The lead attacker stopped. "Don't do anything you're going to regret," he said.

"I want to know what the hell is going on. Are you the police? What?"

"We're after a dangerous criminal."

"I don't think so."

"You don't have all the facts."

"Fill me in."

"I don't have to." The voice came from behind the lead attacker. "Let us pass."

"Not without an explanation."

"Sorry. You're holding us up."

While the leader argued with Sid, one of the other men pulled out a gun and shot him twice in the chest as casually as he might have swatted a fly.

Lindsay gasped, then gasped again as Sid went down, sinking to his knees, then sprawling on the grass.

The shooter ran up to Sid and knelt beside him. Wresting the gun from his hand, he tucked it in his own belt. "Get the bastard!" he shouted.

The other men had already leaped into the woods after Mark. The man who fired the fatal shot followed. But Sid had given his cousin a few minutes' head start.

Shaking, Lindsay buried her face against Jordan's shoulder, but she couldn't blot out the terrible scene. Sid lay on the ground. Blood bubbled between his lips as he tried to speak.

"He's not dead," she gasped. "Oh, Lord. He must be in pain."

Jordan held her more tightly. "I'm sorry," he growled. "I should have let you call—"

"Quiet! He's trying to talk."

To her astonishment, the first word out of his mouth was her name.

"Lindsay . . ." he whispered. "What are you doing here?" His lids fluttered, and she thought he was looking directly at her, although that had to be an illusion.

"Sid. Oh, God, Sid."

"Lindsay, help Mark . . ."

"Sid?"

"Don't let . . . cover up . . ."

He stopped talking and lay still, and she felt the picture in her mind snap off. Because Sid had died. Her link to the place had been severed.

She tried to claw the connection back into existence and knew she was trying to bring Sid Becker back to life.

But that was beyond her power.

She felt her shoulders shaking as great gulping sobs took her. She had kept her emotions under control, but now she couldn't hold back the pain and guilt. "He's dead. He's dead . . . and it's my . . . fault."

Jordan's fingers dug into her arms. "No. Stop it. That's crazy. He was trying to help his cousin."

"Don't you get it?" she screamed. "Sid came to *me!* He asked for help. He asked for it again—just now."

"And his cousin came to *him!* He called you and said he was taking care of the problem. Mark was in trouble, and he agreed to meet him. This has nothing to do with you. Nothing!"

She wanted to believe him. Yet the guilt was like a giant, crushing weight.

"I hope . . . at least . . . Mark got away," she whispered.

"Yeah. Sid gave him a head start. If he knows his way around the park and they don't, he could have made it."

She clung to that, even as she tried to absorb the terrifying scene she'd just witnessed.

"What can we do for him?"

"I don't know. I don't even know where to find him."

THE papers clenched in his fist, Mark ran into the woods, heading for the hiding place he'd prepared—just in case— before keeping his appointment with Sid. Just in case.

Behind him, two shots sounded.

Oh, Christ. Sid!

He felt sick. He should have known that dragging his cousin into this was a bad idea. Probably he had gotten Sid killed. Now he thought about simply stopping, turning around, and letting the bastards get him. But he didn't do it. Because then they'd win the whole game.

So he made for a fallen log and dived into the trough he'd scooped out under the massive horizontal trunk. After stuffing the paper into his pocket, he scrambled to pull a cover of fallen leaves back over the opening.

He could hear men move hastily through the underbrush, coming after him.

He didn't know whether he was completely covered. A toe of his shoe could be sticking out of the leaves. But he didn't dare move now. All he could do was lie in his shallow grave, wondering if they were going to find him, drag him into the open, and shoot him.

* * *

LINDSAY held on to Jordan because that was all she could do. She wanted to believe they could keep each other safe, although she knew that safety was just an illusion.

"Those are the same people who are after us?" she whispered.

His features had been grim. They turned grimmer. "We have to assume they are. Well, not the exact same people, since the time frame would be pretty tight. They probably have several goon squads."

"Wonderful," she answered, struggling to think rationally. "How did they find Sid in the park?"

"Probably they worked backward—and figured out who was most likely to help Mark. Then they could have put a transponder on his car."

"A tracking device?"

"Yeah. And they could have tapped his phone. In that case they'd know he called you."

She felt her throat clog.

Jordan stroked her hair, her shoulder.

"Why did Sid speak to me—at the end?" she managed.

"I guess he sensed your presence." He tightened his hold on her shoulder. "Maybe he did get the message about being careful. But he wanted to meet Mark anyway. Or he didn't believe he was hearing you in his head." He stopped and made a frustrated sound. "Hell, I'm only guessing here. Maybe he didn't actually get the words— just an impression that you were trying to contact him." He sighed. "Neither one of us has much experience with this."

"Who does?"

Jordan turned one hand palm up. "How about Todd Hamilton and Glenn Barrow?"

She sucked in a breath. "You mean, because they broke into Maple Creek and zapped the security guards with some kind of mind ray?"

"Yeah, that." He gave her a piercing look. "If I had to

make an educated guess, I'd say they have the same talent we do. Wait—let me rephrase that. Make that—the same talent we'd have if we figured out how to zap someone's mind with a lightning bolt."

"You think we can attack people?" she murmured. "With our minds?"

"Who the hell knows? We just . . . forged . . . some kind of psychic bond last night. These are early days for us. Todd and Glenn must have practiced their talent."

The way he said it, or perhaps the future facing them, made her shiver.

They were both silent, thinking about the implications.

"The more intimate the contact, the deeper the link," she murmured.

"Um-hum."

"So if Todd and Glenn bonded . . . they must have been lovers," she said slowly.

"Well, Todd was definitely gay. I got that from my research. I have to assume he and Glenn got as close to each other as we have."

She nodded, thinking about the two men. "Before they met, they were probably lonely—like us."

"Probably it was worse for them. In addition to everything else, they had a whole bunch of social-sexual issues to deal with."

"Yes."

"So they found each other—and everything changed."

"Why did they go after Maple Creek?" she asked.

"I have to assume they were peace activists—opposed to chemical and biological weapons. And they were feeling confident enough to attack a secret weapons installation."

"And they got far enough into the facility to get a dose of . . . of Granite Wall?"

"Or they were captured before they obtained their objective. And somebody decided to give them a taste of the nasty medicine they came to destroy."

The theory made her grimace.

"Either way it happened, they got overconfident."

Lindsay was still struggling with the broader implications. She paused, swallowed, then asked, "And how did they get the way they were?"

Jordan gave her a direct look. "Good question. We need to try and answer that."

"Not just about them—about us, too. Do you have any theories?"

She saw his Adam's apple bob. "I'm getting the feeling that Leonard Hamilton knows something."

"Why?"

"Well, because he picked *me* specifically to look into Todd's murder. And . . ." He stopped and started again. "And he's hiding a secret. Something about me. I called him on it, but he wouldn't give it up."

"Can we ask him—together?"

"Unfortunately, we can't risk it. They could be watching him, too. In fact, that might be how they picked up on me. They had his mansion staked out."

She spoke around the lump blocking her windpipe. "So what are we going to do?"

"Well, we're not going back to my apartment—or yours. We have to stay undercover—until we can figure out who's running Maple Creek and how to get them off our backs." He pulled out his wallet and counted the money. "I just went to the bank. I've got five hundred dollars. How much do you have?"

She checked her own wallet. "Just under two hundred."

"We can't use our credit cards."

"What happens when we run out?"

"We rob a bank."

"Oh, sure." She looked down at her hands. "Staying out

of the bad guys' clutches is going to be a problem."

"But we've got an advantage that they don't—the power we've developed."

"Unfortunately, it doesn't always work real well."

"But we'll keep practicing. You don't mind practicing, do you?" he asked, leaning closer and nibbling at her lips.

It was only a light touch. Maybe it was designed to distract her. It did that, all right. Once again she was engulfed by a wave of heat.

God, Lindsay, I never wanted a woman as much as I want you. It's like a craving that won't let up.

Yes.

We shouldn't.

Yes, we should. Because it strengthens the bond between us.

That's not the only thing you're thinking about.

True.

He shifted so that he could cup her breasts, taking their weight in his hands, molding and squeezing.

Flames shot through her. Through him. She knew that as certainly as she felt her own desire.

She was instantly wet and wanting. And suddenly, neither one of them could fight the urgent need clawing at them. It was built of the connection they'd discovered—and the knowledge that someone could snatch away their lives before they had a chance to explore the amazing link.

Jordan took her mouth in hot, desperate kisses as he tugged her clothing out of the way. She did the same, unzipping his fly, freeing his penis, exclaiming when she found him hard and heavy in her hand, loving the feel of him, and knowing at the same time what that intimate touch was like for him.

She shoved away from him. He might have protested, but she knew he understood why she needed maneuvering room. He helped her pull down her pants. As she kicked them away, his hands tore at her panties.

She heard the silky fabric rip and felt a moment of shock that she was with a man who wanted her so much that he couldn't wait another few seconds. She had never understood the wild passion she'd read about in romance novels. With Jordan, the out-of-control urgency drove her to a place of white-hot need.

"Yes," she moaned as his hands clamped onto her hips, so he could lift her up and into his lap. She came down facing him, calling out again as he filled her.

She was the one on top. The one in control. And she began to move frantically, sliding his cock in and out of her, driving them both insane.

Jesus. Lindsay.

I know. I know.

Something flickered in her mind. Information. It was like the other times—when the joining had been more than physical. But she pushed everything else aside to focus on the sweet, urgent need for sexual climax.

It didn't take much to send herself over the edge, because arousal had simmered below the surface every moment they'd been together.

Once again the heat of orgasm burst forth—over her, through her, and she felt him follow her, felt how it was for him, that pumping sensation as he poured himself into her.

She collapsed in a sweaty heap against him, and they stroked and kissed each other as they came back to earth.

She could barely move, but a question bubbled in her consciousness.

Who is Henry Remington?

You picked up his name from my mind? Just now?

Yes.

He's a doctor who ran a fertility clinic. Where Todd was conceived.

What else?

That's all I have. He clipped out the denial. She knew that was true. Yet she sensed his disquiet as her head rested against his shoulder.

She felt his arms around her, and she wished everything wasn't so complicated. She wanted to enjoy the peaceful sensations of sexual release. But they weren't living in a peaceful world.

Maybe when we were in ... hypercommunication, we should have focused on Mark, he suggested.

Hypercommunication. Did you just make that up?

He answered with a soft mental laugh. *Yeah.*

Let's see what we can do together.

He clamped his fingers around hers and cradled the back of her head with his free hand while they both tried to bring up another picture of Mark Greenwood.

Jordan's penis was still inside her—the closest contact she could imagine. She squeezed her eyes shut, trying to focus. But they couldn't find Mark.

We don't know him.

But we saw him with Sid.

She nodded against his shoulder, then tried to cast her thoughts in a wider net. She saw Mark running through the woods. But she suspected she was simply making that up.

Perspiration broke out on her forehead.

She felt Jordan give up on the joint effort.

"Please. Help me!" she cried out, unable to hold back her frustration.

"We can't do it. We're not strong enough yet."

"But . . ."

He stroked her hair, kissed her cheek.

The talent isn't reliable. We need to learn to control it.

She felt his restless need for action. Or was it her own? It was a kind of tingling in her mind and body, a sensation of urgency that she wouldn't have been able to describe to anyone besides Jordan Walker. But she knew that he understood, because he felt it, too.

"We can't stay here," he muttered.

"Where are we going?"

"Darien, Connecticut."

"That's where Dr. Henry Remington had his clinic?"

"Yeah. But it's long gone."

They were in sync with each other now. Talking was simply a polite alternative to direct mind-to-mind communication. Still, she knew there was something he was leaving out. Something neither one of them wanted to acknowledge.

Reluctantly she climbed off his lap. As he put his clothing back into place, she picked up her ruined panties, stared at them helplessly, then stuffed them into her purse.

Jordan looked embarrassed. "I assume you brought underwear in your overnight bag."

"Yes."

He reached back and handed the bag over the seat.

Then, while he stood staring down the driveway, she stepped into the detached garage, rounded a Saturn much like hers, and put herself back together.

When she was dressed again, Jordan walked to a workbench that was pushed against the back wall. Above it, tools were neatly arranged on a Peg-Board. Jordan selected a large screwdriver, then squatted beside the car and went to work.

"Why are you stealing license plates?"

When he didn't immediately answer, she stepped forward and laid her hand against his neck, as she tried to dip into his mind. But an unexpected sensation stopped her. There was no way to describe it. In visual terms, she might have said it was as though she'd walked up to a clear window and started to look through. But before she could focus, the window glass turned opaque.

She tried to slide around the blackened window. To her surprise and dismay, it moved, blocking her again.

She could see Jordan's body had gone rigid. Her own muscles tightened as she tried to fight her way into his mind.

The silent mental struggle sent a sick wave of panic through her.

CHAPTER
TWENTY-ONE

LINDSAY WATCHED JORDAN'S fist clench around the handle of the screwdriver. "Are you trying to break the connection between us?" she managed to say.

"No, but I'm doing my best to block your intrusion into my mind," he answered.

She wanted to firm her jaw and pretend he hadn't hurt her. But that was impossible with this man.

So now what? Walk away? That had always been her fallback position when someone slammed at her.

He kept his head tipped down. "I don't want to hurt you."

"Then why are you doing it?" she asked, trying to keep her voice steady.

"It's necessary."

"Why?"

"Don't you think it's a little inconvenient reading each other's thoughts every time we touch?"

She dragged in a breath and let it out. "Too bad I was . . . so thrilled that we could do it."

"So am I."

"Then why did you stop me?"

He lifted his head so that his eyes met hers. "There are times when we both need privacy."

Her mind flashed back to the unsettled feeling she'd experienced earlier, and she asked, "Because I wanted to ask you questions about the Remington Clinic? And you didn't want to answer them?"

He shrugged. "Partly."

When she didn't say anything more, he added, "But

I . . . should have warned you—instead of just going ahead and trying to block you out."

Determined to keep her voice even, she said, "No, it was the right approach. If I'd been prepared, it would have altered the experiment."

"Yeah." He cleared his throat. "I'm not used to consulting anyone before I act."

"I think we're both like that."

"What's happened between us has been like a speeding train."

"And you want to get off?"

"No." He cleared his throat. "But part of why I'm good at my job is that I'm an excellent poker player. It's difficult to cope with the loss of that ability—with you. There's no hiding my strategy. Or my emotions. They're on direct display."

"I'm hoping you'll find some compensations."

He reached for her hand and folded his fingers around hers. "You picked up on the part about the Remington Clinic. The subject makes me uncomfortable. And I'd like to think about it before I comment."

"I understand."

"Yeah, well, that wasn't the main reason I wanted to hide my thoughts. What you said about illegal activity made me remember something that happened in high school. And suddenly I realized it was something I always hide . . . and you would know about it—if you dipped into my mind."

"I have some pretty gross teenage recollections myself," she murmured. "Like in middle school, when I got my period and walked around half the day with blood on the back of my skirt—and nobody bothered to clue me in. Imagine how a teenage girl would react to *that* little embarrassment."

"Christ!"

"Or the sick feeling of sitting there in chemistry class—shrinking into my seat when nobody wanted to be the lab partner of 'weird Lindsay.' "

He gripped her hand tighter, before deliberately easing the pressure. "I'm sorry."

"Don't be. It made me self-sufficient."

"And lonely," he muttered. He stood and wrapped his arms around her, holding tight for long seconds before saying, "Okay, here's my deep dark secret."

"You don't have to tell me."

"I didn't want you to pull it from my mind. But telling you is my choice. When I was fifteen, I got arrested for shoplifting."

The words were a small shock. "Oh."

"I had a juvenile record, but it was sealed."

"Why were you doing it?"

"Partly because we didn't have a lot of money, and I wanted things the other kids had. CDs, electronic toys, nice clothes. But partly it was a game. A game I played because of my special talent for reading people. I'd go into a store and sense whether or not the clerk was focused on me. Unfortunately, in a big Wal-Mart, I didn't spot all the security cameras."

"What happened?"

"A rent-a-cop scooped me up, took me to the manager's office, and called the law. They hauled my ass down to the police station and booked me. I got two hundred hours of community service—and the beating of my life from my father. Along with a tongue-lashing I'll never forget."

She winced. "Your father was into physical punishment."

"Yeah. Like I said before, I wasn't the son he wanted."

"You couldn't love him," she said in a small voice. "And he couldn't love you."

His hand tightened on hers again. "I guess that's the curse of . . . people like us. We go through life alone because we can't connect with . . . anyone . . . normal. So it means we don't have much practice with handling relationships."

"Yes."

"But with my old man, it was more than that."

He stroked his finger on the back of her hand, and this time his memories were open to her. Memories of a father who ridiculed him for thinking he was good enough to go to college. Sneered at his "top student" report cards. Demanded obedience at home. Made him go out and get a job if he wanted any spending money.

She couldn't hold back a gasp. "I'm sorry."

"I don't go home much. Even though my mom tries to keep in touch."

"I . . . understand why you stay away."

"Dad knew I was . . . different. And he wanted a kid who was like all the other 'regular guys.' "

"At least my mother and stepfather weren't like that. They didn't understand me. But they tried their best to support me and do the right things for me because I was their child." She laughed. "So I had to endure big Thanksgiving and Christmas dinners with friends and relatives, family picnics, dance lessons, riding instruction, trips to Europe. Things that would have thrilled most people. But they just made me feel more like a fish out of water." She paused for a quick gulp of air. "Dad even used his connections to get me a job on the Hill. I've done well, and I'm sure they brag to their friends about it. I just thanked God that they stopped asking about who I was dating."

"You found a way to give them gratification. Good for you."

"I wasn't doing it for them as much as I was doing it for me."

"Right."

She turned her palm up and squeezed his hand. "Your parents should be proud of you. You've carved out a fantastic career for yourself. If they can't see it—that's their loss."

He detached his hand, but kept his gaze on her. "So what would you call us?" he asked.

"Telepaths whose talent blooms when . . ." She stopped because she was embarrassed. "When they . . . find their mate."

His long look made her feel even more embarrassed. "I'm not trying to railroad you into anything . . ."

The sentence trailed off because she knew she wasn't really telling the truth.

"Lindsay, this whole experience is as new to me as it is to you. I never dreamed I'd get so close to another human being. So I'm having trouble coping with it."

"I understand." She gave him the answer she thought he wanted, although it wasn't her answer. She wanted to tell him to relax and embrace this gift they'd been given. But she understood that was difficult for him. Maybe he didn't trust his feelings—or hers. Maybe he never would.

She regarded him from under lowered lashes, glad that they weren't touching. Glad that he couldn't read her thoughts. At least she hoped he couldn't. He'd wanted privacy when he remembered the trauma of getting arrested for shoplifting. She wanted it now, so he wouldn't see the needy part of her that she had always kept hidden.

Being telepathic didn't change the fundamental difference between men and women. Women wanted commitment. Men avoided it. And she was thankful he couldn't see the vulnerability shimmering in her mind.

She was glad when he interrupted her thoughts. "I want to see if you can do what I just did."

"Block you?"

"Yeah. It could turn out to be an important skill."

"With you?"

"With someone like Todd—who can shoot death rays into your head—unless you stopped him."

"If he were alive, would he hurt us?"

"I don't know. But I wouldn't want to be totally vulnerable to him—or anyone else who had the same talents."

"You think there are others?"

"I don't know. But I think it would be a good idea for you to practice shielding yourself."

He held out his hand, and she felt her heart give a small thump.

She had no idea how to do what he was asking.

Give me a clue. What should I do?

Use that window image.

She did as he suggested, imagining a clear window into her mind, then darkening the glass so that there was no way to see through. Only this time, she was on the inside, and he was outside—trying to push his way in.

She felt her muscles tremble as she tried to hold him off. Maybe she didn't have his strength, because she felt tentacle-like probes sliding in around the edges of the glass.

In her hand, she imagined scissors, snipping them off— and felt him wince. "Ouch. That hurts."

She couldn't suppress a grin of triumph. "Serves you right."

In response, he redoubled his efforts, and she felt like she was running from one place to the next, cutting off invaders. Sweat beaded on her forehead. Her breath came in gasps, as if she'd been running a marathon. Raising her eyes to his, she saw that his face was flushed and he was also breathing hard.

Truce.

Had he said that? Or had she?

By mutual agreement, they both stopped, and she fell against him, exhausted.

He gathered her to him.

You did good.

It was hard.

It was worth the effort.

He shifted to speech. "But now I should make that license plate switch so we can get out of here. Before someone goes through the neighborhood looking for houses where the owner is away."

She felt a stab of alarm. "Would they do that?"

"I hope not. But it depends on how desperate they are to find us."

"Like they found Sid," she whispered. She'd been so focused on herself and Jordan that she'd blotted out everything else.

"Maybe we can deflect bullets."

"Oh, sure." She looked nervously down the drive. "Shouldn't we leave right now?"

"Give me a couple of minutes." Jordan turned back to the half-completed job. "If the guys who were after Mark have figured out we're together, they'll look for a Saturn with your license plates. Not these. So once we leave, the most important thing is to stay inside the law and keep from getting stopped by a cop."

"Do you lie around at night thinking up elements for suspense plots?"

He laughed. "Sometimes. Maybe I've got a secret yen to switch from nonfiction to fiction."

He'd said it jokingly. But she caught a serious undercurrent in the admission.

After screwing on the stolen plates, he took a baseball cap off a hook on the wall.

"You're going to wear that—for a disguise?" she asked.

"No, you are." He handed over the cap. "Put it on and tuck your hair inside."

When she'd done as he asked, he studied the effect. "Let's do a little more. Put on my sunglasses—and one of my shirts."

Quickly he opened his overnight bag, pulled out a long-sleeved shirt, and passed it over. She pulled on the shirt over her knit top, then rolled up the long sleeves.

Jordan gave her a long look. "Well, we've managed to erase your polished image."

"Is that good?"

"Of course. Nobody would believe you're a respected

aide to Senator Daniel Bridgewater. Just remember to drive slowly and carefully. But not too slowly."

Totally thrown off stride, she asked, "I'm going to drive?"

"Yeah. They won't be expecting you behind the wheel—if they know we're together. And if they have your picture, they sure as hell won't recognize you."

I hope. Lindsay answered, then watched Jordan climb into the backseat, lie down, and try to make himself comfortable in the cramped space.

KURT liked sitting in his office, waiting for good news. He was like the king of a small country, and his subjects brought him tribute.

But not in the past few days. Of course, he knew it was only a matter of time until his men captured one or all of the fugitives. But it was difficult to contain his impatience.

When the phone rang, he snatched up the receiver.

Jim Swift was on the line. "What about Walker?"

"Nothing at the moment."

"You don't think he's disappeared into the woods, do you? Like that guy who bombed abortion clinics?"

"Not with his urban background."

"Then he should leave a credit trail."

"Unless he's too smart for that." Swift cleared his throat. "I've come up with something interesting."

"What?" Kurt snapped, then silently cursed because he knew he'd given away his state of mind.

"I've been digging into Walker's recent activities. He was at a party last week given by Sam Conroy. A woman named Lindsay Fleming was also on the guest list."

Kurt searched his memory. "I imagine a lot of other people were on the guest list. What do you have on Fleming?"

"She works for Daniel Bridgewater, the chairman of the Senate Armed Services Committee."

"Bridgewater knows when to stay out of trouble. He's mostly left us alone. And if Fleming is on his staff, I'd expect her to know Conroy."

"That's not the main point. I took some pictures of selected partygoers to the desk staff at Walker's apartment. One of them recognized her. She came there a couple of days after the party. And one other interesting fact. I went back to Sid Becker's phone records. He called her—before he went to that meeting with Mark."

"Jesus!"

"She's probably the woman with Walker at Cunningham Falls. They got away in a car. It could be hers. I've got the make, model, and the license plate. I've got cops in a five-state area looking for her."

"Good."

"I have researchers tracing his movements back over the past few months."

"Excellent."

"Any other approach you want me to take?" Jim asked.

"Yes," Kurt answered. He wasn't willing to share everything he knew yet. But he had a theory he wanted to pursue. "I want to find out how Hamilton fits into this. I'm assuming that he picked Walker to investigate his son's death. But why Walker? Why not somebody else? I want you to have a chat with Hamilton. I want you to make sure that nobody else in the house knows you've been there." He paused. "He's an old, sick man. After you get everything you can out of him, get rid of him. Make it look like natural causes. Or an accident."

"I can get in there tonight."

"They probably won't even do an autopsy, if he's under a doctor's care."

"Yeah."

Kurt thought for a minute. "Let me give you a list of questions to ask him."

"Sure."

After he'd dictated the queries and Jim had read them back, they hung up.

His spirits revived, Kurt punched his fist into the air. For the first time in days it looked like things were going his way.

The question was—would he be in time?

He went back to the computer—back to the information he had on Todd Hamilton and Glenn Barrow.

They had apparently met a year and a half before the attack on Maple Creek.

A year and a half before they'd been able to do . . . what?

He still wasn't sure. What he was thinking was so outrageous that if someone else had come to him with the theory, he would have told them they were crazy.

But he had always been flexible. In this case, thinking outside the box might be the only way to go.

He was sitting at the computer when Mary Ann came in. Impatiently he looked up.

She read the expression on his face and hesitated before saying, "I can come back later."

"No. If you've got something important, I want to hear it."

"I was doing what you said, going through the names on that list you gave me." She paused before going on. "Two of the children were twins—named Anderson, Billy and Patty Anderson."

"Yes."

"Their parents were killed in an automobile accident when they were five, and they went into the foster-care system."

Kurt waited for the punch line.

"They changed their name to Trinity. Saxon and Willow Trinity."

He stared at her. "Should I recognize those names?"

"They have an offbeat 'ministry' in Florida."

"How did you make the name connection?"

"They mentioned it once—in a very early interview. Then they dropped the subject."

"Okay. What kind of ministry?"

"Well, their followers swear they're able to work miracles."

"Jesus! Get me everything you can on them."

LINDSAY had driven only a few blocks when she saw a police car.

Her foot bounced on the gas pedal.

"What's wrong?" Jordan asked from where he lay curled on the backseat.

"A cop is on my tail."

"Just keep driving like you belong here."

"Would the bad guys have gotten the local police looking for us?" she asked, hearing the strangled sound of her own voice.

"They might. But they would probably have lied about what they wanted us for."

She wondered what he meant—exactly. It was hard to drive normally with the patrol car in back of her. She kept fighting the impulse to speed up. But she knew that was precisely the wrong thing to do.

When she realized she was in danger of cruising right through a stop sign, she pressed down too hard on the brake and came to a jerky stop.

"Sorry."

Jordan reached between the seats, his hand slipping under the loose shirt and knit top to press against her ribs.

Steady. You're doing fine.

He's looking at me. I'll bet he's checking the plate number. She knew she sounded panicked, but she couldn't help herself.

If he is, he'll find you live around here.

And if he stops me, he'll find out I don't. The silent words were like a shiver quivering at the edge of her thoughts.

Then we'll do an alien mind lock on him.

What's an alien mind lock?

I don't know. I made it up. Maybe that's what Todd and Glenn did.

She knew he was trying to distract her. Still, she felt her throat close as she thought about what would happen if the cop pulled her over. He'd ask to check her license and registration—and ask why a man was lying in the backseat.

The cop stayed behind her as she drove with what she hoped looked like casual unconcern toward the highway.

To calm herself, she turned on the radio. An old Police song was playing. "Every Breath You Take." The words and the rhythm didn't calm her nerves.

Maybe it had the same effect on Jordan because he said, "See if you can get a news station."

She switched to AM and turned the dial, stopping when she came to an interview with a diet guru. After what felt like a hundred years, the police cruiser speeded up and drove around her. He was in front of her for several blocks, then turned onto a side street.

When he was out of sight, she gave a small sigh of thanks.

In the backseat Jordan shifted to a more comfortable position—if there was a comfortable position for him in such a small space.

On the radio the announcer was in the middle of a weather report. Next came a series of advertisements, and Lindsay reached to find another station, then changed her mind.

Something important was coming up. She was sure of that, and she clenched the wheel as she waited for the commercials to end.

Finally the announcer returned with the headlines—starting with the situation in the Middle East.

"Come on," she muttered.

"What?" Jordan asked from the backseat.

"Shush . . ." she hissed. "I have to hear this."

Probably because Jordan caught the tension vibrating in her voice, he sat up and leaned forward.

Finally the announcer said, "Police have a new lead in the murder of retired Army Colonel Sidney Becker, who was found shot to death in Rock Creek Park this morning."

CHAPTER
TWENTY-TWO

JORDAN WATCHED LINDSAY'S hands go rigid on the wheel, her knuckles whitening. He felt the same tension, but all he could do was wait to hear the rest.

"They caught them," she whispered. "Thank God."

The announcer was still speaking. "Evidence points to the involvement of Mark Greenwood, the colonel's cousin. Family members say that Greenwood's behavior became erratic over the past several months. He had demanded money from his cousin, who had agreed to meet him in the park. Greenwood, who is five feet nine, one hundred and sixty-five pounds, brown hair and brown eyes, is armed and dangerous."

"Oh, God. No," Lindsay breathed.

"Jesus!" Jordan leaned against the front seat, pressing his hand to the side of her neck. He could feel the pulse that had started pounding.

"That's a lie," Lindsay whispered. "We saw what happened. We know it's a damn lie."

"Yeah."

Waves of anger and outrage came off of her, threatening to wipe out caution. "We have to set the record straight."

When she started looking wildly around, searching for an exit where they could find a gas station—and a phone—he slipped his fingers under the neck of the shirt, cupping her shoulder. "Lindsay, you can't make a phone call. Not now."

"Don't dictate to me!"

"Just stay with me for a minute. What do you think somebody's going to say if we try to tell what really happened?

You were there? Oh, you weren't there. You saw it psychically. In a vision? Maybe we'd better take you right to the funny farm."

She made a strangled sound. Still outraged, she shouted, "What we heard on the radio is a lie! Mark didn't kill his cousin."

"We know that. But nobody will believe us. And whoever is after us will know where we are. To prove that Mark is innocent, we have to unravel the whole rotten conspiracy."

"How?" she demanded.

"We're going to start by finding out what happened to Todd Hamilton thirty years ago."

He could feel her struggling to calm down. "Okay," she finally whispered.

He looked around and pointed to an Exit sign coming up. "Take the road to Frederick, so I can get back into the front seat. And we can get something to eat."

"I'm not hungry."

"Neither am I. But we skipped dinner and breakfast. Our bodies need fuel."

She didn't reply, but she slowed as they drove into town, eyeing the fast-food restaurants among the businesses that lined the road.

"We might as well have burgers and fries."

"Do you look for excuses to eat junk food?"

"Yeah," he admitted. "Stick with me long enough, and you'll learn all my vices."

MARK gritted his teeth. He hadn't signed on at Maple Creek to become a criminal. But he was a realist. If he was going to survive, he was going to have to keep his freedom. Which meant staying out of the clutches of the men after him—and probably the cops, too.

He'd waited a long time under the blanket of leaves,

straining his ears, listening to birds and small animals taking back the forest.

It was agony to lie without moving. Finally the need to take a leak became a major consideration. Furtively he brushed some leaves away, sat up, and looked around. A sudden noise made him freeze. But it was only a squirrel dashing across the leaves.

A good sign, all things considered.

As far as Mark could see, he was alone. But he still knew he was taking a chance as he relieved the pressure on his bladder behind an oak. Then, moving slowly and cautiously, he slipped from tree to tree as he made his way through the park—listening to the sound of his shoes crunching on dry leaves.

He emerged into a settled city neighborhood where it looked like both husbands and wives went off to work in the morning.

He chose a house that appeared to be closed up for the day, then jiggled the lock on a basement window. When it opened, he climbed inside without needing to break any glass.

After determining that the place was empty, he gave himself twenty minutes inside—max.

Hardly able to believe his nerve, he rummaged in the homeowner's closet and found clothing that fit him. Next he took the quickest shower on record, his ears straining for sounds in the house.

Christ, if someone came in while he was naked and covered with soap, he was in big trouble.

Once he was dressed in clean clothes, he felt better—and secure enough to shave—both his face and head.

As he peered at himself in the mirror, he decided the skinhead look went pretty far toward altering his appearance.

Hoping he could hide his brief presence in the house, he cleaned up after himself, then hid the towel he'd used in a pile of dirty laundry on the floor in front of the washing machine.

The clock on the dresser told him he'd been inside for fifteen minutes. At least he didn't have to look for money. Mr. Macho had been carrying over seven hundred dollars in his wallet. Mark still had most of it.

Knowing he was pressing his luck, he liberated a box of cookies and some fruit juice from the pantry.

A noise at the front door made him freeze. And he flashed back to the nasty confrontation with Mr. Macho.

Relief flooded through him when he realized he'd heard the mailman, dropping letters and circulars through a slot in the front door.

"Get out of here before you get caught again, Greenwood," he muttered as he stuffed the food in the knapsack he'd brought to the park and his dirty clothing in a plastic garbage bag. After jamming sunglasses on his face, he left through the back door. In the next block he stuffed the bag with his clothes into a trash can, then grabbed some of the cookies from the box and munched them as he walked toward Connecticut Avenue, pretending that he was a fine, upstanding citizen.

He got the bad news about his murder-suspect status at a bus stop—from a blaring car radio.

"Evidence in the Becker murder points to the involvement of Mark Greenwood, the colonel's cousin." Made-up details and a description of the supposed murderer followed.

As the announcer explained that he was armed and dangerous, Mark wanted to scream that he was innocent—that the bastards had framed him.

Instead he worked to keep his face from freezing into a mask of anger.

Sid was dead. And he was going to get the fuckers who had done it—and clear his own name.

Figuring no one would think he'd walk around D.C. in the open, he caught a bus downtown. At Dupont Circle he sprang for a cab and asked to be dropped at the corner of Wisconsin Avenue and M Street, in the heart of Georgetown, where the streets were full of shoppers and tourists.

In a little Middle Eastern restaurant near the Four Seasons Hotel, he ordered a gyro sandwich, then ate it at a table in the back, where he could read the papers Sid had given him.

Tears blurred his vision when he thought about his cousin. Sid had come through for him—and lost his life. Because his eager-beaver cousin Mark had taken a job guarding a secret lab. He'd done it because he was comfortable in a military organization—and the pay had been great.

As he read the information Sid had paid for with his life, he wanted to scream out his anger. Instead he began to formulate a plan—something to do besides simply staying alive.

Could he succeed? Maybe. But it would take every drop of cunning and stealth he possessed.

GLANCING frequently in the rearview mirror, Lindsay headed north. At a McDonald's, they ordered burgers and Cokes, which they ate as they drove north.

"We should take an inventory," Jordan said as he stuffed his empty burger wrapper into the bag.

"Of what?"

"Our, um, special powers."

"You make me feel like we're in the middle of a super-hero movie."

"Except that this is real life. Our lives."

She kept her eyes on the road. "Okay. So what can we do?"

"Share thoughts when we're touching each other. And block those thoughts—to some extent. Get hints about the future," he added. "Remote viewing. You're the one who's better at those last two."

"You think we can get better at the things we do?" she asked.

"Yeah. Because Todd and Glenn did—unless they started off with a mind-zapping routine. My guess is that they put a lot of time and energy into figuring out how to break into Maple Creek."

He laid his hand on her thigh, feeling her reaction. *After they bonded.*

That first time—did . . . did you feel . . . like your head was going to explode?

He swallowed. *Yes.*

What does that part mean?

He shrugged. *I guess that bonding isn't a sure thing. I think there was some chance we could have blown our brains out.*

A nice way to phrase it.

How would you put it?

That the process could have driven us crazy? Or given us a stroke?

And now we're left with the good part?

"Very good," he said, his voice thick.

"Yes."

If they hadn't been in a car on the highway, he knew what would have happened next.

"Do you always focus on sex?" she asked.

He sent her a picture. His hand sliding up her thigh, working its way between her legs, pressing against her clit through the fabric of her pants and panties.

"Stop! Unless you want me to crash."

He switched the picture to Van Gogh's famous sunflowers, and she laughed.

Struggling with arousal, he leaned toward the car door, watching her as she drove. When she didn't speak, he asked, *Are you angry?*

"About what?"

My . . . making you hot.

"Making us both hot."

"Like you said—it's a guy thing. We think about sex a lot. I should be embarrassed that you're picking up on it."

Do you always get instantly aroused?

With you, I do.

Should I be flattered?

"Don't fish for compliments. You know you should be flattered."

She kept her hands on the wheel and her eyes on the road, and he knew that this time, she was the one having trouble handling their relationship. He knew that sex had never been a big part of her life. Now she was being bombarded by his sexually explicit thoughts.

Do the multiplication tables, she suggested.

Oh sure . . .

She made another silent comment—which he didn't catch. They needed to strengthen that ability.

Which one?

Talking in our heads—without touching, he answered, then began contemplating a way to do it—being careful to keep his plans to himself.

AS head of the Senate Armed Services Committee, Daniel Bridgewater had his own considerable power base. Still, he'd kept his involvement with the Crandall Consortium to a minimum. Kurt MacArthur was dangerous to anyone who opposed him. Calvin Crandall had been the same.

Dan had seen a sanitized report on the incident at Maple Creek, and he'd been willing to take MacArthur's word for the details.

Now he felt compelled to find out what had really happened, and he'd already figured out the best way to access that buried information. Pulling his chair up to the desk, he called up the office e-mail system and sent a message to George Underhill, his nerd-in-chief.

"Need to talk to you one-on-one about some files."

Five minutes later Underhill shambled in. He was in his mid-twenties, the oddball on the staff. Very odd. He was dressed in a gray button-down shirt that had once been white and faded jeans with a hole in the crotch revealing striped boxer shorts. Thank God it wasn't the guy's cock.

Daniel thought of Underhill as a necessary evil, an adaptation to the computer age. He was the staffer who protected the office network from viruses, worms, and hackers, and he was the best. Still, they kept him in a back room, where he wouldn't frighten small children or other visitors.

"How's it goin', man?" Underhill said, parking himself in one of the guest chairs and slicking back his dirty brown hair.

"Fine," Daniel answered. He'd like to tell the guy to go home, take a bath, shave, and change his clothes. Instead, he got down to business. "I need to dip into the records of a D.C. think tank—the Crandall Consortium."

"Which part of the records?"

"I want information on a break-in at Maple Creek—one of their facilities. I need their internal assessment of what happened there—not just what they've put out for external consumption."

Underhill sat up straighter, looking interested. Obviously, the prospect of hacking into Crandall's computers excited him. "I'll get right on it."

"How long do you think it will take?"

"Don't know. I'll get back to you, man."

"Make sure they can't follow your trail back here."

"What do you think I am, an idiot?"

Underhill exited the room, and Dan stood up. Walking to the window, he looked toward the Capitol Building, admiring the view from his spacious office suite. The park-like ground had a majesty befitting the seat of government. But since 9/11 the landscape had been marred by concrete barriers, machine-gun-toting cops, and other antiterrorist measures. He didn't much like the world he was forced to live in now. Still, he'd stayed in the Senate and he was going to run for the presidency because defending democracy was worth the personal sacrifice.

Which was why he was digging into the Maple Creek flap.

He tightened his fists. That was it. Right?

An image flitted into his mind. An image of the Trinity twins. Saxon and Willow. He'd already gotten some money from people in their church. And more was coming. He wanted their support, and they had . . .

The thought slipped away from him.

They had . . . He tried to hold on to the picture that had formed in his head. But it wouldn't stay.

Suddenly he was desperate to remember something very important. Something he should do? Something he should be worried about?

But the image wouldn't come clear. Feeling frustrated, he turned his thoughts back to the Crandall Consortium and immediately felt less anxious. He had the feeling that Kurt MacArthur had gone too far this time. And he wanted to know what the bastard was up to.

LINDSAY was glad to turn over the driving to Jordan at the first rest stop in Delaware. At eight he pulled off the New Jersey Turnpike, into a community that had grown up around the exit.

When he stopped at a motel chain that featured suites, she looked at him questioningly.

"Can we afford a suite?"

"It's not expensive. Trust me." Stopping in a parking

space across from the door, he said, "I'll go in, so we won't be seen together."

When he came back, the look on his face told her that he was enjoying some private joke. But he blocked it from her—and was careful not to touch her.

All she could pick up was sexual arousal. Nothing new about that.

"We have room three twenty-three," he said as he slid behind the wheel again. "You go up first. I'll park the car and meet you."

He held out the plastic card key.

When she reached for his hand instead, he pulled it back, and she knew that he'd put up the same kind of barrier he'd used before he stole the license plate—only he was getting better at it.

"What are you trying to hide from me?"

He glanced around, then tossed the key into her lap. "We'll talk about it later."

CHAPTER
TWENTY-THREE

LINDSAY UNLOCKED THE door of room three twenty-three and found herself in a small living room. The bedroom and bathroom were through another door to the right. Pretty spacious for two people who were sleeping in the same bed.

While she was inspecting the bedroom, Jordan set his bag down on the dresser.

"You're sure we can afford a suite?"

"It's the same price as a room in a lot of other motels. And I want to read over some of the notes from Leonard Hamilton—and do some Web research. Why don't you get some rest? I'll join you later."

The tone of his voice was casual, but she wasn't fooled. "What kind of research?" she asked.

"Let me see what I can find before we talk about it."

"Fine." Determined to give him some privacy, she turned and strode into the bathroom. After a nice hot shower, she dried her hair and changed into a clean T-shirt and panties.

She might have walked into the living room to see what he was doing. Instead, she climbed into bed.

As she stared at the shaft of light coming from the bathroom, she found herself listening for sounds from the living room. She could hear none. But she sensed Jordan's presence out there.

When the phone rang, she jumped—then snatched up the receiver. "Hello?"

The stern voice on the other end of the line said, "You shouldn't answer the phone when you're undercover."

It was Jordan.

"If I shouldn't answer, why did you call?" she snapped.

"I wanted to talk to you."

"You said we couldn't use your cell phone. So how are you calling me?"

"This hotel has two lines in each room. I did a room to room call—to the other line."

"Oh." She felt a tingle of alarm. Well, not exactly alarm. "What are you up to?"

"Strengthening our skills. This afternoon when we tried mind talking without touching, we couldn't always make the connection. I'd like to work on that. I'd like to see what we can do when we're not in the same room."

"Is that why you got a suite—instead of just a bedroom?" she demanded.

"Yes."

She licked her suddenly dry lips.

"What was the catalyst that opened us up to each other?" he asked in a silky voice.

"Touching."

"Not just touching. Arousal."

The word hung in the air between them. They weren't touching now. He'd put them into a position where they couldn't reach for each other. And suddenly she didn't have to be a mind reader to figure out where this conversation was going.

"I think I'm going to hang up," she finally said.

"Don't!"

"Why not?"

His voice turned grave. "Because communicating without talking may be the key to our survival. It's not just fun and games."

The reminder sent a shiver over her skin. Yet she didn't like being forced into a scenario that he'd obviously been contemplating for several hours. "Don't talk to me about danger—when the game is the payoff for you."

"Lindsay, I wasn't kidding. Our lives may depend on

our being able to work together in ways that most people can't even imagine."

Her fist clenched around the receiver. And while she was trying to come to grips with what he'd just said, she heard him drag in a breath and let it out slowly. That breath was reassuring because it told her he wasn't as calm and reasonable as he sounded.

Before she could put up more objections, he began speaking again. "Extraordinary things happen when we touch. Let's see if we can make them happen without the actual physical contact."

"I'm . . . too conventional for this . . ."

"With me, you're very open, very giving. Very sexy. Let's imagine what would happen if I came in there. We both know I'd start kissing you—touching you—taking off your clothes."

She understood his goal—turning her on without being in the room. And it was definitely working. His voice was like honey sliding over her skin.

He went on with the sweet seduction. "You switched off the light. I'd have to turn it back on so I could see your beautiful naked body. I'd take off my clothes, too, and lie down beside you. And we'd go on from there—kissing and touching until I'd made you as hot as I am now."

It was impossible not to react. Her nipples tightened. And moisture gathered between her legs.

Pausing to let the words sink in, he asked, "So am I making you hot by saying all that?"

"Damn you. You know you are."

"Good."

She should tell him she didn't approve of sex games like this. But the words stayed locked in her throat.

"Thanks for admitting it. I don't have any problem telling you I'm hard as a lead pipe. And we're not even in the same room."

"Because you're a man!"

He laughed softly. "Yes. A man who wants to make love to his woman."

"You could come in here right now and do that."

"And we wouldn't accomplish anything we haven't already experienced."

"I get the feeling you started thinking about . . . phone sex before we got to Delaware," she accused.

"Right. So let's see how much pleasure we can give each other—like this. And let's see if we stop needing the phone to communicate."

She turned her head toward the closed door to the living room. He was just on the other side of the wall.

"Where are you sitting?"

"I'm lying on the sofa, where I can get comfortable."

"Oh."

"Have you ever tried aural sex?" he asked, his voice silky, and she knew that he figured she wasn't going to back out now.

"No. Have you?"

"No, actually. I've lived a pretty sheltered life."

She laughed.

"You have a very sexy laugh."

"Do I?"

"Oh, yeah. I love that musical sound. But that's not the only thing I love about you."

The declaration warmed her. "I'm listening."

"I love getting hooked up with a woman who's my intellectual equal. A woman with a sense of purpose. Who has courage—and integrity—and a great body."

"You always get back to the physical, don't you?"

"Because I want you," he answered in a rough voice.

"Does talking when we're not face to face unleash your inhibitions?" she heard herself asking.

"Of course. I don't have to deal with your disapproving look."

"What disapproving look?"

"We'll change it to a look of stupefied passion."

She laughed again. Jordan Walker was a serious man. It gave her a little thrill to unleash his playful side.

"I want to picture you. So tell me what you're wearing," he said suddenly.

"A T-shirt and panties."

"You didn't pack anything sexy? Even when you knew we were going to a cabin in the woods to make love?"

"I'm too practical."

"But aroused."

She swallowed. She could have denied it. It was a unique opportunity with him. If he couldn't touch her, he wouldn't know for sure. Except that he would—from the tremble in her voice and the rapid in and out of her breathing. "Yes," she admitted.

"So. Are your nipples standing up? If I were there in the bedroom with the light on, could I see them through your T-shirt?"

She looked down and saw the twin points outlined by the soft fabric.

"Lindsay?"

"Yes," she whispered.

"And it would feel good if I ran my hand over those hard tips."

"Yes."

"But I'm not there. So you'll have to do it for me."

"Jordan!"

"Are you embarrassed?"

"You know damn well I am."

"But you're hot, too. So take your hands and just touch yourself there. Do that for me."

"You could come in."

"That's a very tempting offer. But it won't prove anything. We know our minds will open to each other if I'm with you on the bed. Naked. Holding your body against mine. My cock hard against your middle."

She made a strangled sound. "Is that what you want to do?"

"You know I do."

This was crazy. She should stop. Instead she did as he asked.

"Ah, that's nice," he murmured.

"Did you feel me do that?"

"I felt the shadow of it. I think we need to be more turned on to bridge the mental gap."

"Jordan Walker, boy scientist."

"Man scientist," he corrected. "You're lying down, right?"

"Yes."

"Are your legs together? Or spread apart?"

"Together," she whispered.

"Because the pressure makes you hotter."

"Stop!"

"Open your legs for me."

"Why?"

"So I can picture you that way. Open for me. Welcoming me. Ready for me to ease my cock inside you."

She did as he asked and found that it made her even hotter to follow his directions.

God, that's good.

You felt it?

Oh, yeah. I felt that leap of heat inside you. He took a breath and let it out. "If I were in there with you, I'd run my hands up the insides of your legs, up your thighs, and find . . ." He stopped and she knew he was grinning. "There's no convenient word for that part of you, is there? I mean no nice word. What do you call it?"

Down there.

"Hum. That got through to me just fine without the telephone. But it's not much help. Not very romantic. I'd like something more poetic."

"Like what?"

"What about your quiver?"

"Did you make that up?"

"Yeah, I did."

"Just now?"

"No."

"And you blocked that?"

"Well, I was thinking about it after I sent you off to get ready for bed. I was thinking about what I wanted to do with you. And the image came to me. Because when I touch you there, I feel you quiver for me."

She made a strangled sound.

"Do you hate the word?"

"We could do worse."

"A lot worse. I'd love to stroke your quiver. Dip my finger inside, then stroke up toward your clit. Right down the center of that hot, swollen valley."

The words were like a caress against that slick, aching place, robbing her of breath.

"Are you wet for me?"

This time, against all odds, she managed to get out one syllable. "Yes."

"Touch yourself there for me. I can't do it. I'm too far away."

"And you want to picture me doing that?"

"Yes."

"That's too much for me."

"But you're so hot. So needy."

Yes.

Let me touch you. It's me touching you. Only I can't do it in person. You have to help me out. I can feel the need building inside you. I can feel how hot and wet you are.

And she could feel the arousal of his body. That hard shaft, straining at the front of him. Such a foreign sensation to her, yet part of her now, too.

"Lindsay, I ache for you."

She liked the way he said it, as though he were having trouble catching his breath.

"I know." She gulped. "So if you can ask me to touch my breasts, and touch myself down there . . ."

Your quiver, you mean.

"So if you can give me directions, than I can do the same. I want you to touch your penis."

"Oh, yeah," he answered.

"Open your pants, if you haven't done that yet. Take your . . . your cock out. Grasp the shaft. Stroke your hand up and down."

She closed her eyes, picturing him lying on the couch, his head thrown back against a cushion, his hand stroking his red, swollen penis. He was doing it now. She knew that as well as she knew the response of her own body. And she loved the sensation of fullness. Of male arousal.

As she captured his reaction in her mind, she felt heat building in her own body.

Did you like telling me what to do? Did that make you hotter?

"Yes," she whispered.

Then it's my turn. Take off your T-shirt for me. And your panties. We don't want them to get ripped again.

Because she had no choice now, she put down the phone receiver and pulled her clothes off. And she didn't need to pick it up again to hear him ask, *Did you do it?*

Can't you tell?

I want to make sure it's not my imagination. That I'm not just fantasizing about your gorgeous breasts. The beautiful curve of your hip. That tempting triangle of dark hair at the top of your legs.

"You, too," she gasped out. *I want you naked, too.*

"Yeah."

The words might be spoken aloud, but they echoed inside her head, too.

He was back moments later, with more erotically

charged questions. *If I were there, what would you want me to do to your breasts? Lift them in my hands? Circle the nipples with my fingers. Squeeze them?*

"Yes," she breathed.

Do that for me.

She did as he asked, moaning her pleasure, knowing that he felt her response as surely as she felt his.

Her breath came faster as her arousal built.

You need to come, don't you?

You, too.

God, yes. But I can't come unless you do.

You mean you won't let yourself.

Yeah. So stroke your quiver for me. Stroke your finger through those sweet folds. Dip your finger into your vagina. Then play with the rim where you're so sensitive. Are you using one finger? Or two? Is two better?

"Two," she gasped.

She followed his directions, her breath coming in little gasps as she felt her climax building. And his.

She knew he was lying on the couch, naked, his taut cock rising toward the ceiling as he stroked it rapidly with his hand. She knew she wasn't making up the scene.

And she knew he saw her, too.

She should be embarrassed. This was too personal, for them to be watching each other. But because they were both playing the same game, she could do it.

She did what she might have done alone in her own bed, building her own pleasure—until her inner muscles contracted, and climax took her body.

He followed her over the edge, semen spurting from his penis as it jerked in his hand.

Lindsay!

When he silently called her name, she answered as small waves of pleasure washed over her.

She collapsed back against the pillow. Moments later a sound made her eyes fly open.

He had opened the door and was standing naked in the doorway, staring down at her. She saw that he wasn't entirely steady on his feet—that he needed to lean his shoulder against the jamb.

His thoughts couldn't have been more clear if he had been touching her.

It worked. The sexual link is the key.

That's a little inconvenient, isn't it?

He laughed. "Oh, I don't know."

He crossed the room and came down beside her on the bed, gathering her close, and she nestled against him.

You should have told me what you were planning.

Like I said, I thought you would object.

I would have.

So I had to draw you into the game by making you hot.

You could have suggested we play . . . gin rummy, and try to read each other's cards.

He laughed again. *Gin rummy. That wouldn't have been quite so much fun. But, you're right. We might try something like that for practice.*

She stroked her lips against his shoulder, and when he began to kiss her throat and drift his hand down her body, she knew that he was forging the bond between them even tighter—in a way she knew she was going to like.

WHAT did the street people do in winter? Mark wondered. Above him, on the Whitehurst Freeway, traffic whizzed by. Down here among the concrete pilings, he'd found a little community of men with nowhere else to go.

Some of them were on drugs. Some were crazy. Some were dangerous. And some were suspicious of a newcomer in their midst.

"What are you doin' here, man?"

"My former business partner went bat shit. I'm hiding out from him."

"What business was that?"

"We had a nice little import business. Products from Mexico."

His new friend answered with a knowing laugh.

"I'm going to get things straightened out. Contact my ex-wife. She'll help me."

"Never trust a woman."

"I don't." He took a sip from a bottle of Wild Turkey wrapped in a paper bag, then handed over the bottle.

The other man took a couple of greedy swallows.

"So, I heard you might know where I could get a gun— for protection."

"I might."

"I'll come back tomorrow," he said, thinking that there were guys here who would slit your throat for a good pair of tennis shoes.

He left the bottle as a goodwill offering and drifted away. Oak Hill Cemetery seemed like a safer place to sleep. In a nice sheltered crypt.

Most guys down here were too superstitious to spend the night in a graveyard. He'd given up superstition for pragmatism.

THE old man was sitting up in his king-sized bed when Jim Swift stepped into the elegantly furnished bedroom. Apparently, Leonard Hamilton had fancied himself a descendant of the English aristocracy, judging from the furnishings he'd chosen.

A reading light shone down on him. Probably he'd been a holy terror in the boardroom—when he'd been in his prime. Now he was shrunken and stooped, his hands gnarled on the book he held. He made a pathetic figure— wearing a padded jacket to keep his old flesh warm.

After several seconds he looked up, then blinked when he saw that it wasn't a member of his staff.

Still, his voice was strong when he asked, "Who are you? What are you doing here?"

Even in his diminished state, Hamilton was a man used to getting answers.

Jim closed the door quietly behind him, then walked across the thick carpet. When he was standing beside the bed, he said, "I came to talk to you—about Todd."

The old man pushed himself up straighter. "What about him?"

"Why did you hire Jordan Walker to investigate your son's death?"

"I didn't hire anyone."

"Call it whatever you want. Walker's sticking his nose in where it doesn't belong. He was here two days ago, interviewing you."

"How do you know that?"

"Not that I owe you an explanation, but I saw his car turn in at the gate."

"You were watching my house? Interfering in my private business?"

"Yes. And let's get something straight. I'm the one asking the questions. I want to know why you selected Walker—and what he's found out."

"I don't have to tell you anything."

Jim reached down and pulled the covers aside, pressing into Hamilton's liver through his abdominal wall.

He wedged his other hand over the old man's mouth, muffling his cry of pain. "There's more where that came from."

CHAPTER
TWENTY-FOUR

LINDSAY'S HEAD MOVED restlessly back and forth on the pillow, and she moaned in her sleep. Her body was still with Jordan in the motel bed. But she knew that her mind had traveled somewhere else.

To another place. Miles from where she slept.

An old man lay in a vast bed, his face contorted with pain. Another man stood over him. He must have just done something terrible, because the old man gasped and sputtered and fought to catch his breath.

She knew who he was. Leonard Hamilton. She had never met him in person. But she had seen a picture in her mind—of him talking to Jordan.

She shivered because the room was cold, and she realized that she was as naked as she had been under the covers with Jordan.

She wrapped her arms around her shoulders, covering her breasts, trying to ward off the icy wind that rippled across her skin.

She wasn't really in Leonard Hamilton's bedroom, she told herself. She was with Jordan. Warm and safe. Yet the cold sensation of being in that other location was very real.

When the man by the bed turned suddenly and seemed to be looking directly at her, she froze.

"Who's there?" he growled.

She wasn't really in the room with him. Not in person. Her body was back in bed. Could he sense her presence? The way Sid had done?

"Nobody's here." She mouthed the denial, struggling to send him a silent message that she wasn't standing fifteen feet away.

He raised his gun, pointing it at her, and she cringed back. If he shot her, could he hurt her?

She hoped she wasn't going to find out.

He took a step toward her.

She fought the impulse to turn and run. Run where? How did you flee from a vision? If she bolted out the door, would she be in another part of the house?

The question was moot, because her legs had turned to stone. So she stood stock-still, waiting to find out what would happen.

The intruder turned back to the man on the bed. "Is someone in the room with us?"

"No."

"What did I see?"

"Hell, I don't know. The ghost of Christmas future?"

"You have nerves of steel, I'll give you that." He tipped his head to the side, staring at Hamilton. "Do you want more pain like I just gave you?" he asked, his voice turning almost gentle.

"I can't take much more pain like that," Hamilton answered. "A few more . . . of your love pats, and I'll have a heart attack."

"We can find out if that's true," the other man said, his fingers still caressing the old man's wrinkled skin.

Hamilton kept his respiration shallow. "I have a proposition."

"I'm listening."

"You're going to kill me anyway."

Lindsay swallowed a gasp as the man on the bed kept speaking. Was he right? Was this intruder his executioner?

"I want to know about my son. I'll answer some of your questions, if you answer some of mine."

The standing man laughed softly. "You are a delightful

surprise. Too bad we didn't meet under different circumstances."

"You don't get to be the head of a multinational corporation unless you can surprise the opposition," Hamilton answered evenly.

Lindsay didn't want to be in the room, witnessing this conversation. Yet she couldn't turn away from the fascinating and disturbing scene. Neither of the men seemed aware of her presence now. They were too wrapped up in each other.

The younger man was deadly calm. Yet underneath the surface, she sensed a pleasure that made her stomach turn.

What about Hamilton? Strangely, he seemed relieved. He had been in pain for a long time. And he had been on a quest. Perhaps he'd complete his mission and find an end to his suffering very soon.

"What's your name?" Hamilton demanded. "If we're going to talk, I'd like to know who you are."

"You can call me Jim."

"Is that your real name?"

"Stop wasting my time. We'll see how the exchange goes."

"You might as well sit down."

The interrogator sat on the edge of the bed.

"A little too close for comfort. Why don't you pull over a chair." Hamilton gestured toward the brocade chair and pie crust lamp table in the corner.

"Because the marks will show on the rug. I don't want to leave any clues to my presence."

"Ah."

"Let's stop dancing around."

"All right. I get to go first."

Jim crossed his arms and waited.

"What did Todd and Glenn Barrow do that got them killed?"

"They broke into a secure government facility and immobilized the guards—without weapons."

"How?"

"My turn. Why did you hire Jordan Walker?"

"I didn't hire him. I invited him up here for an interview—to see if we could work together writing my authorized biography. I liked his style. I liked what I discovered when I met him. And I knew he couldn't resist a good mystery. So I told him there had been a cover-up on Todd's medical report."

"Did you arrange for Walker to meet Lindsay Fleming at Sam Conroy's party?"

The old man made a small sound. "Why do you think so?"

"It was too much of a coincidence."

"Yes. He might have been invited anyway. But I made sure he was on the guest list. I thought getting them together would be a good idea."

"Why?"

"She works for Daniel Bridgewater, the chairman of the SASC. I figured that if anyone could help Walker dig up information on what Todd was doing, it would be someone with good connections."

"That's your only reason?"

"Yes."

The man named Jim leaned forward. "Who else knows about your investigation into Todd's death?"

"Nobody."

He paused, as though mentally consulting a list of questions. "Did Todd know Saxon and Willow Trinity?"

"I have no idea. He didn't tell me about his friends. Who are Saxon and Willow Trinity?"

"A brother and sister with a ministry that claims psychic powers."

"Interesting. And who do you work for?"

"Since you're not going to tell anyone else, I don't mind saying. The Crandall Consortium."

The old man huffed out a breath.

"What does that mean to you?"

"Covert operations inside the U.S. Dirty tricks. Anything and everything necessary to get the job done—as Kurt MacArthur sees the job."

Lindsay felt the scene waver. Suddenly she was being pulled away as if something physical was breaking the connection.

"No!" she screamed, the sound echoing in the room. Or perhaps it was only inside her own head.

The one named Jim turned and stared in her direction, his eyes wide, and she didn't know whether or not he'd heard her—or seen her.

She didn't care. She couldn't leave now, and she tried to claw her way back.

"Wake up. Lindsay, wake up. You're having a bad dream."

"Let me . . ." She struggled against the hands that held her in place.

"Lindsay, sweetheart, you're safe. You're all right. Nobody can hurt you."

"Stop! Don't pull me back here."

She struck out, connected with flesh and bone.

Someone made a harsh sound of pain. "Stop whacking me."

Her eyes blinked open, and she found herself staring up into Jordan's taut face as he hovered over her in the motel bed.

"Jordan?"

"You were having a bad dream," he said again.

She tried to bring her mind back to this room. Back to Jordan. "No. You don't understand. It wasn't a dream. It was real."

"What?"

"I was in Leonard Hamilton's bedroom. Well—my consciousness was there. It was like what happened before, when Sid met Mark—and you and I saw what happened."

She could tell that he was listening to her with full attention.

"Like before? You were somewhere else?" he asked urgently.

"Yes. Only I wasn't awake. I was asleep. And I was alone. I mean, I was the only one who was having the vision, or whatever you call it. You weren't there."

"What happened?"

"A man named Jim came to Hamilton's bedroom. He wasn't someone Hamilton knew. Not a friend. Not anyone who worked for him." She made a hitching sound. "He came there to get information about Todd and about . . . about us."

"Jesus! Us?"

Yes! But Jordan, he's going to kill Hamilton!

How do you know?

They were talking about it. Hamilton made a deal with him. He said if Jim tortured him, he'd have a heart attack and die right away—without revealing anything. He said he knew Jim was there to kill him—and they could exchange information first.

Jordan swore again.

She gripped his arm. *We have to stop him. It may not be too late. They were still talking.*

How do we stop it?

Call the house.

The exchange of information was fast. They weren't actually speaking in each other's heads now. Ideas and concepts flashed between them in some form she couldn't describe.

He ran a hand through his hair. *It's the same people who are after us. The same people who killed Sid. Probably they've tapped Hamilton's line. They'll find out where we are.*

Then we'll be ready to leave as soon as you make the

call. She leaped off the bed and began pulling on her clothing. "Hurry."

She knew he felt her urgency as he began doing the same. When he was dressed, he dashed into the living room and packed his computer, then pulled a small book from his carry bag, found the number, and dialed.

The phone range twice. Then a man answered. A man with an English accent. Not Hamilton or Jim.

"Who's calling, please?"

Ignoring the question, Jordan said, "Mr. Hamilton may be in danger. There may be an intruder in the house. Call the police."

"Who is this?"

"Someone who wants to help."

"Is this Jordan Walker?"

"Shit," he growled, then slammed down the phone. "Come on." Grabbing Lindsay's arm, he pulled her out the door, and they pounded down the steps.

They were in the car and onto the highway again in less than a minute, and she admired Jordan's ability to drive at a normal pace.

"Why did he ask if it was you?" she whispered.

"If it was the butler I met twice, I guess he recognized my voice." He snorted. "Or he's psychic, too!"

"If someone recorded the conversation, then they know you have information."

"Yeah. Unfortunately."

"What are we going to do?"

"Tell me exactly what you found out when Hamilton and the other guy were taking."

She might have started to speak rapidly. Instead, she laid her hand on his muscular arm and closed her eyes, opening herself to him, trying to show him the vision exactly as she had experienced it.

She knew he was getting it from her because she felt the mental response.

Jordan took his hand from the wheel, reached for her fingers, and squeezed. "It must have been pretty horrible for you—being there."

"Yes."

"But it helped us."

"How?"

"We found out a lot. We know that the guy named Jim was sent to find out about the Maple Creek incident with Todd. We know who he works for—the Crandall Consortium."

She shivered. "Why was he asking about us?"

He swallowed. *Maybe they suspect that we're like Todd. Maybe that brother and sister—Saxon and Willow Trinity— are another pair.*

A brother and sister. She made a strangled sound. "You think they . . . developed powers . . . the way we did?"

"I'd be interested to know."

"And are we going to turn on the radio and find out that billionaire Leonard Hamilton is dead—like Sid Becker?"

"I hope not."

"Maybe his butler is a bodyguard."

"Maybe."

She pulled her hand away, and they drove in silence through the night. She caught flickers of thoughts coming from Jordan, and she knew he caught the same flickers from her. But they had apparently both decided to put up shields.

It was dawn by the time they reached Darien.

"Can we call Hamilton's house again?" Lindsay asked, even when she knew the answer. It was too dangerous.

"I don't think we can risk it."

She wanted to scream that she had to find out if another innocent person had died.

But, deep down, she already knew the answer.

"I think the best thing to do is check into a motel and get a few hours' sleep. Then we can try to find someone who worked at the Remington Clinic. And see if they're willing to tell us anything."

"You think they wouldn't talk about a clinic that went out of business thirty years ago?"

"If it was a hush-hush operation—maybe not."

IT was too early in the morning for a business call. But when the phone rang at six, Daniel Bridgewater looked at the number on the caller ID and snatched up the receiver.

"Yes?" he asked, trying not to sound as if he'd been wrenched from a restless sleep.

"I have what you want," George Underhill said.

"Not over the phone."

"Of course not," Underhill snapped. "I can meet you at the office."

"Not the office," Daniel answered, thinking. "There's a Starbucks at Four Corners in Silver Spring. We can meet there."

"You want me to come all the way from Mt. Rainier?" the computer nerd asked, naming a small community just across Eastern Avenue from the District.

"Yes. You have the information on a disk?"

Underhill sighed. "Yeah. And I've got some of it on paper. But it will take me about forty minutes to get there."

"The shopping center is right on the corner of Colesville Road and University Boulevard. On the right as you're coming from the Beltway."

Daniel was there early, trying not to look like he was balanced on a knife edge of tension as he sipped a cup of today's special blend at a table near the front. Underhill came in fifteen minutes late, with a thick manila envelope under his arm. He looked like he'd been up all night and hadn't shaved, taken a bath, or changed his clothing. SOP for Mr. Clean.

Daniel stood and said, "Let's go for a drive."

"I busted my chops getting here. You should at least buy me a cup of coffee," the computer nerd answered.

Stifling the impulse to point out that the guy got a fat paycheck every two weeks, Daniel let him order a latte with banana syrup.

The combination made him want to gag. But he paid for the evil concoction and led the way outside to his parking slot.

He circled around the back of the shopping center, then into the tree-lined Silver Spring neighborhood that was tucked away between the major roads. "So you hacked into the Crandall computer?" he asked.

"They've got the mother of all firewalls. But I got in." He laughed. "They're responsible for some pretty crazy stuff."

Daniel considered how to respond. "We'd better keep this under wraps, until we decide whether it's to our advantage to take it to committee."

"Yeah. Sure."

"So what about Maple Creek?"

"They're continuing with chemical and biological weapons testing programs that the Defense Department said were shut down years ago. But Crandall kept some of the stuff in the hopper—to fight terrorists."

Daniel nodded and let his staffer keep talking.

"According to their internal report, some guys broke in there and tried to disrupt the place. Maybe they even thought they could screw up the whole deal. Anyway, the guards neutralized them. But the men who came in contact with the intruders claimed they were hit by some kind of death ray. Most of them died later. Maybe from the combination of what happened at Maple Creek and the drugs a Dr. Colefax gave them to stimulate their memories."

"Jesus."

"Or maybe some of the stuff they were working with was hallucinogenic, and they got high on their own dope." He laughed.

Daniel wanted to tell him it wasn't funny. Instead, he

said, "I appreciate your getting the information. Maybe it's enough to shut them down." A further thought made him ask, "What happened to the guys who broke in?"

"They're both dead—from a dose of a chemical weapon called Granite Wall. Only Crandall covered it all up and made it look like a boating accident." He tapped the envelope. "It's all in there."

"I appreciate your getting this so quickly."

"I enjoyed it," Underhill answered, then offered some more information. "Something interesting. Kurt MacArthur has a personal file on the situation. Lindsay Fleming's name turned up in there."

Daniel blinked. "Our Lindsay Fleming?"

"He identifies her as on your staff. Apparently she's been conferring with Jordan Walker."

"Jesus. The investigative journalist."

"I assume so."

His eyes narrowed. "I'd better find out what's going on." He gave Underhill a direct look. "This can't go any further. Until we can make an official inquiry."

"Yeah," the hacker agreed, and Daniel wondered if he could trust the man with news that was bound to ignite a firestorm of controversy. Well, it was a little late for second thoughts—particularly when he didn't have a choice.

Back in the parking lot, Underhill ambled back to his car.

As Daniel drove up Route 29 toward the Beltway, he thought about his next move.

Was a special investigation the best route? Or should he talk to one of his contacts at the *Washington Post* or the *New York Times*?

It was in the nation's interest to expose what the Crandall Consortium was doing at Maple Creek.

Shit! Scratch that.

He wasn't going to the news media. He wasn't going to any of his colleagues. He was going back to Florida—as soon as he could let his staff know that he'd be out of the office again.

He considered bypassing the office and going directly to Reagan National Airport. But that would look suspicious. He needed to find out what was going on with Lindsay Fleming. And he needed her and the rest of his people to think he'd been called back to Florida for a meeting with important constituents. Well that wasn't a lie. Who was more important than Willow Trinity?

His foot bounced on the accelerator.

What the hell was he thinking? Confidential government information didn't belong in the hands of Willow Trinity. He needed to share it with the members of his committee, so they could take appropriate action.

No. This wasn't going to his committee. It was going to Willow.

And when he saw her again, he would finally make love with her. Just the two of them. Without the damn brother who was always hanging around.

She was young and unmarried. He wondered if she'd like the idea of being a senator's wife.

He let that fantasy swirl through his brain. A senator's wife. No, a president's wife. Because the Trinitys had something special. And with their help, he could surely capture the White House.

Doubts swam around in his mind like little fish nibbling at his brain cells. But he ignored them. It was much more pleasant to think about making love with Willow.

CHAPTER
TWENTY-FIVE

THE COLD SWEAT had dried on Jim Swift's forehead by the time he pulled out his cell phone. Glad that the instrument didn't transmit a picture of his features, he called his boss.

"Where the hell are you?" MacArthur asked.

"I'm on my way back down there—like you told me," he said. He never lost his temper. He never got impatient. But the session at Leonard Hamilton's had frayed his nerves. This whole assignment had been a circus from the first. And it wasn't getting any better.

"You should have called me right away. I've been waiting for you to report."

Catching the edge in MacArthur's voice, he asked, "You know something I don't?"

"Did you hear the phone ring while you were there?"

"Yeah. But not in Hamilton's bedroom."

"The person who called was Jordan Walker."

"Christ!"

"We have it on our wiretap," MacArthur continued. "Not that I would have recognized the voice. He didn't say who he was. And he wasn't calling from his cell phone. He was in a hotel room in Somerset, New Jersey."

"Did you get a team there?"

"Too far away."

"He's heading north."

"Yeah. When the butler asked if it was Jordan Walker, he hung up."

"Could it have been somebody else? The butler could have been confused in the middle of the night."

"Maybe."

Before Jim could proffer another theory, his boss asked, "What happened after that?"

"The butler came in to check on Hamilton."

"Did you have to kill him, too?" MacArthur asked in a matter-of-fact voice.

"I would have. But I was already across the room. So I slipped into the dressing area. The butler was focused on Hamilton. He examined him and found out he was dead. Then he didn't know what to do and went to wake up the other servants. I got out through an upstairs window."

"Walker was calling to say that Hamilton was in danger. That's odd, don't you think?"

Jim felt the hairs on the back of his neck prickle. "Yeah, odd," he agreed. His mind flashed back to the scene in the bedroom. He'd been sitting on the bed, talking to Hamilton, and he'd felt like someone had opened a window and let a blast of cold air into the room. Only, when he'd turned around to look, nobody had been there. Well, nobody real. He'd thought he'd seen a dim figure in the darkness. A naked woman. But when he'd started to get up, the image had vanished, and he'd put it down to nerves.

Which had never been a problem before. He'd carried out plenty of assignments like the Hamilton interrogation. Nothing had ever spooked him, but somehow this had been different.

"Okay, we'll talk about Jordan Walker later. Did you get any useful information out of Hamilton?"

Jim was glad to be back on comfortable ground. "The old bastard sucked Walker into the investigation by offering to cooperate on an authorized biography. And your hunch was right. He arranged for Jordan Walker and Lindsay Fleming to meet at Conroy's house. He claimed it was because she works for Daniel Bridgewater—which would give Walker access to information about Maple Creek."

"What do you think?" MacArthur demanded. "Was that the only reason?"

Jim waited a beat before answering. "If you want my gut feeling, I'd say there was more to it."

"What? Did he know something about Walker and Fleming?"

Do you? Jim wondered, picking up on the way his boss kept coming back to the couple. But he didn't ask about it. If MacArthur wanted to give him information, he would.

"You're a skilled interrogator. You couldn't get anything else out of him?"

"I showed him what I could do to him. And he had the balls to tell me he wasn't going to stand up to torture. I decided he was right. He was too old and sick to take what I was prepared to dish out."

"You let him set the rules?"

"Sometimes you have to go with the flow. I think he *wanted* me to kill him."

"That's fucking weird."

"We know he was in physical pain—and mental pain, over his son's death. He said he wanted to know what happened to Todd before he died. I told him we'd killed Todd and made it look like an accident."

"What?" MacArthur sounded totally incredulous. "*You* gave *him* information?"

"Not much. Nothing he was going to tell anybody else, and it turned out to be the best way to get him to talk."

"Yeah. Okay. Did he know how Todd pulled that trick at Maple Creek?"

"He said he didn't."

"And you believed him."

"Yeah. I did."

MacArthur continued to ask questions, digging for information that Jim couldn't give him. Finally the director sighed. "Okay. He was a loose cannon. At least he's out of the way. But that phone call from Walker may trigger a police investigation."

"How the hell would Walker know Hamilton was in danger?" Jim asked, interested in hearing the answer.

"Maybe he has superhero powers," MacArthur suggested.

The observation hung in the air, and all at once Jim was thinking again about the naked woman who had seen him with the old man. No, not a woman. A ghost, from the looks of her.

He felt goose bumps rise on his skin.

MacArthur was speaking again. "Did he know anything about Saxon and Willow Trinity?"

"I don't think so."

They talked for a few more minutes. Finally Jim asked, "Do you want me to head back there and help with the search for Mark Greenwood?"

"No. I may want you in Darien, Connecticut."

"You think that's where Walker is going?"

"Yeah."

LIVING without a credit card was a damn nuisance, Jordan thought as he sat in bed in their latest motel room—this one a bargain special. It was amazing how fast cash evaporated when you couldn't rely on plastic. More than that, the mere act of paying cash at a motel created a certain amount of suspicion.

He'd gone with the subtle suggestion that he and Lindsay were meeting for a tryst. But he was glad she hadn't been standing beside him at the counter when he'd made the reference to her "husband."

While she slept, he sat propped against the pillows, going through the papers he'd gotten from Hamilton. One file contained a list of other children besides Todd who had been conceived by Dr. Remington's techniques.

Some of the names were blacked out with heavy marker. Holding the sheet up to the light, he tried to read the redacted information, but because it was a photocopy, he couldn't do it.

Were Willow and Saxon Trinity among the unreadable names? Why had the old man scratched them out? Were they children who had died? Or was it a privacy issue?

Feeling Lindsay stir beside him, he tensed. When he saw her lids flutter open, he steeled himself for what was coming next.

Before he could move out of reach, she grabbed his hand. He didn't even try to block her. She was going to have to find out about Hamilton. And if it didn't happen now, she'd only get his computer and go to one of the news Web sites.

Still, when he felt her silent scream, it was like a physical stab of pain.

He's dead.

I'm sorry. The condolence sounded hollow as it echoed in his mind.

Like Sid.

No!

Two men dead, because of us.

He tossed the papers on the floor and slid down in the bed, reaching for her and folding her into his arms. He felt a sob take her. Just one sob, and he knew she was struggling to hold back a flood.

You've got it backward, sweetheart. Two more men are dead because of Todd Hamilton. He set this whole thing in motion by attacking a secure government installation. Then his father tried to find out what really happened. That sealed his doom. Sid got involved because he tried to help his cousin—who was a guard at the place.

He tightened his hold on her. *We have to put together the whole puzzle—so they don't get us, too.*

She had recovered enough of her equilibrium to ask, *By they—you mean the Crandall Consortium.*

Yes. But I want to find out about Todd. We have to start with him.

Why?

You don't feel it . . . ? He dragged in a breath. *You don't feel something gnawing at you? Something just out of reach?*

She didn't bother to lie to him because their minds were working together now.

Yes, she answered, even as she began to focus on what they needed to do.

"You have a list of people who worked for Dr. Remington."

"Yes."

"We should start making calls."

"It's early yet. First we're going to have breakfast."

I'm not hungry.

You need to eat. You haven't had a decent meal in days.

You think we can get a decent meal around here?

There's a pancake place down the road.

He was pleased to see a stack of blueberry pancakes leap into her mind.

He let her take a shower first, thinking about joining her as he listened to the water run. But he knew she wouldn't welcome sex while she was still grieving over Hamilton. Well, not grieving exactly. She hadn't even known the man. But she'd been in his bedroom very close to the end of his life.

It was frightening. Her voice came into his mind, and he knew that she had been following his thoughts. *The question is—why just me?*

Apparently we can't choose how this psychic thing works.

You're better than I am at projecting your consciousness to remote places.

A talent I wish I didn't have.

But it got us important information. He was sorry immediately that he'd said it, because the pain of watching the Crandall operative interrogate Hamilton came swooping down on her—and him.

Sorry.

Yeah.

He came into the bathroom, wrapped her in a towel, and tenderly dried her off.

You don't have to coddle me.

I'm not coddling. I'm . . .

Being considerate. Thank you.

He held her for a few moments longer. *Better?*

Yes.

He knew it was only partly true. But he knew she had to come to terms with Hamilton's death on her own.

While he was in the shower, his mind started working on their problems again.

But maybe we can choose what talents we want to focus on, he said as he stepped out and started drying off. *When we're not fighting for our lives.*

He heard her silent wince from the bedroom and wished he hadn't put it in those terms. Too bad it was impossible to guard his thoughts about their dangerous situation.

Lathering his face, he asked, *The man who was interrogating Hamilton. What can you tell me about him?*

She paused to think. *It was dark. But from what I could see, he was in his late twenties or early thirties. The scary part was how he went about what he was doing. He knew he had the power of life and death over Hamilton. It was just a matter of what happened first.*

He could have hurt him.

He was being pragmatic—not merciful. Let's hope he doesn't have the chance to be pragmatic with us.

He wanted to tell her to focus on what they could do for themselves, but he had never been good with other people's feelings. Now he was trying to soothe Lindsay while he couldn't offer her any real reassurances.

Just as he finished shaving, she came up behind him and laid her head on his shoulder. "Did you ever read a Hemingway story called 'The Short Happy Life of Frances Macomber against'?"

"Yeah. In a lit course in college."

"That's where I read it, too."

They both thought about the story—about a man on an African safari who had lived like a milquetoast all his life. Then his world opened up when he found out he had more courage than he'd thought. Unfortunately, his wife didn't like the transformation and shot him in a "hunting accident" before he could enjoy his newfound confidence.

Jordan turned and took Lindsay in his arms, cradling her body against his. "That's not going to happen to us!"

"You don't know it for sure."

"Together, we're stronger than they are."

He felt her nod, but he sensed her doubts as well. And he couldn't lie to himself. They were in a hell of a fix.

BRIDGEWATER arrived in Orlando on the first flight of the morning. In a routine that had become familiar, he took the monorail to the main terminal, rented a car, and exited onto Route 528.

The rush-hour traffic slowed him, but he was at the Trinity mansion before eleven.

He hadn't bothered to call ahead, because he knew that Willow would be as eager to see him as he was to see her. But there was some trouble at the gate.

That asshole who worked for them, Michael his name was, wouldn't let him through until he conferred with his bosses.

Finally the gates swung open, and he roared up the drive, then had to cool his heels again when the jerk left him in a small reception room.

He was too restless to sit. Instead he paced the Oriental rug, waiting for Willow.

When she came through the door, it was obvious that she'd been sleeping in. She was wearing a silky green robe, her hair was tousled, and he could see creases on her cheek from where she'd been lying on her pillow.

The sight was endearing. He knew that was how she would look when they woke up in the morning together, and he felt a rush of love for her.

He wanted to cross the room and take her in his arms. But once again, she was joined at the hip to her damn brother.

Daniel felt a surge of jealousy. It subsided when she hurried forward and took his arm.

"Dan, this is so unexpected."

"I came as soon as I could arrange it. I have some important information for you." He held up the manila envelope like an offering to a pagan goddess.

"What have you brought me?"

When her hand played with the back of his neck, he felt himself go instantly hard.

"I had my computer geek break into the files of the Crandall Consortium. I know what was going on at Maple Creek."

She beamed. "Wonderful."

"And I have the director's notes on the investigation. Remember I told you about Lindsay Fleming, the woman on my staff who asked about the matter?"

She nodded.

"Apparently, she's hooked up with an investigative reporter named Jordan Walker."

He saw Willow's eyes sharpen. "What do you mean—hooked up?"

"Well, see, first Walker started poking into the case. Then Lindsay joined him. But nobody knows where they've gone."

"Wouldn't she have to inform the office of her whereabouts?" Saxon interjected.

"She should," he muttered. "But she just disappeared. Nobody's heard from her for a couple of days. I wonder if she's all right," he said, then dismissed the thought immediately. Lindsay wasn't important.

Only Willow could hold his attention. She was standing very still now, gripping her brother's hand.

"Let's go upstairs," she said.

His heart leaped as she led him up the curved staircase, then down a hall and into a bedroom. Not her bedroom. A guest room. He knew that right away, because the bed was still made. But he didn't care. He just wanted to be with her. When Saxon followed them into the room, he turned and glared at the creep. Then Willow pushed him down on the bed, and he forgot about the brother.

She pressed her hand over his cock, the way he wanted. But when he tried to unbuckle his pants, she stayed his hand.

"No, Daniel. You need to sleep now, while we read the papers you brought us."

He felt the brother slipping off the loafers that marred the bedspread.

But his focus was on Willow. She was still speaking in that beautiful voice of hers. "Thank you, Daniel. Thank you so much for being loyal to me. I'll get back to you as soon as I absorb the material. You sleep now. Just sleep," she murmured as she stroked his forehead.

He tried to stay awake—to stay with her. Because he wanted so much to remain connected. He wanted to be everything to her. Lover. Husband. Father. Brother.

No, he wanted the damn brother out of the picture. He wanted to take Saxon's place in her life.

But he couldn't fight the soothing effect of her voice and her touch. Against his will, his eyes closed, and he slept as she'd told him to do.

CHAPTER
TWENTY-SIX

AFTER A QUICK breakfast Jordan drove to a service station with a couple of pay phones, and they started on the list Hamilton had given him, with Lindsay posing as his assistant.

Some of the people they were calling had died. Some had moved. But after fifteen minutes Jordan got a positive response—from a woman named Frederica Vanderlin.

When the conversation was over, he hung up slowly, fighting a tight feeling in his chest.

"What's wrong?" Lindsay asked.

"She knew exactly who I was. It was like she was waiting for me to call."

"Maybe the source of all psychic power is Darien, Connecticut," she answered, then went pale. "Could it be a trap?"

"We'll be careful."

They both got back into the car. When he glanced at Lindsay, he saw her sitting rigid in her seat. Reaching out, he touched her arm. She kept herself completely open to him.

You see an ambush?

I don't think so. But I'm nervous about meeting her. I feel like we're going to find out something we don't want to know.

He felt the same thing and didn't bother to hide it from her. He kept his eyes on the road, but an image had come into his mind, and he couldn't dislodge it. An image he had secretly been fighting for days. Himself as a toddler, sitting in a waiting room with his mother—surrounded by other mothers and children.

He had been there more than once, waiting for one of the nurses to call his mother's name.

They reached Mrs. Vanderlin's clapboard duplex but drove past and slowly up the street, looking at the cars. No one was paying any attention to them.

"Let's get it over with," Lindsay murmured.

As though both were reluctant to make contact, they didn't touch as they made their way up the walk, past neatly tended beds of irises and peonies, to the front porch.

Jordan fought the tightness in his throat as he rang the doorbell.

"Just a moment," a woman's voice called out.

When she opened the door, the breath froze in Jordan's lungs as he stared into a familiar face. It was older and more lined than he remembered, but he knew who she was without being told. One of the nurses from the clinic where he'd gone as a boy.

He hadn't known the name of the clinic on those long-ago visits. He hadn't known why they'd kept going back there. He'd just known he was going to see a doctor he didn't particularly like.

But he realized with a flash of insight that he shouldn't have been surprised that he and Todd Hamilton had something important in common. He should have picked up on the clues. Apparently he hadn't wanted to know what was right in front of his face.

Beside him, he heard Lindsay gasp. "You're . . . you're Vandi . . ."

The woman beamed. "Oh. How charming. And you must be . . . Lindsay . . . Powell. I'm Mrs. Vanderlin. That's right. I'd forgotten. But you used to call me Vandi, didn't you."

Beside him, Lindsay nodded dumbly.

"You've grown into a fine young woman. But why couldn't I ever find out about you?"

Lindsay spoke haltingly. "My . . . my parents divorced when I was two. Then my mom remarried and my stepfather adopted me. I'm Lindsay Fleming now."

"Yes, that would explain why you dropped out of sight. What do you do—for a living?"

"I'm an aide to a U.S. senator."

As Jordan listened to the conversation, he felt like he had stepped into a Mother Goose fairy tale.

"That's wonderful," Mrs. Vanderlin was saying. "So many of the children never fulfilled their promise. But you and Jordan obviously did."

"Their promise?" he asked.

"Yes, but what am I thinking, keeping you standing out here on the porch? I'm getting old. Come in and sit down." She stepped aside and led them down a short hall into a fussy living room where an overstuffed couch and chairs squatted on a faded Oriental rug. The room looked like something out of the nineteenth century, except for the television set on a low table in one corner.

"Please, have a seat," she offered. "Can I get you anything. Tea? Coffee?"

"No, thank you," Lindsay answered, and Jordan heard the tension in her voice.

They sat on the overstuffed sofa—neither one of them wanting to share their own private thoughts.

"I've kept track of my children. I thought of them as my children, you know. I kept a list of everyone. All two hundred and twelve babies who were conceived by the clinic's methods. The charity patients and the babies from the couples who could afford to pay."

"And our names were both on the list," Jordan clarified.

"Well, Jordan Walker and . . . Lindsay Powell."

Making a mental leap, he asked, "Did Leonard Hamilton get the list from you?"

Apparently that was too much for Lindsay because she

reached out and grasped his hand. *You're thinking Hamilton got us together—to see what would happen?*

Yeah.

The silent conversation had taken place in a flash. Mrs. Vanderlin was speaking. "Mr. Hamilton and I talked about the children. So many of them have met . . . untimely deaths."

Trying to cope with this new information, Jordan stared at her, "How many?"

"Well, at least fifty-seven of you are dead. Including Todd and Glenn Barrow."

"Glenn, Todd's friend, was one of . . . us?" Jordan asked.

"Why, yes."

So Leonard Hamilton found out I was Lindsay Powell. That meant he had to do some digging.

Why didn't our parents tell us how we were conceived?

It wasn't common back then. Maybe they were embarrassed. You know—egg and sperm meeting in a petri dish.

Or maybe they signed a confidentiality agreement.

Mrs. Vanderlin broke into the silent conversation. "Mr. Hamilton had such high hopes for Todd. He thought that the doctor's method would get him a superintelligent heir."

"Wait a minute," Jordan interjected. "You said Dr. Remington was running a fertility clinic—for couples having trouble conceiving."

"Well, most of his patients were couples who could only conceive by in vitro fertilization, of course. But that wasn't the secret purpose of the program. He took so many charity patients so he'd have more embryos to work with."

Both Jordan and Lindsay leaned forward. "What *was* the purpose?" he asked.

"To create children with exceptional intellect. Dr. Remington offered his fertility services so he would have access to eggs and sperm. Except in the case of a few parents like Mr. Hamilton who were willing to pay for an intelligent child. Basically, after the doctor carried out the in vitro fertilizations, he operated on the blastocyte, to enhance brain development. It's a shame he didn't live to see the project through."

Jordan felt like somebody had aimed a jackhammer at his chest. So he and Lindsay were part of some nutball mad scientist's brain experiment.

"What happened to Dr. Remington?" Lindsay asked, her voice high and breathless, and he didn't need telepathy to know she was experiencing the same shock that he felt.

"He died of a heart attack. I think because he couldn't take the disappointment when the Crandall Consortium canceled his funding."

Jordan already knew the heart attack part. He hadn't known about the connection to the same organization that ran Maple Creek.

Crandall! The silent exclamation echoed from his mind to Lindsay's and back again.

"How did you know the Crandall Consortium was funding him?" Jordan asked, managing to sound amazingly calm.

"That nice man from the agency would come to the clinic for progress reports."

"Do you happen to remember his name?"

She thought for a moment. "I believe it was Kurt MacArthur."

More shocks to absorb. He knew from his computer research that Kurt MacArthur now headed Crandall. That was one of the few facts he'd uncovered. So back then—had he been a hit man?

"What was their interest in the experiment?" Lindsay whispered.

Mrs. Vanderlin looked uncertain. "I think it had something to do with the Russians—beating us in the science race. But Mr. Crandall wasn't satisfied with the IQ results. That's a shame, because some of the children have been outstanding in their fields." She beamed at Jordan. "Like you. You've done so well for yourself. And you, Lindsay. Working for a senator—that's an important job."

"So how did you end up with the clinic's records?" Jordan asked.

"Oh, no. You have the wrong idea. I don't have all the records. Not the scientific information. I think Mr. MacArthur took that away. But I had lists of the families and the children. I kept those."

Lindsay's fingers gripped his.

She seems nice. But is she trying to sell us a bill of goods?

We could try to find out.

Turning all his focus on Mrs. Vanderlin, Jordan strove to penetrate her mind. He'd only tried the process with Lindsay. Mrs. Vanderlin was an unknown quantity to him.

He couldn't tell what she was thinking, maybe because she'd knocked the stuffing out of him with her revelation. He was still trying to come to grips with the information that they hadn't randomly been born with a special talent. Dr. Remington's experiments had given it to them—by accident. If Mrs. Vanderlin knew what she was talking about.

Her thoughts remained inaccessible to him, but he did get the sense that she was telling the truth—as she knew it. At least he was picking up a sense of integrity from her.

She was still speaking. "Sometimes I wonder if the doctor made a mistake with what he was doing. Some of the children have gotten into such awful trouble. I know some who drank themselves to death or who took drugs."

Yeah, to blot out the buzzing in their brains. Jordan sent the silent message to Lindsay.

"Some of them deliberately committed suicide," the old woman mused. "The saddest was when two of them killed themselves together. That happened a few times. It was strange—don't you think? That two of my children would get together, but they'd decide to take that awful step."

Jordan winced. He and Lindsay were both remembering when they had first made love, remembering the sensation of walking a tightrope between ecstasy and madness. They'd come out of it with their sanity. It seemed that others had not.

He was feeling shaky now. So was Lindsay.

"This is a lot to take in," he told Mrs. Vanderlin.

"Of course. But it's wonderful that you're doing a book on fertility technology."

He'd forgotten all about the excuse he'd given. "Perhaps we'll come back and talk to you later," he muttered.

"I'm so glad to find the two of you doing so well."

"Thanks."

"Why don't you tell me where you're staying—in case I think of something else important?"

Jordan hesitated. "I can't remember the name of the place," he fibbed. Instead, he gave her his card, knowing he wouldn't be home anytime soon.

He and Lindsay stood. "It was wonderful seeing you again," they both said.

"Yes." The old woman started to heave herself out of the chair.

"No need to see us out. We can do that ourselves," Jordan said.

They gripped hands, as much to steady each other as anything else. Walking back to the car, he felt as though only the connection with Lindsay was anchoring him to reality.

They both collapsed into the front seat.

He felt sick and angry. He knew Lindsay felt the same. Well, not as bad. He was supposed to be an investigative reporter—but he'd completely ignored clues that should have set off alarm bells.

You didn't know, she murmured in his head.

I damn well should have been able to fit the pieces together.

Don't beat yourself up. Help me understand what's going on. How did the Crandall Consortium get mixed up in this—thirty years ago—and now? she asked.

"I think Todd figured out what we couldn't."

"He had more time. He dug into his past and connected the dots. Probably he and Glenn did it together."

"Okay. I'll give you that."

"He found out what was wrong with him because his father told him about the Remington Clinic. And our parents kept it to themselves."

"How do you know?"

"I'm guessing that Leonard Hamilton threw it in his face. 'I paid all that money to get an heir worthy of the Hamilton fortune. And you failed me.'"

Jordan nodded. Lindsay's theory made sense. "So Todd dug into the background of the diabolical clinic. Maybe to get ammunition to use against his father."

"Don't call it diabolical."

"Do you prefer unethical? Based on a lie? An experiment that delivered children who couldn't fit into society?"

He started the car. "Let's get out of here."

"I want to ask some more questions about Todd," she said as he headed back to their motel. "Either his father told him about the Crandall Consortium's funding of the Remington Clinic, or he dug that out for himself. Then he started investigating what Crandall was funding now?"

"Right."

"I assume that he wanted to strike out at Crandall for what they'd done to him. Maybe he was even striking out at his father."

She reached for his hand. "At least he found Glenn. I have to believe they were happy together."

"But it got them killed." Jordan cleared his throat. "Christ, it's a tragedy that we can't talk to him."

"Yes."

"I'd like to ask how it was for him—the buzzing in his brain and then finding Glenn Barrow."

"Two men who were as close as you and I are. I wonder what the chances were that he'd find another homosexual in the group."

"Probably not high."

The talk with Mrs. Vanderlin had shaken them both. He felt manipulated by Dr. Remington, by the Crandall Consortium, by Leonard Hamilton. Yet at the same time he was profoundly grateful that Hamilton had brought him together with Lindsay.

"Yes," she murmured, pressing her hand over his.

Once they were inside the room, she turned and held out her arms, and he went into them. When she lifted her face, his lips came down on hers for a savage, hungry kiss.

They devoured each other, the need between them building, even as they exchanged urgent information.

What are we going to do?

Get the Crandall Consortium off our backs.

Do you think they know we were on the list?

Probably they know about me. Maybe not you.

But they know I'm involved now.

He caught her desperation—her need for sexual contact. It mirrored his own. The longer they were together, the tighter the link that bound them. And the more unthinkable was separation.

Leonard Hamilton had brought them together.

Too bad we can't thank the man. In the next second he wished the thought hadn't flitted into his mind, because he felt her guilt when she focused on Hamilton.

Sorry.

It's hard to censor thoughts.

Her answer wafted below the surface, submerging in the need for physical contact. He tore at her clothing, getting her naked as fast as he could. And she was intent on doing the same.

The bed was too far away. He wanted her, needed her now. When he lifted her naked body in his arms, she wrapped her legs around him, and he braced his shoulders against the door as he dove into her.

Orgasm was like a quick rush of joy. Of affirmation. Of relief.

When he thought his legs were working properly, he pulled out of her, then cradled her in his arms as he carried her across the room and laid her on the bed.

She snuggled against him, and for long moments they both drifted in feelings of contentment.

For a little while they relaxed together. Then he sensed her thoughts.

I have an idea.

He didn't have to ask what. It was there in his mind.

Todd and his friend decided to go up against Maple Creek by themselves. What if we don't have to do it alone? You said that we might have to protect ourselves against other people like us. But what if they want to work with us? What if we can find the others and tell them what happened? Get their help?

It was a plan. And for the first time he felt hope rise in his chest.

Do you think there are others who have bonded—who are already living their lives—together?

The Trinity twins. We know about them.

Jordan climbed out of bed again, brought his computer from the desk, hooked it into the phone line, and booted up.

While they waited for the machine to run through its initial routine, Lindsay asked, *Do they have a Web site?*

Everybody has a Web site.

I don't.

Your boss, the senator, does.

He used Google to find the twins. Then clicked on the link. The front page opened with a starburst of color that faded to a picture of a dynamic looking man and woman standing shoulder to shoulder. Both had blond hair. The man wore an expensive navy suit. The woman was dressed in a demure white jumpsuit. He was handsome in the Nordic god sort of way. And she was an equally striking woman, her blond hair shimmering around her heart-shaped face. They looked cool and confident.

Linsday climbed off the bed and started gathering up her clothing. Jordan puttered around the site.

First he looked at the twins' biography and laughed.

"What's so funny?" Lindsay called from across the room as she pulled on her panties. Then pulled a T-shirt over her head.

"This piece of fiction." When her head was visible again, he gestured toward the screen. "Come get a load of their bio. It's totally made up. They talk about being descended from a long line of psychics who lived in Hungary and cultivated the 'old ways,' then passed on their gifts from generation to generation."

"Maybe they are," she countered, laying his clothing on the end of the bed.

"Are you keeping house?" he teased.

"Right. Even in a motel room." She cleared her throat. "Maybe they do have Hungarian blood."

"Come on. We know they got their psychic abilities the same way we did."

"Maybe they have both. That would certainly give them an edge on everybody else."

"I think the fact that they were together from birth gave them an edge. They bonded early."

"Became sexual partners early?"

"I guess so."

"It's a little creepy. But I can see how it happened."

He was about to make another observation when the screen rippled like a pool of water into which someone had thrown a stone.

"What the . . ."

"Jordan?"

Before he could finish the sentence, a blue-tinged hand emerged from the screen and grabbed him around the neck, choking off his breath.

CHAPTER
TWENTY-SEVEN

LINDSAY LOOKED AT Jordan, who had only moments before been speculating cynically about the Trinity twins.

His face was contorted. The skin red and blotchy.

Fear leaped inside her. "My God, what's wrong?"

He didn't answer. When he tried to speak, no words came out. Lindsay watched in horror as he raised his hands toward his throat and pulled at something she couldn't see.

Jordan, what?

His lips moved, and she heard him scream in her mind.

Oh, Christ . . . The computer . . . The silent words choked off as he raised his hands—clawing at his own throat.

Something was choking off his life with horrible speed.

When his hands fell back to his sides and he slumped sideways, she knew that he couldn't even defend himself— and she had only seconds to save him from death.

In those moments of terror her mind made crucial connections. He had gone to the Trinity Web site. And this horror was coming from them.

It didn't make sense. But she knew on a gut level that if she looked at the screen, they would get her, too. What if she touched the computer? Was that just as deadly to her?

They could both die in the next few seconds. But what did it matter? Without him, she would only drift through her lonely existence. It hadn't been so bad before. Now she knew the difference.

When she reached for the laptop, she felt a jolt of electricity travel up her arms.

The shock made her gasp, but she didn't let go. Keeping her gaze averted from the machine and ignoring the horrible sizzling sensation that crackled through her body, she fumbled to spring the catch on the little clip that attached the phone line.

It wouldn't move. She couldn't do it with her hand because her fingers were too numb.

She wanted to scream in frustration. Instead, she focused her mind on the catch, squeezing the plastic with her thoughts instead of her fingers.

Maybe it took only nanoseconds. But it felt like centuries before the phone connector came free.

It was like slamming a metal door on a firestorm. The sizzling stopped. Jordan gasped in a breath.

She pushed the computer out of the way and turned back to him. He had sunk down against the pillows, sucking in air.

"Jordan? Say something, Jordan. I need to hear your voice."

"I think . . . we'd better not consider Saxon and Willow Trinity best buddies."

He said it with such deadpan sincerity that she couldn't stop herself from barking out a hysterical laugh.

"You mean because they almost killed you?"

"Yeah, that."

She had been afraid to embrace him, lest the pressure against his chest interfere with his breathing. But when he held out his arms, she came into them with a small sob.

"Thank you for saving my life," he whispered.

"I was terrified."

Likewise.

What happened?

My guess? They found out about us, and they don't want to share the psychic stage.

They'd kill you for that?

Apparently, they're not very nice people.

How do they know about us?

I'm guessing again. Somehow, they've found out about Crandall and Maple Creek. His thoughts came rapidly now. *Suppose they never knew that anyone else like them existed? Suppose they thought they were unique. And now suddenly they get the news that there's a whole bunch of us out there. Maybe they want to ensure that they're the only ones with that kind of power.*

She nodded, trying to wrap her mind around the concept of using psychic power to do evil.

"Not everyone's going to have the same reaction to finding out they have special gifts," he murmured, his voice raspy. "Some people will grab for all the goodies they can get."

She burrowed into his warmth, and he held her against himself, stroked his hands over her shoulders and into her hair. The physical contact and the mental contact helped ground her.

She swallowed. *So my idea of getting a big happy family of us together was a little naive.*

Sorry. It was a good idea. We just didn't know what these people would be like—as individuals. And we have no idea how bad it was for the Trinity twins—how they got to be what they are. If the twins felt they had to make up their background, maybe the real story is so horrible that we can't imagine it.

That could be true, but it's no excuse for trying to kill you.

He held her more tightly. *They would have done it, if you hadn't been brave enough to grab the computer and yank out the phone cord.*

I knew I couldn't look at the screen or it would get me, too.

What did it feel like to you?

Like grabbing a live wire.

You didn't see . . . a blue hand coming out of the screen?

No! Oh, Lord. That's how it was for you?

Yeah.

She heaved in a breath and let it out. *One more thing you should know. I . . . I couldn't work the catch with my fingers. They were paralyzed.*

He moved so he could give her a direct look. *What are you saying?*

I . . . I used my mind—to uncouple the catch.

He stroked a hand through her hair. *Good for you! Something else we need to practice.*

She felt a shiver go through her. "I just want . . . to be left alone . . . with you."

"Soon."

She tipped her face toward him. "You mean after we escape from the Crandall Consortium, from the police, and from the Trinity twins."

"We will."

"Jordan—how can we fight the world?" she whispered.

"I think we have to be keep working on our gifts."

"That didn't do Todd and Glenn much good."

"I think they went off—if you'll pardon the expression—half cocked. We have the advantage of knowing what happened to them."

"Yes," she managed as she struggled for strength she didn't know she had. She felt a question from Jordan flickering at the edge of her mind but she blocked it.

"What are you thinking?" he demanded.

"You're always coming up with clever ways to practice. There's another skill we have to try."

"You're getting better at blocking me," he said, his voice not quite steady. "What is it that you don't want me to know?"

"I want to tell you in the regular way." She gulped. Getting off the bed, she moved a few feet away from him.

"We have to practice fighting off an attack. A mental attack."

"Jesus," he whispered, because he grasped the implications immediately.

"Do that to me. What they did to you."

She saw his hands clench and unclench. "No!"

"Now that we know what kind of power they can call on, we have to be prepared," she insisted. The hardest thing she'd ever done in her life was launch a sudden spear of energy at Jordan. But she made herself do it. Imagining a small thunderbolt—and hurling it toward his head.

He cried out, then threw up a shield. Not a pane of glass. A metal wall. She was about to praise his quick thinking when his eyes turned fierce.

He'd given her a moment of warning. Still the force of his counterattack was a steel spike ramming into her head.

Gasping, she struggled to call up a shield—the way he had done just moments earlier, but it was hard to do *anything* when the pain in her head made it difficult to think. She'd sent him a thunderbolt. But it was like a girl kicking a football. And he'd launched a man's attack.

"Stop," she gasped, even as she tried to fight him off.

His face contorted, and the pain mercifully cut off.

She collapsed onto the bed, her skin cold and clammy. The headache receded, and she was pretty sure he had taken pity on her—not that she'd fought him off by herself.

When he stroked her hair, she could feel his hand trembling. "I'm sorry. I didn't like hurting you."

"Back to you."

He held her and stroked her, but she knew he was thinking about the attack launched through the computer.

Her gaze darted to the laptop. "Is it safe to use that machine? Is it safe to use your own e-mail address?"

"Shit. I didn't think of that. I just don't know. Maybe it's safe if I stay away from their Web site."

"Or maybe not. Now that they know who you are—and that you were poking around on their site."

They stared at each other, and he cursed again. "We are in one hell of a fix. Because if I can't use the Internet, I might as well be on an atoll in the South Pacific."

"Maybe that would be safer."

"For a while."

She felt like someone caught in a terrible psychological experiment. As if a diabolical scientist was testing her, but she didn't know why—or for what.

She rolled onto her side, looking like she was weak and defenseless. Before he could reach for her, she attacked him again. Despite the emotional cost of hurting Jordan, she had a flash of satisfaction at seeing the shock and surprise on his face, even as she felt beads of sweat form on her own forehead.

While she still basked in the glow of her small victory, he gave her back what she'd sent him. She gasped and struck out again. And for several minutes, they engaged in a battle royal that no one else could see—or understand.

She wasn't even sure how long it went on. But finally her mind and body were as limp as a beached jellyfish. Maybe Jordan felt the same way, because he stopped.

She lay on the bed, her breath shallow, and he moved beside her, clasping her hand, stroking her damp hair back from her face. *You are very strong.*

No.

Stronger than I am.

Are you sure?

Yeah. I gave up because you were winning. That's the truth.

I was sure I was losing.

I guess we both were.

He opened himself completely and let her see for herself. *Can your male ego take that?*

I hope so.

They lay quietly for several minutes.

Finally she asked, *So where are the other children Dr. Remington created? What's happened to them?*

You mean Dr. Frankenstein.

Don't call us monsters.

What would you call us?

"People struggling to cope with powers beyond ordinary human conception," she murmured.

Okay. I'll go with that for now.

He settled down beside her, and they both dropped quickly into an exhausted sleep.

Sometime later she woke up. Panic surged through her when she realized he wasn't in the bed.

Jordan?

He stepped out of the bathroom, fully dressed.

"Where are you going?"

"To get us some food."

It had been hours since breakfast, and eating hadn't entered her thoughts. But apparently he was being practical again.

"Let me come with you."

"It's better not to go out together," he answered.

"You think they know we're here?"

"I'm not making any assumptions." He crossed the room and laid his hand on her shoulder. "Okay, so you're not very hungry, but you could try and choke down a double cheeseburger with special sauce, french fries, and a Coke."

"Right. More junk food."

While he was gone, she dressed in slacks and a knit shirt, because having her clothing on made her feel less vulnerable. Then she made the bed and straightened the room.

He looked around when he came back and smiled. "Housekeeping again?"

"We both like a neat environment."

"Yeah."

They ate at the table by the window, but she sensed his restlessness during the meal.

You need your own space.

Yeah. Sorry.

She shifted in her seat. *Don't apologize. We're both trying to work this out.*

He nodded.

"Go to the library."

"Huh?"

The befuddled look on his face made her grin. "Libraries have computers. Maybe you can get into the Net that way."

"You don't mind my leaving you again?"

"You know I mind. But we both need a togetherness break." She said the words. They were a social lie. He needed a break. She wanted to be with him. But she'd vowed to give him as much independence as she could.

She forced herself to eat half her double burger and most of the fries.

He polished off his french fries, then asked, "You're sure about . . . my leaving?"

"Yes," she said, keeping her voice strong as she helped him clean up, then wrapped and stuffed the rest of her burger into the minibar.

"Be careful," she added as he went through his notes, selecting what he wanted to take.

"I'm a macho guy. I can handle the library."

She forced a laugh.

"I'll be back in a couple of hours."

When he left the room, she sent her thoughts outward, trying to follow him down the hallway, then out to the car.

She had suggested that they take some time away from each other, but when she lost contact, she had to fight down her panic.

Trying to focus her mind on something else, she lay down and began practicing some of the relaxation exercises she'd learned to use as stress relievers.

JORDAN felt the connection with Lindsay stretch, then snap, and it was all he could do to stop himself from going back to the motel room, gathering her in his arms, and hanging on tight. He was feeling guilty because he needed the time away from her—and she had given him permission to take that time.

More than that, she'd come up with the perfect excuse. He stopped at the motel desk and asked where he could find the nearest public library with computer access.

Fifteen minutes later he stepped into the building. It was a modern facility, with a computer room that patrons could use. Glad that he had an alternative to his laptop, he used one of the terminals to do a Web search. When he hit the button to call up the reference, he felt his throat tighten painfully. But nothing reached out to choke him as he read an article in a small religious magazine about the twins' faith healing abilities. Did they really have that power? Or were the brother and sister using their psychic mojo to convince people that they felt better?

He read more references to the Trinitys. A minister with a national following had denounced them. Their newly built church was featured in an architectural magazine.

As he read through the article, he kept fighting an uneasy feeling that something bad was waiting to leap out of the shadows at him.

He almost got up and called the motel room. But he hoped Lindsay was sleeping, and he didn't want to wake her up.

Still, the nerve-tingling sensation wouldn't go away. Finally he had to stand up. Once he was on his feet, they carried him toward the door and back to his car.

                              * * *

LINDSAY knew she was asleep and dreaming. But that didn't stop the fear crackling through her.

This time she saw Mrs. Vanderlin sitting in her fussy old lady's living room, watching a soap opera.

Lindsay saw the woman smile. She had no idea that while she was enjoying *Another Dawn*, evil forces were gathering around her.

"Run. Get out of the house!" Lindsay shouted, but Mrs. Vanderlin didn't hear the warning, and Lindsay had the sick, awful feeling that she was helpless once more in the face of terrible danger.

In the vision she heard a knock at the door. Mrs. Vanderlin looked up, her face filling with annoyance as she pushed herself awkwardly out of the chair.

The knocking came again, and she called out, "Just a minute."

"No! Don't answer it," Lindsay screamed, but the old woman ignored her. She peered through the spy hole in the door, then turned the bolt.

"Can I help you?"

"I was hoping you could help me find Lindsay Fleming and Jordan Walker."

"They were here this morning."

Without being invited, a man stepped into the hall. "Where are they now?"

"In town. But I don't know which motel."

When the man spun her around and grabbed her arm, she screamed in pain and terror. Ignoring her reaction, he herded her back into the living room. Behind him, another man entered the house.

"You're hurting me," Mrs. Vanderlin whimpered. "Please stop."

"Ease up," the new man told his partner.

"Our orders . . ."

"Be nice to the lady."

Lindsay clawed her way to consciousness. Waves of nausea rolled through her as she sat up in bed, clutching handfuls of the sheet. "Oh, God, no," she gasped.

This was like what had happened with Sid—and with Leonard Hamilton. She'd seen they were in trouble. Only this time, she was sure it hadn't happened yet. It was in the future. She could still save Mrs. Vanderlin, if she got there in time.

Jordan! she screamed inside her head. *Jordan, can you hear me? I have to go over there and get her out of the house.*

Snatching the phone off the bedside table, she called the desk. "I have to leave the motel and take care of a sick friend. I'll be downstairs in a few minutes. Can you call me a cab?"

"Certainly, Mrs. Luck."

For a moment she blanked on the name. Then she remembered that was the last name Jordan had used when he'd registered.

She was about to jam her feet into sandals. Then she pictured herself holding Mrs. Vanderlin's arm and hurrying her away. So she dug out socks and tennis shoes and got them on.

She was downstairs minutes later, pacing back and forth under the covered entryway, wishing she could just steal a car and leave. If she could have run to Mrs. Vanderlin's house, she would have done it. But she was too far away for that.

THE sense of dread increased, making Jordan's mind feel like a lump of plastic explosives about to detonate. He was halfway back to the motel when he thought he heard a scream inside his head.

His foot jerked on the gas pedal, then pressed down

hard as he sped back to Lindsay. But he had to slow down abruptly when he saw a cop car from the corner of his eye.

Keeping within the speed limit was agony. Then he blinked as he turned into the motel driveway. A cab was several hundred feet in front of him. Lindsay leaped across the sidewalk and climbed in.

He wanted to roll down his window and shout at her, but it was already too late. The vehicle lurched off, leaving him sick and shaky.

Lindsay!

She didn't respond.

What the hell was she doing?

Lindsay? Lindsay? Where are you going?

Either she couldn't hear him, or she didn't want to answer. He stayed behind the cab, then lost the vehicle as it roared through a yellow light.

"Christ!" He sat in her car, gripping the wheel, every nerve in his body screaming with tension. What was she doing—running out on him?

Even as he asked the question, he knew that was impossible. She wouldn't run away from him. They needed each other.

When the light changed, he sped in the direction in which the cab had disappeared. The landmarks looked familiar, and all at once he was pretty sure he knew where she was going in such a hurry—back to Mrs. Vanderlin's house.

But why?

Lindsay! he shouted in his mind. *Lindsay!*

To his relief, he got back a faint reply.

Jordan?

What are you doing?

Mrs. Vanderlin. They're coming . . . They . . .

The words cut off, and he screamed aloud in frustration. "Lindsay—what? Tell me!"

Wait outside for me. I'll bring her out. We have to get her away.

Ahead of him the cab pulled to a stop. Lindsay jumped out and rushed up the steps.

Wait.

I can't. Don't you understand, we put . . . in danger. Like we . . . Sid in danger . . . Like . . . Hamilton. The words were disjointed, and he knew he wasn't getting everything she was thinking at him. But he got the gist.

Leonard Hamilton put himself in danger! he silently shouted back at her. But she wasn't paying attention.

His heart in his throat, he pulled into the driveway and slammed out of his own car. No way was he waiting outside.

He was pelting across the lawn when he heard Lindsay scream. Not out loud. In his head.

God, no! Lindsay? What's wrong? Sweetheart, answer me!

Fear threatened to swallow him whole. Desperately he ran toward the side door of the house and charged inside.

A man was standing in the kitchen, holding on to Lindsay's arm.

He leaped toward them, the only thought in his mind to get her out of there. Before he reached them, another man charged into the kitchen.

He raised a strange-looking gun and fired. Something hit Jordan in the shoulder. Not a bullet. Something with a red streamer attached. He kept going, trying to get to Lindsay, but instead he dropped to the kitchen floor—then dropped into blackness.

CHAPTER
TWENTY-EIGHT

JORDAN WAS IN a warm, safe place. A cabin in the woods, like where he and Lindsay had first made love.

Only this was better. It was their home. A place far away from civilization, where they could focus on each other and practice their gifts. He had a lot of money saved. And a new career. He was writing a spy novel under a pseudonym. And his agent had already gotten him a huge advance—based on a proposal.

But right now he was thankful to be lying in Lindsay's lap so she could stroke his aching head.

He had . . . hurt himself. He didn't know how. But her touch was the only comfort in . . .

. . . in a dark, cold place. His throat tightened. He wasn't in a cabin in the woods. He was . . .

He was somewhere . . . bad.

But Lindsay was with him. Stroking his head. Calling his name. Desperate for comfort, he curled into her warmth.

Jordan, are you all right? Jordan, wake up. You have to wake up. You have to let me know you're all right. Her voice sounded urgent—and far away.

He was still asleep. And he wanted to stay that way. Because sleep was his refuge.

Jordan, I need you. The sheer terror in her voice focused his attention.

Still, it was difficult to make himself come back to the world, because he knew he was going to hate what he discovered. He was lying on a cold, hard surface. Like a shelf.

Jordan. Please. Oh, God, Jordan.

He forced his eyes open a crack—because he couldn't let Lindsay down. The light was dim, and he tried to figure out where he was.

Some instinct told him not to move. Not to let anyone know he was awake. He wasn't sure why that was important, but he sensed the truth.

His brain processed the unfamiliar surroundings. He was lying on a narrow bunk—in a small concrete room. A cell. And he was alone, he realized with a start. Lindsay wasn't there. He had just dreamed her presence because he needed her so badly. As he took in her absence, stark emotions clawed at his insides.

Instantly she caught his feelings. Again her voice came to him.

No. I'm here. In your mind.

Thank God! The relief was enormous, but he couldn't allow himself to relax. *What happened?*

He felt the voice inside his head falter. *Men . . . captured us at Mrs. Vanderlin's house. It's my fault. I'm so sorry. I thought I was in time . . . but I wasn't.*

Not . . . your fault.

I should have known I couldn't save her.

Christ! She's . . .

Maybe dead. I don't know for sure. They hit her. Probably the news will say we robbed and beat her. That poor lady. She was so thrilled to see us. And we brought the devil's spawn to her door.

He winced at her words. Memories came back like a rush of dirty water down a drainpipe.

They shot me . . .

With a tranq gun, I think.

Yeah. That sounds right.

The fog was lifting from his brain. With the clarity came amazement. He and Lindsay were speaking mind to mind, and he didn't even know where she was.

Emergency powers? she suggested.

He knew better than to laugh—since any movement made his head throb.

Doggedly he forced himself to think. He wanted to sit up and stretch, but he stayed where he was, because probably someone was watching to see when he woke up—so they could come in here and . . .

He caught the gasp in Lindsay's mind.

We won't let them kill us. Even as he offered the reassurance, he wondered what their chances were.

"Shit!" he murmured. *I wish I could lie to you.*

Yeah. Inconvenient to be joined at the . . . brain.

Now who's cracking jokes?

They could joke to cheer each other up, but they were in deep kimchee. He winced again as she picked up the thought.

He was parched with thirst, but he ignored the sensation.

You know who has us?

Crandall, I think.

She had come into his mind, helping him return to reality. Now he felt her deep, gut-wrenching fear.

You're doing good.

I'm scared.

We both are. But together we're stronger than they are. That's our ace in the hole. They both knew he was trying to comfort her. But they could both pretend that the death squad wasn't going to swoop down on them. *How come they didn't tranq you?* he asked.

I think they figured that putting you out was good enough. I think they figure they're safe if they keep us separated.

That means they suspect that Todd and Glenn were linked.

Yes.

Do you know where we are?

The D.C. area. I recognized some landmarks as we drove by—like the Washington Monument. But I don't know our exact location—the building.

Where are you?

In a cell—like yours.

Fear rose in his throat. *Did they hurt you?*

No. I'm fine.

He thanked God for that answer, then probed to make sure she was telling the truth.

Instinct and experience had him shouting urgent instructions—from his mind to hers. *Lindsay, don't let them know we can communicate without touching. Whatever you do, don't give that up.*

Why?

He tried to explain the combination of intuition and information that went into his conclusions. *They went to a lot of trouble to scoop us up, because they think we're dangerous. They think our power comes from touching—because that's what they saw when Todd and Glenn invaded Maple Creek. We have to convince them they're right. We have to convince them they have some control over us.*

He felt her struggling not to whimper.

We have to make them think they can use us. That we're valuable.

For what?

Shit—I don't know. He sighed, wishing he had thought about what to do if Kurt MacArthur caught up with them.

Don't beat yourself up. We didn't realize what resources they had. We didn't know they'd find Mrs. Vanderlin and go after her.

Yeah.

He gritted his teeth. He had been trying to comfort her. Now he knew he had to talk tough. *Job number one is staying alive. We've got to fool them. Or we're going to end up like Todd and Glenn and Sid and Leonard Hamilton. We have to keep those bastards from winning. For us—and to avenge them.*

Before she could respond, he heard a clank of metal. Suddenly lights flashed on in the cell, making him blink and throw his arm over his eyes.

"You're awake."

When he could see, he peered up at a hard-looking man. A guy who appeared to be in his thirties. One of Kurt MacArthur's henchmen, he assumed. But not the guy who had shot him.

Inwardly he cursed. He hadn't even thought to ask Lindsay how long he'd been out.

Five or six hours, she answered in his mind. Thank God she was still there.

He hoped his face hadn't reflected that jolt of recognition.

"Yeah. I'm back from the dead," he answered, knowing for sure now that someone had been watching him on a television camera.

"Come on."

"Where?"

"We're asking the questions."

"Well, if I don't have a drink of water, I'm not going to be able to answer them."

His captor only grunted. Another man stood by the door—his sidearm in his hand.

Jordan wondered if he and Lindsay could send a bolt of energy into these two guys' brains. Maybe. But only as a last resort. Better to get the lay of the land before they tried anything.

Better to save it for MacArthur. The comment came from Lindsay. Apparently she was thinking more clearly than he was.

The guards who had come into the room hustled him up a flight of stone stairs. As they stepped through a stout door, the decor changed abruptly from modern dungeon to luxurious office complex.

He fought a feeling of unreality as they marched him

through a palatial reception area where a sleek-looking blond was working at a computer.

She looked like she was busy, but he sensed her interest in the guy from the basement as the prisoner was escorted across the thick carpet.

Was MacArthur's secretary used to seeing poor jerks brought in at gunpoint?

The guard paused and knocked at a closed door.

"Come in," a male voice called from within.

Jordan fought to pull himself together for this crucial meeting. Everything could end in the next few minutes. His life. Lindsay's. The connection they had forged—that they hadn't had a chance to explore. Maybe they never would.

We will. Lindsay's voice echoed in his head, but he didn't know if he believed her.

He followed his guard into the room, struggling to keep his composure. But as he stepped through the door, he felt fear leap inside Lindsay.

Men had come for her, too. They were in her cell. They were taking her out into the hall.

He had told her that they must keep the connection between them secret. Now he wondered how in the hell he was going to pull that off.

Forget about me. Focus on MacArthur. The brave words echoed in his head. He struggled to obey them, because he knew that these first minutes with the head of the Crandall Consortium could mean the difference between life and death.

Reminding himself that he had always been a good judge of character, he studied Kurt MacArthur. He saw arrogance and self-confidence, the marks of a man with power—who had just pulled off an important coup. Yet something lurked below the surface. A layer of fear that the director of the Crandall Consortium was struggling to hide.

To Jordan's vast relief, he had some idea of the man's thoughts. Todd Hamilton and Glenn Barrow had pulled off an impossible attack. These new captives had come from the same hatchery. What could Walker and Fleming do? And how much risk was he taking by being in the same room with this guy?

The thought flickered in MacArthur's mind that he'd like to have a transparent shield between himself and the prisoner. But he could keep his doubts from showing on his face—or in his body language.

Jordan picked that moment to speak, exaggerating the rough timbre of his voice and emphasizing his normal humanity. "I need a drink of water. And I need to use the toilet."

"We're here to talk," MacArthur snapped.

"Are you planning to use a full bladder as an intimidation tactic?"

When MacArthur only shrugged, Jordan continued in what he hoped was a forceful but nonthreatening tone. "I've interviewed plenty of people who were subjected to stressful interrogation. There's no shame in wetting your pants when the interrogator won't let you go to the bathroom. But I'm betting that some of the pee drips down my leg and gets on your expensive carpet. It might be tough to get the smell out."

The Crandall Consortium director jerked his head toward the right. "The bathroom is over there. Keep the door open. And don't try anything funny."

Jordan glanced at the guns that were now in both guards' hands. "I'm not suicidal," he answered.

Keeping his arms at his sides, he walked to the bathroom. The temptation to send a mental jab into the heads of everyone in the room was overwhelming. But he didn't dare try it—since the likely result would be his getting shot.

Turning his back, he used the toilet, giving himself time to prepare for the confrontation with MacArthur.

After flushing, he washed his hands, then cupped them under the faucet, getting himself a long drink and rinsing out his mouth. For good measure, he washed his face.

"What are you doing? Taking a bath?" MacArthur called out.

"I'd like to. After waking up in your Black Hole of Calcutta."

Wondering if he was ready, Jordan crossed to one of the guest chairs. Without being invited, he sat down.

DANIEL pulled his Lincoln Town Car into the parking area at the Maine Avenue Wharf, where fresh fish was sold from boats tied up at the dock. He'd always been sure that the guys selling the fish weren't the ones who had caught it. But the scene at the dock added to the local color in the nation's capital.

Most of the fishmongers had gone home for the night. But the smell of their wares came through his air-conditioning system.

He switched to interior circulation only, just as a man and woman stepped out of the shadow cast by a parked truck.

Quickly they crossed the tarmac and climbed into the back of his car.

Saxon and Willow. Together—as always. He wanted to embrace her. He wanted to feel her body pressed to his.

She was his lover. They had made sweet love many times in the past.

Or . . . was that right?

He had come back to Washington alone. And she had promised to meet him. He remembered that much. But the rest of his memories of their time together was hazy. Like a dream. But when she reached across the seat to press her hand onto his neck, the recollection became sharp and clear again.

"Thank you for meeting us," Willow murmured.

"You said you had to discuss a matter affecting national security."

"Yes. It's about Jordan Walker and Lindsay Fleming. They're a danger to the United States of America."

"Lindsay? She works for me."

"Yes, remember, she was pumping you for information about the U.S. chemical weapons program."

He nodded, remembering a conversation with her. But was that what she'd asked?

"She and Walker are responsible for the break-in at Maple Creek."

Daniel goggled. "But why?"

"She's a spy for foreign powers," Saxon said.

Daniel tried to take that in.

"Kurt MacArthur thinks he can handle them," Willow added. "But he's wrong. You can get us into his enclave—to lay out the facts."

"Yes, of course." The words were firmly spoken, hiding his confusion.

"We'll go there now," Willow said.

"Not now. It's late. They won't let us in," he protested, wanting to explain how business was conducted in Washington.

"They'll let *you* in. You're an important man."

"Yes. Right."

"The head of the Senate Armed Services Committee. That makes you MacArthur's boss."

Did it? He had never thought of it quite that way.

He started to throw the gear lever into reverse. Then he stopped. He wanted to do this—for Willow. But he couldn't just go charging into the Crandall Consortium after ten o'clock at night.

"How do you know MacArthur has Walker and Lindsay?" he asked.

Saxon sighed. "We have been monitoring Crandall's

activities. We know that they brought the two spies back from Connecticut."

Daniel winced. Lindsay had worked for him for two years. She had access to a lot of military information.

"It's all right," Willow soothed.

"We'll sort it all out. Just get us through the gate. Tell them it's urgent," Saxon added.

"Yes. All right."

THE director of the Crandall Consortium gave Jordan a long look. "You seem pretty cocky for a guy in a very tight spot."

"I'm not cocky. I'm adaptable." He said the sentence in an even voice while he sent MacArthur a silent message. *Despite your preconceptions, you find you like me. You respect me. You will believe it when I tell you that Lindsay and I cannot communicate unless we're touching.*

The director kept sharp eyes on him, assessing, evaluating. Jordan wanted to look for hidden cameras, but he didn't want to give his concerns away. Instead, he maintained eye contact.

MacArthur answered, "I'm thinking you have a secret weapon."

"Maybe," he allowed. "Nothing I can use here and now." *You believe me. You believe I can't do anything to hurt you. I can't do anything unless Lindsay and I are touching.*

"Because we've got your girlfriend downstairs?"

He answered with a clipped, "Yeah," then silently added, *You believe that. You believe I can't do anything without Lindsay.* He wasn't sure what effect he was having on MacArthur, but he had to keep trying. And he was thinking that they had covered an amazing amount of territory with a few sentences. He struggled not to react when the director signaled to one of the armed men. The guard walked around the desk so that he was facing forward, watching the prisoner.

MacArthur's features were hard, but he was doing a fantastic job of hiding his jumping nerves. Jordan did the same, feeling like he was in a high-stakes poker game, only instead of chips, he was playing for his life—and Lindsay's.

"How did Todd Hamilton and Glenn Barrow get into Maple Creek?" MacArthur asked.

"I don't know for sure. I never met either of them. I only found out about them when Todd's father asked me to investigate his death."

"And what do you know about that?"

Dark images flickered in his brain. Bodies wrapped in tarps. Taken to Kent Island and dumped in the Chesapeake Bay.

"The official story was a bunch of bull, but I understand the need to keep information secret—if it's for the good of the country." *You believe I'm a reasonable guy. You believe what I'm saying.*

MacArthur's eyes narrowed. "In your book, *In the Halls of Power*, you busted open some national security secrets."

Jordan shrugged. "Nothing you couldn't have gotten from the Freedom of Information Act." He kept his face impassive. *You think I'm a reasonable guy, caught in a terrible situation.*

MacArthur circled back to an earlier topic. "And do you know how Hamilton and Barrow got past the guards?"

"I have some theories—as I'm sure you do."

The director made another rapid change of subject. "What did you find out about the Remington Clinic?"

Better stick to the truth—as much as he could. "Obviously, you've dug into my background enough to know I'm a pretty good investigative journalist. I found out that Remington hatched a plan to produce superintelligent children. It didn't appear to work."

"But Remington's experiments created children with special talents," MacArthur pointed out.

"When they get together with someone else who was part of the experiment."

The Crandall director leaned forward. "What happens?"

Jordan had already considered how to answer that question. "Their nascent paranormal powers surface."

"What powers?"

"My guess is that it's different with different couples."

"What happens with you?"

"Lindsay and I can communicate with each other—without speaking. But we have to be touching." *You believe that. You absolutely believe it,* he projected, hoping he was striking some vulnerable place in the director's brain.

"Interesting." MacArthur's voice was mild, but a flicker of intent in the man's mind warned Jordan that despite all his attempts to project a perception of honesty, something bad was coming. The director's gaze flicked down, and Jordan knew from his surface thoughts that he was about to play his ace in the hole—by pressing a hidden button under his desk.

Nothing in Jordan's imagination could have prepared him for the image that leaped into his mind. The same image MacArthur saw on a television screen below the level of the desk.

CHAPTER
TWENTY-NINE

TO HIS UTTER horror, Jordan saw Lindsay strapped to a chair with a man in a white lab coat standing over her.

The man slapped her hard across the face, and she screamed. Not in his ears. In his mind, and somehow—incredibly—even when she was in pain, she lent him her strength and her determination.

Don't let him know!

Her silent words and her strength were the only things that kept the shock from showing on his face.

He didn't know how she projected such iron resolve—right into his brain. But he knew without doubt that she had decided she wasn't going to give in to the bastards who had taken them captive. Because she believed what he had told her. If they let MacArthur know about their long-distance connection, they were dead. And if she could keep that information to herself, *he* had to try to do it, too.

Against every savage impulse raging through him, he sat quietly in the office of Crandall's director, pretending he didn't know anything about the horror downstairs.

In his mind he was screaming, but he made the scream into a mantra and flung it at the bastard sitting across the desk, looking down at a small television screen hidden from view.

I can't hear her. I can't see her. You believe I can't hear her. I can't see her. I don't have a clue about what you're doing to her.

As he chanted, he fought to keep his expression from

changing. MacArthur's gaze flicked from the hidden screen to him as though he expected a reaction.

"What?" he asked. To his own ears, his voice sounded like a coarse croak.

MacArthur said nothing.

"I guess I need some more water," Jordan said, starting to stand.

"Sit down," the director growled, and Jordan obeyed.

I don't have a clue about what's happening to Lindsay. I'm just sitting here wondering what's going on.

"You wanted to ask me more questions?" he offered.

"In a minute," MacArthur snapped. The phone on his desk rang, like he'd arranged for it to interrupt, and he picked up the receiver, listening, answering with a clipped "yes." And Jordan knew he was talking to the man with Lindsay.

She was downstairs, in a small, colorless, windowless room. Bound to a chair. He saw her, and he needed to focus all his attention on her. He needed to figure out how to free her.

No. We can't do it yet.

Her warning was sharp and clear in his mind.

I'm fine. I'll be fine. You can't let him know you're with me.

The man standing over Lindsay leaned down.

She tried to flinch away, but she couldn't move.

Using both hands, he casually ripped her blouse open.

She made a whimpering sound, but her voice in his head was steady. *He's testing you. Don't let him know you can see this. Don't let him know a damn thing.*

He wanted to grit his teeth. He wanted to scream. All he could do was sit there and pretend he wasn't in agony, watching as the bastard pulled down the cups of her bra, took her nipples in his fingers and twisted.

She cried out as though she were terrified—and humiliated. But he didn't sense fear. He sensed iron resolve. He understood that only part of her consciousness was in her body. The rest was with him, telling him to be strong. Adding her power to the message he aimed at MacArthur.

I don't know what you're doing to her. I don't have a clue. I don't know what's going on. I'm wondering why you don't continue this damn interview, since you called me up here. So why don't you tell your guy that there's no point in going after Lindsay again.

He focused on that thought, even when the room around him blurred. He fought not to strike out with a bolt of mental energy. Instead, he shifted in his seat.

Over the buzzing in his ears he heard MacArthur say something into the phone. He wasn't sure what. But the man downstairs threw a blanket over Lindsay's ruined blouse, and she breathed out a sigh of gratitude.

He unstrapped her, hoisted her up, led her out of the room, and down the hall to the cell where she had been earlier.

She flopped onto the hard bunk, waiting until the door was closed before she allowed tears to leak out of her eyes.

I'll kill him.

No. We're winning. Don't blow it now. I have an idea.

When she told him what she was thinking, he bit back a smile.

"What?" MacArthur demanded.

"Actually, I'm in a very unique position. A very good position."

"Oh, yeah?"

"You're interested in developing inimitable weapons."

"What's your point?"

"It appears that Todd Hamilton and Glenn Barrow developed a weapon, but they didn't really think through what they were going to do. What if Lindsay and I could do something similar? What if you could use us for some important job?"

"Can you do something similar?" MacArthur snapped.

"Not yet. But we can work at perfecting our new ability—under your supervision." *You like that idea. You want to be able to use us. You want to present the Pentagon with the scientific triumph that you set in motion thirty years ago.*

"How would I supervise you?"

"I don't know. Lie detector tests? Observation by a psychologist?" *This guy's trying to be helpful. He wants to work with you.*

"And what guarantee do I have that you wouldn't turn a weapon on me?"

"I guess you'll have to work out how to control the experiment."

MacArthur considered the plan, then nodded.

Jordan slowly let out the breath he was holding. "And while you're mulling it over, I'd appreciate not being stuck in a dungeon. Do you think you could get me a decent room? And I assume Lindsay is downstairs, too. I'd like her to be as comfortable as I am."

MacArthur stroked his chin. "If we're going to be working together, I guess that's a fair request."

Jordan didn't have any illusions. The director still hadn't decided what to do.

Limit the way they can touch. Have a barrier between them and an interior partition you can drop between them in a split second if it looks like they're trying to pull anything funny.

The director's expression turned thoughtful. Jordan hoped he was considering the idea that his prisoner had planted in his head. And he was thinking he'd come up with it on his own.

Jordan prayed it would buy them some time. Because the alternative was attacking a house full of armed guards with no idea of success.

But if MacArthur gave them a few days, that was better than nothing.

The man behind the desk reached for the phone again and gave terse orders—for the prisoners to be brought to rooms on the top floor.

Not the presidential suite, Jordan assumed, but better than the basement.

And he was picking up something from the man now. His computer password, Jehovah101. Maybe that would come in handy.

"Come on," one the goons ordered.

Jordan got up and followed him out of the room.

KURT waited until the door had closed behind the prisoner.

Leaning back in his contour chair, he tried to ease the tightness in his shoulders.

"Sit down," he said to Swift.

His most trusted aide came around the desk from where he'd been observing the session and took one of the guest chairs—not the one where the prisoner had been sitting.

"So what do you think about Jordan Walker?" Kurt asked.

"I think Walker is lying through his teeth."

"Why?"

"He was too cool. Too calm. He thinks he has an edge."

Jim had a point, although Kurt was inclined to be less judgmental.

"The man's in a jam. Of course he's willing to cut a deal."

"That doesn't make him reliable."

The door opened, and Frank Wainwright came in. He was the man who had put his hands on Lindsay during the interview with Jordan.

"We were discussing Walker," he said. "What do you think about the broad?"

"She acted like I'd expect. She was frightened. She was in pain. She tried to distance herself from me. We have her on video. Want to see it?"

"Yeah."

Frank crossed to the television, inserted a tape in the VCR, and rewound it.

They all watched with interest as Lindsay was strapped into position in the chair.

"She's scared," Kurt pointed out.

"But determined not to give up anything," Swift countered.

Kurt nodded, watching as Frank slapped the subject, then ripped her blouse and manhandled her breasts.

She looked sick. Terrified. Withdrawn.

"What I'd expect," he repeated.

"Too calm," Swift argued.

"Like Frank said, she's withdrawing mentally. You don't have to be a telepath to do that. That's the way a lot of rape victims handle the abuse."

Kurt considered the video. "I don't think Walker could have known about what was going on downstairs and stay so cool."

"Unless he had some kind of pact with her," Swift suggested.

"I don't buy it," Kurt murmured.

"Since when are you so trusting?" Swift asked.

"Since I think we have a chance to use these people," he shot back. "Maybe they can help us find Greenwood."

"He could be hundreds of miles away. How would they know where to find him? I don't think keeping them around worth the chance," Swift said.

"Sid Becker, Greenwood's cousin, contacted her. She may know something."

Swift shifted in the chair. "One other thing you should consider. Maybe Walker is trying to sell you a complete bill of goods. Maybe he's a lot more powerful than he's letting on. Maybe he planted the idea in your mind that you should trust him."

Kurt kept his expression neutral.

"Just do me a favor and consider that possibility," Swift said. "Study the tape you just made of Walker. And keep an eye on them."

"Do you know something I don't?"

Swift swallowed. "No."

"Spit it out!"

"I have a bad feeling about her. Just watch them. See how they're behaving. Her in particular. Nobody's interviewed her. She had to be frightened. She has to be wondering what's happened to Walker. Unless he's communicated with her."

Before they could argue further, he turned and left.

LINDSAY lay curled on her side, her arm across her face and her mind turned inward as she huddled on her hard bunk. The bastard who had torn her blouse had thrown her a man's shirt to wear. She had put it on because being covered was better than being exposed. But buttoning the shirt had sapped all her energy. She didn't have the will to reach out to Jordan. She didn't have the energy to do more than lie like a mindless lump of flesh, trying to steady herself.

She'd put up a brave front with Jordan. But she hadn't been prepared for this kind of captivity.

A shiver raced over her skin. What if those horrible men came for her again? What if they did more than strip off her blouse and grab her breasts? She wasn't sure she could take that. And she didn't want Jordan to see her weakness. So she had turned away from him. Turned away from this horrible place—inside herself.

Outside in the hall she heard footsteps.

Her heart leaped into her throat, and she clenched her fists, bracing for another assault.

She sensed Jordan struggling desperately to get back into her mind, and she tried to fight him off. But he forced his way past the barrier.

Lindsay, stop. Let me in. I have to tell you something important.

It felt like he was shouting inside her head. And she was too weak to fight him off. He came into her mind, sweetly, swiftly.

It's all right. The men who are coming for you won't hurt you. I convinced MacArthur to put us in better rooms. They're just moving you upstairs. That's all. They're not going to hurt you, he repeated, then went on, *I want you to know that. But you still have to act like you're afraid.*

She pressed her knuckles against her lips.

That won't be hard.

Lindsay, you were magnificent when he had you in that torture chamber. You gave me your strength. You made it possible for me to pretend I didn't know what was going on downstairs. Don't let them get the better of you now.

She swallowed. He was right. She had scored some important points. She had to keep scoring them—to stay alive.

Yes.

We're going to get out of this. We're smarter than they are. And together we're stronger, too.

The voice in her mind rang with conviction, and she wanted desperately to believe him. But she knew she couldn't trust the assurance. Neither of them had control of this situation, and it could turn very bad—very quickly.

The lock clicked, and Lindsay tensed.

Ask them about me. As far as they know, you have no idea where I am.

Yes. Right.

Jordan had asked her to act frightened. Despite his reassurance, there was no need to pretend. When two men stepped through the door, she felt her heart start to thump inside her chest as she cowered on the narrow bed.

"Come on," one of them said in a gruff voice.

"Where?" she asked, unable to hold her own voice steady.

"To a room you'll like better."

"Where's Jordan?" she asked in a voice that came out high and shaky. "What's happened to him?"

"He's upstairs."

"Are you telling me the truth?"

"Yeah. Come on."

"Don't touch me. Please." Stiff-armed, she pushed herself up, wavering on her feet, staying as far as she could from the guards.

They won't hurt you, Jordan reassured her.

One of the men stood behind her, the other in front, and she felt her chest constrict as they proceeded down a dark hallway, toward the room where she had been tortured for Jordan's edification.

She couldn't breathe until they had walked past that door. Then she gasped out her relief. Some of the tightness in her chest eased as they started up the stairs. They kept climbing, past the first floor—to the upper reaches of the building.

The men led her to the end of another hall, unlocked the door, and ushered her into a small bedroom. When they left her alone, a shudder went through her. Leaning back against the door, she closed her eyes, struggling to get back her sense of balance.

Are you all right?

Yes, she answered, hugging Jordan's presence to herself as she wrapped her own arms around her shoulders and rubbed her icy skin.

Struggling for calm, she looked around the room. It was comfortable, with dark wood furniture, a double bed, brocade curtains, and a private bath.

Like an upscale hotel room.

Except that the door is locked.

She paced to the window, which was covered with decorative bars. When she looked beyond them, she saw that the building appeared to be on a high bluff above the Potomac River.

You can see the river? Jordan asked.

Yes.

You must rate. I can see a parking lot—and the Dumpster.

She pressed her lips together to keep from laughing, because she was afraid that if she laughed, merriment would shade off into hysteria.

Steady, Jordan murmured in her head.

I'm okay.

You can't be. And neither am I. But we're going to focus on getting out of here. I assume we're at opposite ends of the house.

Yes. She heaved a sigh. *He's keeping us away from each other.*

Not for long.

DANIEL pulled his Lincoln Town Car to a stop at the gate. As he reached to activate the intercom speaker, he could feel waves of tension radiating from the man and woman in the back of his car.

The speaker clicked.

"Yes?" a man asked.

"This is Senator Daniel Bridgewater. I need to speak to Kurt MacArthur."

"Tonight?"

"Yes. I have urgent—private—business with him."

It's about Jordan Walker and Lindsay Fleming, Willow's voice murmured in his head, and he repeated the line, then repeated the rest of Willow's silent words.

"It's about Jordan Walker and Lindsay Fleming. I know you have them there. If you don't want me to call the police, you'd better let me in."

"Just a minute."

Daniel waited with his heart pounding. Finally the gate swung open.

"Proceed to the front of the house," the disembodied voice ordered.

He steered the car up the driveway.

Stop, Willow ordered.

"But we haven't reached the house."

That's all right. Sax and I are getting out here. When we're out of the car, keep going. Speed up. Head for the cliff. Drive the car over the side of the cliff. That will focus all their attention on you and the car. Repeat what I just told you.

"I'm supposed to drive over the side of the cliff."

That's right, Daniel. And we'll be together soon. I'll be waiting for you down in the river.

"How is that possible?"

You'll see. We'll be together the way you want. But you have to drive off the cliff to reach me. Now go on, before they wonder why you've stopped.

They closed the car and disappeared into the shadows at the side of the driveway.

WITHOUT the link to Jordan, Lindsay didn't know how she could survive in this room. In this house. *So when we get away, we'll escape to your cabin in the woods?* she asked, trying not to sound desperate.

Yeah. We'll be alone. Away from people. Just the two of us. But first things first. Like—you'd better assume that there are microphones in our rooms. So no talking out loud to me. And there may be cameras, too.

Lindsay couldn't hold back a strangled sound.

Unable to stand the confines of the room, she cast her mind outward—and discovered something that made her gasp.

What? Jordan asked urgently.

There's a car coming up the drive. She answered. *Senator Bridgewater is driving.*

Bridgewater? What's he doing here?

I don't know. . . .

The thought trailed off as she saw something else. Before the gate closed, a man slipped inside. A man on foot, crouching low.

Someone came in after the car?

Yes.

Who the hell is it?

He stepped under an overhead light, and she blinked as she caught a good look at his face. It was grim and anguished—and determined. She thought she had seen him before, but she didn't know who he was. Not one of MacArthur's men out for a stroll. Not the way he ran, then ducked for cover.

DANIEL roared up the driveway. He could hear someone in back of him shouting. But he ignored the frantic voice. He was going to meet Willow. The woman he loved. And she loved him, too. They would be together. Without that bastard of a brother.

They would be together soon.

She had said to head for the edge of the cliff. She was down there at the bottom, waiting for him. In the river.

In the river? That didn't make perfect sense. Maybe he had remembered that part wrong. But she had promised. And she had never broken a promise to him. So he kept going.

The big car broke through a flimsy barrier. A chain-link fence. He roared toward open space. Across the river he could see traffic moving on Canal Road.

He plunged off into space, flying through the air for several seconds before the car nosed downward.

Terror gripped him by the throat. And in that frozen moment he knew that it had all been a lie.

The promises. The loving relationship. The feelings.

He fumbled for the door handle, then screamed as he hit the water.

* * *

IN the hall an alarm bell rang.

And Jordan's voice echoed in Lindsay's head—sharp and frantic.

Can you open the lock on your door? If you can, get the hell out of your room. I'm coming.

Before she could think about the lock, her door burst open, and a man with an automatic pistol stood facing her. Not one of the men she'd seen earlier. It was Jim. The man who had killed Hamilton.

She gasped.

"You know me, don't you?"

"No," she lied.

"I knew you were dangerous. How did you get to Hamilton's house?"

Lindsay acted instinctively. In one furious flash of fear and aggression, she shot a bolt of energy toward the man who leveled the gun at her chest.

He screamed, pulled the trigger. But she had bought herself precious seconds. She lunged for the floor, then realized she'd increased her vulnerability.

She tried to roll, tried to aim another mental bolt at her captor. But then she found she had been through too much this evening to manage more than one attack.

As Jim adjusted his aim, she braced for the impact of bullets.

CHAPTER
THIRTY

BEFORE JIM COULD fire, he screamed and dropped the weapon.

She didn't understand what had happened until Jordan stepped into her line of sight, and she knew he was the one who had lashed out with his mind this time. They might not be experts, but they had enough power to do damage.

As Jim lay crumpled on the floor, Jordan went from the psychic to the physical, aiming a hard kick at the man's head, battering him unconscious.

Jordan bent to pick up the weapon, keeping it in his right hand as he gripped her with his left. The contact was like a sweet reunion—and a jolt of power surged inside her. She felt as if someone had given her a blast of some powerful stimulant.

He was going to kill me. Because he saw me at Hamilton's house. Somehow he saw me.

Yeah. Come on, let's get out of here.

She realized the alarm bell had stopped ringing. Not because the emergency was over, she assumed.

"Wait," she cautioned. She wasn't sure why she had issued the terse order. She only knew that it felt like the right thing to do when she turned back to the room—then narrowed her new surge of energy to the window curtains.

When they began to smolder, then burst into flames, she gave Jordan a satisfied grin.

A diversion?

Yeah.

Then maybe we'd better turn off the sprinkler system.
Oh, right. Sorry.

Their brains in sync, they mentally followed the pipes back to a valve in the basement, which they closed.

"Good work," Jordan said, giving her a quick, passionate kiss, then leading her toward the stairs. Before they'd gotten ten feet, another man came around the corner of the hall. As she saw him, Lindsay gasped. The man's image had burned itself into her brain. He was the bastard who had slapped her, then put his hands on her breasts in the torture chamber. And somehow she knew his name—Frank Wainright.

Wainright stared at them. "What the hell?" Even as he spoke, he reached for a gun.

Before he could pull the weapon from a shoulder holster, she and Jordan acted together again—sending a bolt of pain into his head, bringing him to his knees. Anger fueled Jordan's attack, and she knew they had burst blood vessels. She wasn't sorry.

Jordan's grip tightened on her hand. *These guys are going to kill us on sight—unless we get them first.*

Yes.

They made it down to the next floor.

The office level, Jordan informed her. He pulled away from her, toward a closed door.

Come back. We have to get away. Now.

JORDAN heard Lindsay's warning in his head. But he ignored it because he knew they would never be safe unless he had documentation of Kurt MacArthur's illegal activities.

He wanted proof of what had happened to them here. And proof of what the Crandall Consortium had done in the past.

He had the man's computer password, Jehovah101.

So he could get into the computer fast—then out again.

The train of thought was logical, given the circumstances. But as he walked toward the office door, he realized that the idea wasn't his. Someone else had planted it in his mind.

Someone who wanted him and Lindsay to stay inside the building.

In some small corner of his mind, he understood that he must ignore the outside interference if he wanted to get out of this horror house alive.

Instead, he walked through the reception area, then into the office—even as he heard Lindsay's frantic voice.

"Jordan? Please, come on."

He wanted—needed—to turn back toward her. Instead, he kept walking.

"Jordan, why are you blocking me?"

When he tried to speak, he felt his throat tighten. He hurried into the darkened room and stopped short. A man and a woman stood beside the computer. Two strikingly beautiful blondes. Brother and sister.

Saxon and Willow Trinity.

Good of you to join us, Saxon murmured in his mind. *We need your help. You've got the password—and the skill to get the Remington records off the computer, don't you?*

SENSING something badly wrong, Lindsay started after Jordan. They needed to escape—as fast as possible. She could already smell smoke coming down the stairs from the upper floor where they'd been locked in.

Jordan! Come back.

He didn't answer. Why was he shielding his mind? There must be something he didn't want her to know.

Fear clawed at her insides. Because she sensed on some deep, gut level that he was in trouble.

Someone's footsteps pounded up the stairs.

God, another one.

She leaped toward the door where Jordan had disappeared. But before she reached it, Kurt MacArthur himself came charging around the corner.

When he saw her, he stopped short—his face contorting with anger. Like everyone else she'd encountered in the past few minutes, he was armed.

"Well well, a telepath on the loose. Did you kill Bridgewater?"

She gasped. "No. What do you mean?"

"The senator called from the gate and asked to be admitted."

She knew that much.

"Then he roared up the driveway and drove his car off the cliff."

She couldn't hold back a strangled exclamation.

"Did you call him here?" MacArthur pressed. "Is that why he showed up unannounced?"

"No!"

"Swift and Wainright went upstairs when the others went out to the accident site. What happened to them?"

Swift? That must be the guy named Jim.

"I don't know," she lied.

"How did you get out of your room?"

"The door was unlocked."

"I don't think so."

As she spoke, she silently screamed for Jordan. But he didn't respond, and she wondered how she was going to get away from the Crandall director.

The smell of smoke was stronger now, coming down from the floor above.

MacArthur coughed. His expression was savage as he flicked his gaze toward the stairs—then back to her. "The place is on fire. What the hell is going on?"

She licked her dry lips and fell back on her innocent refrain. "I don't know."

"You're lying."

Her body tensed as she struggled to gather her power. Somehow, she managed to continue the conversation. "What do you want me to tell you? That I torched my curtains?"

"Did you?" he growled.

"With what? I hope you didn't leave a box of matches in my room."

His expression hardened, and she knew she had stalled as long as she dared.

MacArthur gave her an assessing look. "I don't know what happened upstairs, but if you're out of your room, then I guess Jim was right. You're too dangerous to live."

He brought his gun up, aiming for her heart. Her vision contracted to a narrow tunnel. All her attention was focused on him.

Desperately she summoned what power she was able to muster. She didn't have much hope, but she had to try. Because the alternative was her own death.

Before she could attack, a shot rang out from behind MacArthur, a shot that whizzed past her head—too close for comfort.

Responding to the new threat the Crandall director whirled. Two more rounds split the air—and MacArthur fell to the ground.

The man who had gunned him down was still standing, his shaved head glistening with sweat and his face contorted into a grimace of satisfaction as he walked toward the body on the floor and knelt.

Struggling to catch her breath, she gaped at him. What in the name of God had happened?

Could this be one of the security men here? Someone with a grudge against the boss—taking advantage of the chaos caused by the senator's car going over the cliff?

No. Someone had rushed through the gate—using the car for cover. And she was pretty sure it was this guy.

Eyeing the gun still in his hand, she edged slowly away, wondering if she could get into the office and find out what was wrong with Jordan.

He made a grating sound in his throat, stopping her in her tracks. But he wasn't speaking to her.

"I got him for you, Sid. I got him."

Lindsay's mouth fell open, as the contorted features and the bald head resolved themselves into a pattern she recognized.

"Is he dead?" she managed to ask, hearing the raspy quality of her own voice.

"Yeah. Mr. Big Shot won't go after anyone else now," he spit out.

"Mark? How did you get here?"

His eyes narrowed, and he seemed fully aware of her for the first time. "Who are you? How the hell do you know who I am?"

She scrambled for a coherent explanation. "They were holding me captive here. I escaped."

"Oh, yeah? Why?"

"I . . . I work for Senator Bridgewater. Your cousin, Sid, came to me. He asked me to help him find out what had happened to you."

He trained the gun on her. "Explain what's going on."

She swallowed hard, knowing that it would be dangerous to say too much. Mark had just killed a man. Now his gun was trained on her. And he didn't exactly look friendly. "I was helping Jordan Walker dig into the Maple Creek break-in."

"Who the hell is Jordan Walker?"

"An investigative journalist. You might have read some of his books. Or—"

"I don't read that kind of crap," he snapped, and she knew he wasn't in good enough shape for a logical conversation.

"Okay. Well, he's legit. MacArthur was hunting us down.

He . . . he caught up with us and brought us back here. He was going to get all the information out of us he could. Then he was going to kill us."

"Why should I believe any of that?"

"Because it's the truth." As she spoke she tried to project the message into his head, the way she knew Jordan had done in the office with MacArthur. *It's the truth. You believe me because it's the truth.*

He stared at her, and she wondered if the silent directions were sinking in. She knew he held her life in his hands—and his decision could go either way.

Mark, please. I need your help. I—

She never got a chance to finish because the office door opened and a blond woman stepped out.

Lindsay's breath stilled in her lungs. The woman was Willow Trinity.

Willow gave her a passing glance, then focused on Mark, and he crumpled to the floor, screaming, his hands clamped to his shaved head.

Aghast, Lindsay tried to go down on her knees beside him. But her muscles went rigid. An outside force had frozen her in place. She could feel static crackling inside her head. It hurt, but it was obviously nothing compared to what Mark had experienced.

Questing fingers probed her mind as Willow lifted her head, sniffing the thickening air. "You fool. Did you torch the place?"

Lindsay pressed her lips together, but she couldn't hold back her answer. "Yes," she moaned.

"That makes it simpler. We can leave you to burn up in your own fire."

She yanked Lindsay forward, and she stumbled as her legs suddenly unfroze. Willow gave her a shove, propelling her into the office—where she saw Jordan and a blond man.

Saxon Trinity.

With a sick feeling, she focused on Jordan. He was sitting at the desk, his hands on the keyboard. She sent her thoughts toward him, but his brain might as well have been a block of wood. He didn't look at her, and she felt her guts clutch.

"What have you done to him?" she moaned.

Saxon ignored her. "Get the data out of there," he growled to Jordan.

Willow slammed the door behind them, shutting out the worst of the smoke.

"The bitch set her curtains on fire," she said.

"We've still got time."

Willow pushed Lindsay backward onto the couch, where she flopped like a bag of grapefruits.

Again she tried to reach out to Jordan with her mind, but the way was blocked by a powerful force that made the flimsy shields they'd constructed in their practice session seem like tissue paper. Obviously, they had been fools to think they could fight these two experienced telepaths with their own fledgling powers.

Willow must have caught the thought, because she turned and gave Lindsay a satisfied look.

Yes, your miserable little life is going to end right here—in a burst of flames. You'll never have what Saxon and I have found together.

Willow's focus was divided. Part of her attention was on Lindsay. But she was also helping her brother direct a beam of raw energy on Jordan—forcing him to sit at the computer and work. Below the surface of his mind, Lindsay could sense him struggling to break free. She wanted to help. Maybe together they could do it—if she could figure out a way to reach him.

When the printer began to chug out papers, she knew their time was almost up.

She couldn't link with Jordan. She couldn't hurt Willow

or Saxon. But was there anyone else here who could help them?

She cast her mind outward, frantically searching for someone who might come to their rescue.

She detected men and a woman out by the cliffs. And another man, making his way toward the house.

When she caught his thoughts, she lowered her gaze and tried to keep her expression and her brain waves neutral. She wasn't even sure what that meant. But she knew she was struggling to do it.

Hurry, she called out. *We're in the office. Saxon and Willow are going to kill us. Can you stop them?*

Lindsay risked a glance at Willow, but most of her attention was focused on her brother and Jordan now.

"We don't have time for a printed copy. Just take a disk," she said.

"I want to read it on the way home," Saxon answered.

They exchanged a look that told Lindsay the twins didn't always think in lockstep.

All the time she kept up her call for help. *In the office. Can you get to the office? Hurry. We need you.*

Time ticked past with horrifying speed, and at the same time she felt like she was in some kind of slow-motion, underwater bubble.

From the corner of her mind she caught the knowledge of a new presence. A man was just on the other side of the door—not the door to the hallway. The back way into the office.

It was the man she had summoned, creeping forward in the shadows, and she had to keep Willow's focus away from him.

Around the buzzing in her brain, she managed to say, "We can work together. We have the same goals."

"I doubt it."

"We want to learn from you. We hope you can teach us what you know."

Willow's gaze bored into hers. "We don't need you. We don't need anyone but each other."

In back of Willow a bloody hand gripped the doorjamb. Slowly a face came into view.

CHAPTER
THIRTY-ONE

SAXON WAS THE first one of the twins to sense the intruder. Whirling to face the newcomer, he stared in shock. "Christ! You're supposed to be dead."

As Saxon spoke, he momentarily lost his focus on Jordan. And Lindsay knew that gave Jordan the opening he needed. He might not be able to fight the Trinity twins on a psychic level, but he had another option. With a mighty push of his feet against the desk, he sent the rolling chair hurtling backward—and into Saxon, who cried out as he tumbled sideways, his thoughts now totally disrupted.

Lindsay's gaze flicked from Saxon and Jordan to the doorway, where Daniel Bridgewater leaned against the jamb, holding a pistol in a two-handed grip.

"You bitch. You'll never mess with my head again." His voice was a dead man's wheeze as he fired at Willow, fired again. She and Saxon both screamed as she toppled to the ground.

Saxon was already on the floor. Hoisting himself to his hands and knees, he dragged himself toward his sister.

Lindsay felt the life leaking out of Willow. And Saxon felt it, too. Howling like a wounded animal in anguish, he crawled toward his sister. Jordan reached for a brass paperweight on the desk and brought it crashing down on the blond head, caving in Saxon's skull and putting him out of his misery.

Lindsay rushed toward Bridgewater. "Senator . . ."

He coughed. "The bitch did ... something ... to ... my mind." He blinked and gave Lindsay a startled look.

"What are you doing here?"

"Kurt MacArthur captured us."

"Did you have something to do with the break-in at Maple Creek?"

"No. We were investigating it."

"Oh, shit. More lies from that bitch."

He gave her a commanding look—a look she recognized from the office when he was exercising his authority. "Get out of here."

"I can't leave you."

"You have to get out."

"You, too."

"I was tough enough to make it up the side of the cliff. I'm tough enough to haul my ass out of the building."

Jordan ignored him. "We're leaving together. Now." *Now. Before the whole place goes up in flames.*

Jordan reached for Lindsay's hand, holding tight as he continued sending a message to the senator, hoping it would work, now that he had broken free of the Trinity twins. He had put up defenses against them, but not against her and Jordan. *You didn't see us here tonight. You can say you came to question MacArthur about the cover-up of the Maple Creek break-in. You'll tell the press how MacArthur was using Defense Department money for his own dirty work. But you won't remember you saw us here.*

Lindsay thought of something else. *But you do remember Mark Greenwood. He came to talk to you about Maple Creek. He was with you in the afternoon three days ago.* She named the date. *He came to your house. You remember Mark was with you. He told you about Maple Creek. You were talking about the break-in. So when the police try to put him in the park where his cousin Sid was shot, you'll know he was set up. You'll help him.*

In the corner of her mind she picked up on what Jordan was doing. Turning, he opened the bottom left desk drawer and took out his wallet—along with her purse.

The action jogged her brain, and she put the computer disk into her purse and grabbed the papers from the printer.

"GOOD thinking," Jordan murmured.

After manually flicking the switch below the desk that opened the gates, he wiped that clean, too.

We have to get Mark.

Yes.

When she opened the door, the reception area was filled with smoke, and she began to cough. Crouching on the ground, she and Jordan crawled to Mark. Jordan took the gun from the unconscious man and stuffed it into his waistband. Together, they hauled Mark into the office. He was like a dead weight, but she felt him returning to consciousness as they pulled him out of the smoke-filled hallway and into the office complex.

The senator was staring down at Willow and Saxon. Jordan grabbed his arm, too, leading him back the way he'd entered the room—down a flight of stairs and out a side door.

You won't remember we were here, she said again, joining her thoughts with Jordan. This time they addressed both Mark and the senator.

Jordan added his reinforcement to the message, speaking to Mark. *But you will remember going to Senator Daniel Bridgewater's house. You know Sid was killed, but you weren't there. You were with Senator Bridgewater. You were in his house. In his den.*

Lindsay kept talking to him, giving him details about the house, about the room where he was supposed to have met the Senator, stopping when they stepped outside into a smoke-filled night.

Bridgewater pulled away, staggering across the lawn. Lindsay let him go, reminding him silently that he hadn't seen her or Jordan here tonight. She had a good chance of affecting his thinking, she told herself, because she was telling him something he would want to believe.

She was still coughing as they dragged Mark to one of the cars and threw him in the backseat. Lindsay climbed in after him. There was no ignition key, but they didn't need it.

Jordan started the engine, and they sped down the drive. When she turned around, she saw flames shooting out of the upper windows. Then a roaring sound leaped toward them, and she was pretty sure the upper floor had just collapsed.

As they screeched onto a side street, she heard sirens in the distance. Someone had called the fire department. She wondered if the bodies in the office complex would burn. She wondered how many people knew she and Jordan were in the house. Would they talk about it?

Probably not, since their capture and confinement had been illegal.

Mark moaned, and she stroked his shoulder, sending him soothing thoughts.

"My . . . head . . . hurts. It's like . . . Maple Creek."

"No. You're all right. You're all right," she said aloud, sending him the same message with her mind, knowing Jordan was adding his reassurance. "Where were you staying?"

"Oak Hill Cemetery."

Lindsay shuddered. *Can we take him to the cathedral? To the Bishop's Garden?*

I don't think we should, Jordan answered. *If we do, he'll be even more confused. He probably left some stuff in the cemetery. And he'll wonder how he lost it if he wakes up somewhere else.*

You're right.

Jordan headed across Key Bridge and into the city. They drove up Wisconsin Avenue and turned onto R Street. All the way they talked to Mark, asking him questions, giving him the information they wanted him to remember.

As Jordan pulled up near the cemetery gate, she asked, "Are you sure you can get back inside?"

"Yeah. I know a back way in."

They gave Mark final instructions. "Tomorrow, go to Senator Bridgewater for help. He'll remember meeting with you. He'll stand with you."

"Yes," Mark croaked.

She couldn't be sure it would work out the way she and Jordan wanted. But they had done as much as they could.

After Mark disappeared into the darkness, Lindsay moved into the front seat of the car.

"What about us?" she whispered. Jordan reached for her, and they held each other for a long moment.

"MacArthur's no longer a problem. And any of his guys who are left are going to be a little busy. I'd say we're in the clear. But just to be sure, we'll stay out of sight for a while."

She nodded against his shoulder, then eased away so he could drive. But she kept her hand on his arm and knew where he was going.

He drove to the garage at Reagan National Airport, where they wiped their fingerprints from the car.

"Your face is a little smudged," he murmured as he gave her a good look.

"So is yours."

"Maybe we should clean up."

She was too dazed to think clearly. So she let Jordan take charge. He led her to the concourse, where some of the shops were still open. There he bought a couple of Nation's Capitol T-shirts.

"Wash up in the ladies' room, and I'll do the same in the men's room."

They each disappeared into a rest room. When she looked at her hair and face, she was thankful that she had her purse along. Glad that the place was almost empty, she washed, changed her top, then put on the clean T-shirt and threw her borrowed shirt in the trash before combing her hair.

Jordan had also washed and changed his shirt.

She was still too discombobulated to function on any kind of intelligent level as he led her to the cabstand.

"Where are we going?"

"A hotel. Until we know that everything is okay."

He asked to be taken to the Embassy Suites on Pennsylvania Avenue. On the ride over they huddled together in the backseat. And she closed her eyes, praying that they would be alone soon.

Incredibly she drifted off to sleep. When the cab stopped, she woke with a jolt.

We're . . . safe. Everything's fine, he spoke into her mind.

As they stepped into the lobby, he tightened his hold on her hand, then strode to the desk, where he asked for a room for the night. After a moment's hesitation he handed over his credit card.

As soon as they were alone in the room, he wrapped her in his arms, and she knew this was what she had been waiting for since their escape.

The intensity of his feelings, of his thoughts almost shattered her.

Oh, Lord, Jordan. I thought we wouldn't get out of there.

We did it—together.

With a little help from Mark and Bridgewater.

They clung together, swaying on their feet. And when he lowered his lips to her, she opened for him, drank him in, the kiss simmering with passion and promise.

I love you.

God, yes. I love you.

Panting, they tore at each other's clothing, sinking to the rug—only half naked because they were too impatient to wait.

Stark, desperate emotions shimmered between them. His hand shoved her T-shirt and pants out of the way while she struggled with his zipper, moaning with satisfaction as she freed his cock.

She felt the pleasure of it—hers and his. But she needed more. Much more. And he knew exactly what that was. Exactly.

His hands found her breasts, stroking and squeezing before his thumbs and fingers tightened on her nipples, giving her the precise pressure she craved. And when he replaced one hand with his mouth and sucked, she thought she would shatter.

All the time her hand clasped his cock, moving up and down with light strokes, not too hard, just enough. Because she didn't want him to come until he was inside her—until he could ease the throbbing between her legs.

She was balanced on a high wire of need, swaying with each surge of hot wind blowing over her body. He knew it, too, because he yanked her pants farther down, helping her free one leg to give him access.

Then he was inside her, and they both cried out with relief. He drove into her, and it took only a few frantic strokes to send her over the edge. She came so quickly that her head was spinning. And he followed her seconds later.

They lay gasping in a heap on the rug, until he helped her up and somehow got them both naked and into bed, where they clung together.

Half-formed thoughts bounced between them as they drifted into sleep. She woke hours later to find the sun streaming through the window.

At first she didn't know where they were. Then the horror of what they'd survived flashed through her mind.

Through Jordan's mind, too.

IT'S okay. We're okay, he reassured her.

We need to find out what happened.

Let's start with cable news.

Jordan picked up the remote from the nightstand, so he could turn on the television across the room. They didn't have to wait long for news. CNN had a report of the fire at the Crandall Consortium—and chaos among the staff—caused by the arrival of Senator Daniel Bridgewater, who had come to demand information about a national security matter.

A number of Crandall employees—including Kurt MacArthur—were dead. Someone had driven a car into the river. A couple of religious leaders named Willow and Saxon Trinity were also dead. Apparently they had been hatching some kind of conspiracy with Kurt MacArthur. And Senator Bridgewater was promising a congressional investigation into the recent activities of the consortium.

"No mention of us—or Mark," Lindsay murmured, then turned her head toward him.

"Score one for the home team," he answered, feeling tension easing out of himself. He'd been wondering what the morning would bring. The CNN report was reassuring. But he'd have to tap some of his sources and make sure it was all true.

Beside him, Lindsay nodded, obviously following his thoughts. He'd have to get used to that.

She cleared her throat. "I don't think the law would say Mark killed MacArthur in self defense. Or Bridgewater—when he killed Willow."

"In both cases I'd say it was as justified as our taking out Wainright."

"What about the operative named Jim Swift? He's the man who killed Hamilton."

"I don't know. They didn't mention him."

"I assume Bridgewater's not going to talk about the Trinity twins controlling him."

"I assume not."

"So what do *we* do now?" she asked.

"For starters, we need to call the Mountain View Lodge and see if they have my car. Then we drive up to Darien and get my computer—and visit Mrs. Vanderlin in the hospital."

That poor woman. But she's on the mend. I can sense it.

Jordan caught her next silent question and said, "I may abandon the Hamilton project. But I think I can get a book out of my recent investigations. Correction—our recent investigations. How would you like co-authorship?"

He had his answer from her mind before she could speak.

"Okay, you can keep a low profile. But you get a big credit in the acknowledgments."

"You really think Bridgewater will talk to me about it?"

"Yeah. I think he's feeling guilty."

He sensed her reluctance to get near the man. *I'll be with you.*

What about my job?

You don't need it. Whether or not your name's on the book, we're going to get a big advance. And when we sell our condos in D.C., we . . .

He stopped short.

"You were going to say we'd have enough to buy some property in rural Maryland or Virginia—somewhere out of the way, where we can . . . practice. And you can write."

"Yeah. Then I remembered, you don't need to sell your apartment. You have a trust fund."

She nodded. "Does that bother you?"

He wished he could lie.

She smiled. "Probably we can make good use of the money."

He scanned her thoughts. "You want to take the risk of getting other couples together?"

"Cautiously. On a limited basis."

"Very cautiously. I'm good at research. Maybe that can be my job. Investigating suitable candidates."

"Yeah."

She found his hand under the covers and locked her fingers with his. "And will you come meet my mom and dad?"

He knew exactly what she was getting at. "So you can introduce them to your future husband?"

"They'll be delighted I fell in love with a big-shot author."

"A big-shot author who loves you passionately."

She closed her eyes and snuggled against him, and he reveled in the feeling of completeness.

Yet after a moment he sensed the edge of uncertainty in her thoughts.

What?

Will you be upset if they want a big wedding?

Is that what you want?

No. But I know it will make my parents happy. Their little girl finally landed a man. I'd like to give them that gratification—because they stood by me all these years.

"I can go with that," he said in a thick voice. "Maybe my parents will even show up."

He gathered her close, marveling that Jordan Walker was making wedding plans. And he knew that she felt the strangeness of it, too.

I never thought I'd find Mr. Right.

He laughed. "I hope I am."

"You're getting used to being . . . open to me?"

He struggled for honesty. "I may need to go off by myself sometimes. Would that bother you?"

"Yes. But I understand why. Maybe we can find a property with a separate house you can use as an office—or if there's a freestanding garage, you can convert it."

"Good idea."

He slid down beside her and turned her in his arms, then began to show her with his hands and lips and mind how much she meant to him.

Turn the page for a special preview of
Rebecca York's next novel

SHADOW OF THE MOON

Coming soon from Berkley Sensation!

THE THICK UNDERBRUSH of Rock Creek Park made the perfect cover for the gray wolf who hunted in these woods where no wolf should be.

He hadn't invaded this stretch of urban wilderness to stalk deer or rabbits or any other wild animal. He was a werewolf, and he was after much more exotic prey.

Laughter drifted toward him through the darkness, and he moved closer to a hulking building that perched at the edge of the woods. A fantasy of stone and concrete, it was built to look like a medieval fortress with turrets and small, arched windows designed for privacy—or to prevent escape.

His supersensitive hearing picked up footsteps to his right and the strong scent of a man who hadn't bathed in a couple of days.

Blending back into the shadows, the wolf watched a security guard pass on his rounds, then crept toward the front of the building.

It was called the Eighteen Club, and he knew the main floor housed a nightclub. Above and below it were much more interesting private rooms—set up to accommodate any sexual fantasy that the elite of the nation's capital could imagine.

A long black limousine pulled up, and a man got out. A U.S. senator, his broad smile and craggy eyebrows instantly recognizable. Tonight he bent his head as he hurried toward the front door.

The wolf watched as the senator was swallowed up by

the massive stone building. Then something subtle caught
his attention. At first, it was simply an unfamiliar scent.
Something that didn't belong out here in the woods. Not
perfume. But skin washed with scented soap.

He looked to his right, peering into the darkness, then
blinked as he saw a shadow detach itself from a tree. A
person. Someone slender, probably a woman, judging from
her height and the feminine scent of her. She wore black
leggings, a long-sleeved black top, and her hair was tied up
in a black bandanna.

Like her body, her face was delicate. With his night vision, he could clearly see her light eyes, her little nose, her
lips that might have been sensual if they hadn't been
pressed into a thin line.

A wisp of blond hair had escaped from her bandanna,
adding an endearing touch.

But the overall effect was no-nonsense. He saw anger,
determination, and more. Emotions that made his chest
tighten.

What had the Eighteen Club done to her? Alienated the
affections of her lover?

Something dangled from a strap around her neck. A
camera.

So what was she doing here? Was she part of a special
security patrol? Had she come to take pictures of the people who entered the club—so she could blackmail them?
Or was she stalking this place for the same reason as he?
And what were the odds of that?

More cars pulled up, and she snapped away. First she
caught a man and a woman. He wasn't a political celebrity.
Far from it. This guy kept his face out of the media. But
he had a reputation for getting things done—for a price.
The woman with him was a looker, wearing a barely there
little dress that clung to her body. She was slender, except
for the large breasts that had probably been purchased from
a plastic surgeon's catalog.

The woman in black caught another patron. A matron in her late forties or early fifties with auburn hair and a face that looked like it was just on the verge of sagging.

The photographer moved closer to get a better angle with her camera. He might have growled a warning—but it was already too late. One of the guards had spotted her.

"Hold it right there!"

She whirled, poised to run as the guard moved quickly toward her.

"Freeze. Hands in the air—or I'll shoot."

FROM where the wolf stood in the darkness, he couldn't see the woman's face, but he felt her terror—smelled it wafting toward him in the night air.

"Take off your camera and put it down on the ground," the guard ordered in a voice that was edged with steel.

With unsteady hands, she followed directions.

The guard snatched up the camera and slung the strap over his own shoulder.

"Come on," he ordered.

"Where?"

"Inside."

She looked like she wanted to run. But the gun kept her standing in place.

"Let me go. I didn't mean any harm."

"Then what were you doing?" He gestured with his weapon toward the camera that now hung from his shoulder.

The wolf waited for the answer, and gave her points for guts—and fast talking. "I'm an amateur photographer. I was in the woods taking pictures of the natural environment. And I was curious about the lights of that building. I didn't see any NO TRESPASSING signs."

"Do you expect me to believe that? When you snuck up on us at night—dressed like a damn ninja. Move. Down there. Around the back."

The man started toward his victim, obviously enjoying himself.

The wolf watched the drama. This woman's fate was none of his business. That was what he told himself. But he couldn't make himself buy into that truth.

Over the past weeks, he'd discovered a lot about the Eighteen Club. He was pretty sure that if the guard took her inside, she might never come out again alive. And death might not be the worst thing that happened to her.

The wolf could feel his heart pounding, his adrenaline pumping as his body tensed to strike. Once the thought of attacking entered his mind, the savage need to hunt gathered inside himself.

He was in back of the guard, and the man was focused on his victim, sure that a lone woman in the woods wasn't going to get the drop on him.

He pulled out a pair of handcuffs. "Hands behind you," he ordered.

With a snarl, the wolf sprang forward, leaping on the man's back, taking him down. The handcuffs clanked to the ground. And the guard's finger squeezed the trigger of his gun.

As the wayward shot rang out, the wolf went for the gun hand, chomping down until the man screamed in agony and fear as he lost his grip on the weapon.

The woman screamed as well, but she didn't stay around to find out what would happen next.

She turned and ran, sprinting through the woods as other guards came pounding toward the sound of the shot.

Before the security force could catch him, the wolf leaped up. Snatching up the camera strap in his teeth and pulling it free, he dashed after the woman, his body bracing for the thud of a bullet piercing his flesh.

But he was lucky. The guard was in no shape to fire his weapon, and the other men were too far away for an accurate shot in the dark.

The wolf disappeared into the darkness, following the woman's scent, the camera thudding against his chest.

"What the fuck?" he heard someone shout.

"Get the damn girl," another voice gasped.

"And the dog."

He kept moving. He couldn't see the woman now. But he could hear her crunching across dry leaves, desperate to get away from the men with guns.

And from the creature who had come to her rescue. He knew that as well as he knew anything else.

She was in good shape; she could run fast. And she must have made sure of her escape route, because she seemed to know where she was going.

Too bad she hadn't done a little more research before coming here in the first place. The Eighteen Club was a well-guarded playground for the rich and powerful. And anyone who tried to get too close was taking an enormous risk.

She fled through the woods, up an incline, then slipped partway down again. Scrambling for purchase, she righted herself and kept going toward a residential neighborhood on the other side of the stream valley.

When she chanced a glance behind her, she spotted the wolf and made a headlong dash for the street. He saw her hand go into her pocket, probably fumbling for her keys. She pulled out a remote control, pressed the button, and lights blinked as a car lock opened.

The wolf was more surefooted than the woman. He reached the edge of the woods in time to hear a car engine roar to life.

Leaping onto the blacktop, he put on an extra burst of speed. The car jerked, and pulled away from the curb. Exhaust roared in his face, making him cough.

But he focused on the license plate, taking in the letters and numbers, committing them to memory as the woman sped into the darkness, not bothering to turn on her lights.

USA Today bestselling author

REBECCA YORK

Crimson Moon

Needing a fresh start, a young werewolf
heads west and changes his identity. As Sam
Morgan, he meets Olivia Woodlock, a woman
of many secrets, whose life is in jeopardy.
If he can't protect her, he'll never have a change
to explore the passion that promises to bind
them together for eternity.

0-425-19995-9

"Rebecca York's writing is fast-paced,
suspensful, and loaded with tension."
—Jayne Ann Krentz

"A true master of intrigue."
—*Rave Reviews*

B093

Cravings

ALL-NEW SENSUOUS STORIES FROM FOUR OF
TODAY'S HOTTEST AUTHORS

○

Feeding the Ardeur
An all-new Anita Blake, Vampire Hunter preview
by *New York Times* bestselling author
Laurell K. Hamilton

○

Burning Moon
by *USA Today* bestselling author
Rebecca York

○

Dead Girls Don't Dance
by the bestselling author of *Undead and Unwed*
MaryJanice Davidson

○

Age Difference
by *USA Today* bestselling author
Eileen Wilks

0-515-13815-0

**Available wherever books are sold or at
penguin.com**

J863

What Dreams May Come

ALL-NEW STORIES OF MAGICAL ROMANCE

Knightly Dreams
by *New York Times* bestselling author
Sherrily Kenyon

Road to Adventure
by award-winning author
Robin D. Owens

Shattered Dreams
by *USA Today* bestselling author
Rebecca York

0-425-20268-2

Available wherever books are sold or at
penguin.com

BERKLEY SENSATION
COMING IN SEPTEMBER 2005